A PATIENT MAN

Inspector James Given
Book Three

Charlie Garratt

SAPERE
BOOKS

A PATIENT MAN

Published by Sapere Books.

20 Windermere Drive, Leeds, England, LS17 7UZ,
United Kingdom

saperebooks.com

ISBN: 978-1-913518-91-2

PROLOGUE

The air is alive with wasps, buzzing and escaping half-drunk from fallen apples. The sun scorches my face as I stride, whistling, across the orchard towards the copse at the edge of the field, which offers me coolness. I can't refuse, pulled forward with no control over my legs.

At the edge of the undergrowth it goes dark. Immediate and total. Not shade dark but dead-of-night dark, as though someone has flipped a switch on the sun. I turn my head and the blackness covers everything, in front and behind. Where there had been rows of fruit trees seconds earlier, I can now see nothing. Far away a church bell chimes, and there's the chatter of pickers as if they have the light to work by. I push on into the shrubbery.

To my right, candles flicker to life. They illuminate a clearing where swastikas and glittering crucifixes hang from the trees. At its centre stands a dark-haired man who I recognise but whose name won't come. He mops blood running from a gash on the crown of his head and his face splits with a sly, evil grin. I want to ask who he is, but the words freeze on my lips.

The apparition shimmers, replaced by a girl in a battered straw hat, a bright red rose in her teeth. Then the candles extinguish as abruptly as they'd lit, succeeded by more, far inside the woodland. Something tells me I must run toward them, before these too disappear, but my feet cling to the ground. I grab a bush and drag myself free, then I'm hurtling, crashing, face whipped by leaves and branches and getting no closer to the light.

Then I am there.

A scream comes from deep inside. Bubbling up through my chest, the pressure building, escaping my lips when it explodes. It echoes across the woodland and away into the fields basking in August sunshine.

ONE

I slammed the filing cabinet drawer with a bang which would have rattled the windows if this twelve by fifteen cellar room had any.

'Everything all right, sir?' Constable Tom Smith looked up from the mound of papers on his desk.

'Everything's fine, Tom. Just fine.'

I hadn't disagreed with the boss when he'd insisted I take a break from the heavy stuff after what I'd been through. Three deaths and two attacks on me. Superintendent Dyer told me to take it easy and asked me to consider a piece of work he had in mind. He'd suggested that the day to day grind of the paperwork involved would take my mind off things, would help me forget. He was right, up to a point. It had helped me to cope. But now my outlook had become grey, the walls and the cabinets were closing in, and I was finding it brain-numbingly boring.

Superintendent Dyer had wanted me to devise a new filing system. Every case, from time immemorial, had a file, of sorts, and for years we'd stored them in alphabetical order by victim surname. This only worked well for individual crimes but made no sense if you were looking for connections. Also, some coppers are better at keeping records than others, which made matters worse. Dyer had suggested we needed a better method, one which would make cross checking more efficient. So, he'd put me with Constable Tom Smith in this dungeon, the walls reeking with the smell that only old, damp paper can generate, and he'd told us to get on with it. Every surface groaned under heaps of manila folders: thin ones, thick ones, torn ones. I now hated the lot.

Smith was young — three years in the force — and appeared to relish this daily grind. Some people are like that. They love putting things in order, be it collections of stamps, coins or birds' eggs. In his case, it was thousands of dusty papers. For the first month I'd put my heart and soul into devising a way of correlating the material so a detective, like me, could find links. We'd provided every folder with a code which, at a glance, showed the date and type of crime committed. Then we'd revamped the card index system to cross reference the folders. With these two small changes in place, we could track suspects across crimes and pull several elements together to paint a bigger picture.

I'd found it interesting for a few weeks. We'd had a little success when the system threw up new lines of investigation, but the work soon settled into the tedium of filing and retrieving. I'd thought I was ready to return to detective work, so I'd spoken to Superintendent Dyer.

'Stick with it, James, stick with it. It's too soon. No need to rush these things. You've had two nasty endings in a row, bound to take its toll.'

I'd telephoned him several times since and always had the same answer, the latest this morning, minutes before the drawer slamming tantrum. At first, my request had fallen on deaf ears again and, even when we'd finished arguing, the boss was far from happy.

'I'm still inclined to say "no", Inspector Given. However, I'll see you in my office tomorrow morning at eleven o'clock and we'll talk about your future then. Now you get back to your work and let me finish mine.'

Smith was back into his papers by the time I'd walked back to my chair. He had a smile on his face, and I saw him still at that desk, older, bald, and just as content, in twenty years. That future wasn't for me.

The next morning, I fidgeted at my desk for an hour before I could stand it no longer and left early for my appointment with the boss. This gave me time to wander through town to collect a gasmask from the distribution centre in the church hall, not appreciating there'd be a last-minute rush in response to the latest news.

When I arrived, the queue ran around the corner from the gates of the brick and timber building and I winced when I glanced at my watch. It looked like every man and his dog in Kenilworth had come out to form the line in front of me. I suppressed the temptation to flash my warrant card to get to the front, and I settled in my place to study my companions. Forty to fifty individuals, who'd never find themselves so close in normal life, made up the snake. But this wasn't normal life.

Jim Grimshaw, manager of Williams Deacon's Bank waited beside Benny Brady, who claimed to be a professional musician. Brady sang in an occasional charity concert, though everyone knew him to be an illegal bookie.

Most people were quiet, alone with their own thoughts, most likely of the war to come. One or two chatted, like the mother with babe-in-arms ahead of me, talking in a low voice to a bus conductor and rocking her crying child.

A hand tapped my shoulder, and I turned to see an elderly gentleman in a trim flat cap. He wore far more clothes than were necessary on this balmy late-August day.

'Do you think it will happen, son?'

'I don't know. Perhaps,' I replied.

'I can't see how it won't, regardless of what Mr Chamberlain tells us. The wireless says the Russians have abandoned their neighbours and German tanks are threatening the Polish border.'

'I imagine you're right.'

The old man shook his head. 'I hope I'm wrong, though. I was in the last one.'

The last thing I wanted, or needed, was another depressing conversation about the horrors of the Somme. It was all anyone talked about these days, as if reminding themselves how bad the Great War had been would somehow avert this one.

We shuffled towards the entrance each time someone left with their brown cardboard box, nodding their thanks to the ARP warden on the gate. All the while, my new-found friend regaled me with stories of his life in uniform. I was almost on my knees with despair by the end of the half hour it took to shuffle indoors, then the further five minutes to the trestle table and the sour faced man behind it.

'Name?'

'James Given.'

'Address?'

I gave it and he handed me the box.

'Standard issue gasmask. Instructions inside. Keep it with you at all times.' He waved me away. 'Next'.

So this is how it would be. On the verge of a war to fight against oppression and there were already tiny tyrants in uniform staking their claim on power they'd never experience in peacetime.

I only had ten minutes to spare when I left the church hall and I dashed to the car, then drove, just above the speed limit, through country lanes to County headquarters.

Superintendent Henry Dyer's office had become chaotic, although, like everything about him, in an orderly fashion. He was preparing to retire within the month and so was spending his days sorting through fifteen years' accumulation of papers, with the help of WPC Susie Fallon. She'd been his secretary for the last five.

They were both on their knees on the carpet when I walked in, with a heap of folders between them. Stacks of similar folders covered the floor and every surface. Each one had a sheet of coloured paper listing the contents on top. In the middle of this mess was his desk, polished and bare, save for a photograph frame on one side and a single file at its centre.

He raised an arm in greeting. 'Morning, Inspector, take a seat.' He stood, dusted off his trousers, and asked Susie to leave us for a while. He relaxed the formality when she'd closed the door behind her, clearly in a better mood than the previous day. 'Hell of a job, James, trying to decide what to keep and what to throw away.' He pointed to the biggest stack of papers. 'My predecessor left that lot, stuff that should have gone when he did and ninety-five percent of it not looked at since. His rubbish, and a good bit of mine, will go down to the central files to add to the material you and young Smith are sorting out.'

I groaned. Was this why he'd called me in? It would take weeks to go through it all, and he'd already said the material was useless. 'Are you telling me my future is in filing, sir?'

For a moment he knitted his eyebrows. Then he realised what I was talking about.

'My God, James, no. You're too special a detective for that. Letting off steam, that's all. The prospect of this damned retirement is getting me down. I thought I'd be looking forward to it, but going through this —' he swept the room with the back of his hand — 'has reminded me how much I've enjoyed the job. Lots of exciting and tough cases in there. I'm not sure pottering round the garden and the odd day's fishing will make up for it. Don't get me wrong, I'm ready to go, just apprehensive I suppose. A police career is all I've ever known, and with that has come a lifetime of mixing with good men, but also with terrible men. Villains and coppers included. I'm fed up to the back teeth with that side, so I'm going with mixed emotions.'

I'd never heard Dyer speak about his thoughts in this way, even though he often made his moods obvious. If he were mad, he'd certainly leave you in no doubt.

He shook himself, pulled his chair closer to his desk, and opened the folder. 'I've asked you over here because you've been nagging me to get back in the saddle. This came in today and might ease you into it. Nothing too taxing. A suicide on your patch, unpleasant but straightforward. Discovered earlier this morning. The body's in the mortuary so look at the scene, tie up the loose ends and write the report. Shouldn't take more than a day or two, and we'll see where we go after that. I've had your old office cleared, so you can move in whenever you're ready.'

Dyer passed me the folder, shrugged, and said he needed to continue the job in hand.

I whistled as I walked to my car, much happier than I'd been in a long while.

TWO

From the pavement, 57 Beeches Lane looked the same as every one of its neighbours in that part of Kenilworth: a plain terraced house with bay windows and a small, tidy, garden behind a discrete low wall, the closed curtains being the only clue to anything out of the ordinary. I assumed they'd always be that way, protecting customer reputations as much as the sensibilities of those living close by.

I knew the place, or rather, knew *of* it. All the coppers in town did. Several of my colleagues even frequented the establishment when they were frisky, or lonely. Young and separated from their loved ones, or older, where love had departed home ages ago. The neighbours never complained, and the girls were decent enough in their own way. As a result, the boys in blue left them alone to carry on their trade.

Three doors away, a passage led through the row to a walkway which ran from one end to the next. Similar passages punctuated the length of the terrace, the same for the houses opposite. I counted the entrances until I came to the yard I was looking for.

An outhouse was a few steps inside the white painted gate with a uniformed man, Barry Cranmer, leaning against a wall having a smoke. It was a common red-brick building, with a slate roof, patched in places. The woodwork, not touched since they'd built the place, was rotten where years of weather had attacked it. Cranmer was there to make sure no-one disturbed the scene. I suspected he'd upset his sergeant and so drawn the most boring job of the day. I gave him a look, and he crushed his cigarette under his heel then opened the door for me.

They'd found the Reverend Duncan Beattie inside the building that morning, hanging from a rope tied around a beam, wearing full clerical dress, dog-collar, the lot. Mary Fisher, a prostitute, who went to clean the room before it was used, raised the alarm. The building was never usually locked up, but when Mary tried the handle she couldn't get in. She fetched Eddie, the heavy who kept the customers respectful of the girls. He put his not insubstantial shoulder to shattering the lock. They'd discovered the vicar, slammed the door, and Mary scuttled round to the police station.

Inside looked better than out. The walls had been plastered then distempered, and the floors laid with green linoleum, giving it a homely feel. The owner must have decided there'd be more profit in the room if the clients thought they weren't being taken to a shed in the yard. A bed with whitish sheets and brown woollen blankets filled half the space. The grubby settee and small dining table completed the impression that this was just a normal room, with a little more privacy than the ones in the house. What broke the spell was the one-inch rope dangling from a roof-beam, its noose cut to release the body it had choked a few hours earlier. A dining chair lay on its back beneath the rope. The only other furniture was a washbasin and stand, and a corner cupboard with two beer bottles and glasses on top.

Other than the obvious cause of death, there was little I could glean from the room. It appeared nothing more than a convenient spot the clergyman had found to do away with himself. The cupboard was empty and the bed unruffled, so I assumed not used by the vicar and a lady friend. I spent a few minutes making notes then told Constable Cranmer, who was still leaning against the wall outside, to make the shed secure.

'Do we need to do that, sir?' he asked. 'I've already had the boss man wanting to know how long we'll be — says he's losing money over this.'

'Tell him my heart bleeds. He'll have the room back when I'm finished with it. Clear?'

'Yes, sir. I'll get on to it.'

'What's his name?' I asked.

'Grainger, sir, Benny Grainger.'

'Well, tell Mr Grainger I'll be round to talk to him later about the business he's running here. That should keep him quiet.'

Walter Naismith looked up from scrubbing his hands when I walked into the Coventry mortuary. I assumed he was fresh from lifting vital organs from the woman on a white slab at the centre of the room, and I hoped he wouldn't offer to shake hands. He likes his little jokes like that, does Walter.

The pathologist cocked his head towards the door in the corner leading to the cold room. 'Yours is in there. Second bay. Not started on him yet.'

That was a relief. It's not that I was queasy, I just preferred them to look more like a person than a butcher's window. I lifted the steel handle and pulled open the heavy door, shivering as the cool blast hit me.

'We've stripped and washed him though. His effects are in the box with his name on the side. Second shelf down, if I remember right.'

The stainless shelves lined one of the tiled walls, and I suspected these shiny surfaces made it easier to hose away the blood, guts, and gore when Walter finished his day's work.

Duncan Beattie looked in his early fifties, bald except for a wreath of dark hair greying above his ears. He'd have been an attractive man though, if he'd any natural colour left in his swollen cheeks. Before the noose scarred his neck and forced the tongue from his lips. Even through the antiseptic, the whiff from him confirmed he'd been dead for a while.

Walter spoke from the doorway. 'Not a pretty sight, is it, James?'

'Prettier than the one you've sliced in there though, don't you think?'

He laughed. 'Expect it is. Depends on your perspective.'

'How so?'

'Well, it's my job and I couldn't do it unless I found beauty in the workings of the human body. For you, what you see is a life snuffed out and your only further interest is in catching whoever caused it. I go to places you wouldn't want, and vice-versa, but we're both attempting to answer the same questions. How, who, and why?'

'That's very philosophical, Walter.'

'Perhaps. It's the way I'm thinking at the moment.'

'Any reason?'

'Partly this war hanging over us, partly because I'm retiring soon. Not sure what the future holds, I expect, making me weigh up what I've achieved in my life. Cutting up bodies all day can get to you sometimes, James. It's probably what's put me on the sauce from time to time.'

I muttered a few encouraging words to let him know what he did was crucial to solving crimes and that it made the world a better place. I wasn't sure we were winning this battle, but Walter had been a great support in my down times, and he deserved as much from me.

'Any thoughts on this one? Time of death?' I asked.

'Not yet, other than the obvious. You can tell yourself he's been that way a day or two, but I won't commit more till I've done some tests. Took a quick look at him at the scene and the skin and eyes showed it was the hanging that killed him.' He grinned. 'That, and the noose round his neck, of course.'

I'd noticed the same thing. The burst blood vessels were a sure sign he'd died from strangulation. Not a nice way to go. In the legal hangings I'd witnessed, the executioner calculated the drop with precision to snap the prisoner's neck and end life as quickly as possible. An amateur affair like this would have left the vicar kicking for long enough to regret what he'd done but be in no position to undo it.

Reverend Beattie's things were where Walter said. On top was a good quality wig. So the dead man was vain enough to try to take a few years off. Beneath this lay a letter in a neat copperplate hand, addressed to his wife. The usual pattern. Apologies for "taking the coward's way out". Regrets for what brought him to this and how he wished he'd not brought shame on her. I'd seen a few of these in my time and was never sure what they achieved. I was certain they gave no consolation to the bereaved relatives.

Next in the pile was a white smock, a surplice — part of the vicar's regalia, and I wondered why he'd have been wearing it if he was out for a night of clandestine pleasure. I took it out, followed by his dog-collar, black shirt, and trousers.

The gleaming cross below made me step away, slap the lid on the box and leave without a goodbye to Walter.

All the way back to Kenilworth in the car I was shaking with anger and fear. Anger that I was letting myself get into this state. The fear was the same I'd been experiencing for weeks. It was only after the trial of the murder of Paúlu Demma — the man who raped and killed my ex-girlfriend, Heather, many years ago, and then viciously beat me before he was killed — that the nightmares started. They were always the same. A phone call, a shadow at the window and a young body with a crucifix round her hands. A smashed clock in a pool of blood. Cigarette burns on my fingers. The bruised and broken corpse of Heather telling me it was my fault for leaving her alone. I don't know why it took so long for the nightmares to come out. Perhaps the dam only withstood the pressure long enough to make sure the wheels of justice kept rolling and I stayed fit until I put my cases to bed.

The duty sergeant began to crack one of his jokes as I walked past, but then saw my face and changed his mind, returning his attention to the stack of paperwork in front of him.

I took the stairs two at a time, slammed my office door and sat on the edge of my desk, panting, waiting for the red mist to clear. When it had, I slumped into my chair and lifted the phone.

I thought I was ready to return to the job, but I had not a clue how to tell Dyer now that desk work was all I was fit for. The superintendent had always been good, supporting me through my early days in the force, encouraging me to go for promotion when it came along. Although he could be difficult at times, keeping one eye on what the bigwigs upstairs want, underneath he's sound and as keen as I am in getting a result.

After the trial, I'd lost interest in the job, struggling through every day, and taking to my bed as soon as I got home. There, I'd lie curled under the covers until sleep dragged me off to dark dreams through to morning to begin the cycle again. So apathetic that even boozing held no serious attraction. Not that I wasn't tempted. The first night I walked past The Queen towards my cottage, I pushed through the swing door. The sight of three sad men sitting at the bar, and the landlord's raised eyebrow, turned me on my heels, knowing there'd be no comfort in there.

After two or three weeks it showed and Dyer hauled me over to headquarters in Warwick, where he ticked me off but he knew what I'd been through. He'd been office-bound too long to understand it, though he could see I wasn't right, that I needed time to get over what had happened, and he'd shifted my work sideways. Dyer brought in a replacement inspector, Phil Trimble, and pressured John Sawyer to take the step of becoming a detective. I don't know what he said, but he'd had more success with Sawyer hanging up his uniform and moving into town than I'd had. It was one bit of good to come out of the whole affair.

Trimble and Sawyer made a good fist of clearing anything run-of-the-mill that turned up while I was out of action. I'd known the new man a few years back when I'd been below him in the ranks, and he'd seemed a good copper. Thorough. No great flashes of inspiration, just plodding though the evidence until he found an answer. It was enough on ninety per cent of cases to put the villain away. Sawyer was cut from the same cloth, and together they made an effective team most of the time.

The two of them should be able to handle this latest one if it was as straightforward as Dyer suggested. If he insisted on me picking it up, then I always had my letter to fall back on. I lifted it out of my drawer, read through my words again, put them back in the envelope and put it away. Just as I had every one of the last few days.

Dyer refused to discuss my objections on the telephone and dragged me back over to headquarters.

All the way over in the car I was chuntering to myself about how he wouldn't get away with bullying me into a case I didn't want to work on. I'd tell him I'd work on anything else but not this one. I'd even resign over it if he insisted. Then, with the sun catching the colours of the browning leaves, and the gentle hum of tyres on the road, I'd relaxed for a few minutes, deciding it couldn't be as bad as I imagined. We'd have a proper discussion, and either he'd see it my way or I'd see it his.

By the time I'd waited outside his office for fifteen minutes, thinking about why I'd fled the mortuary, my mood had switched back again.

The boss sat me down, asked WPC Fallon to bring us some tea, and then launched into why he thought I should take this case. I refused, saying I wasn't being disrespectful but there were factors about it I couldn't deal with. This fell on deaf ears and he repeated his reasons.

'Listen, James, you were begging for something like this last week and you're right. It's clear you're wasted at that desk all day. You're the best detective inspector I've got, and we have you filing interview reports.'

When the boss had cut my duties, saying I needed a break from violence and murder, I expected to need just a week or two to get me back in the right frame of mind. But then it had dragged on. He'd had me in several times in the early days and I'd made excuse after excuse as I struggled to make sense of the previous three months. Now, when I'd thought the time was right and the boss was keen for me to come back, that cross in Beattie's effects had turned me back on my head. Gleaming golden, and as potent a reminder of death as I could envisage.

The boss insisted this was a simple suicide, where the man had become full of guilt about his lifestyle and ended it all. To tell the truth, I'd stopped listening.

'Come on, Given, pay attention. What's your opinion?'

I looked out of the window at the larches bending in the autumn breeze. Dyer banged his desk.

'Damn it, James, you need to shake out of this. It's not a difficult case. All you've got to do is oversee the boys making the enquiries and write a report when the pathologist's done his work. You'll finish in no time.'

Those trees were becoming more interesting every minute. The wind blowing the first leaves like confetti onto the grass fascinated me, and my eyes focused on the sky darkening with storm clouds in the distance.

I hated being confined to the clerical work and it was driving me mad, but I now knew I just wasn't ready to get involved in another death, regardless of how the end had come.

'Sorry, sir, I can't do it. You must ask someone else. Now, is it all right if I get back to Kenilworth? I've work to be getting on with.'

'No, Inspector, it isn't all right, as you put it.'

He started again on the whole thing. A big mistake. That's when I leapt up on my size nines.

'What else can I say, sir? I'm not doing it and you can like it or lump it.'

I shook my head and left.

I came home to find a letter had been posted through my letterbox. Lifting the envelope from the mat, I ripped it open as soon as I spotted the French stamp. The postmark dated it a week earlier and it could only be from my father's brother, Gideon. His last correspondence said he and his family were fleeing across Germany, trying to get to Switzerland or France. My uncle had been writing once a fortnight, then the letters stopped and we feared the worst with the reports in the news every day of Hitler's activities.

After I read it, I telephoned my father.

'Hello? Dov Geffen here.'

'Papa, it's James.'

'Jacob. How are you?'

He'd never accepted my change of name.

'I've received a letter. From Uncle Gideon. Posted a week ago, and it says they've escaped Germany and they're safe in Paris.'

There was a loud exhale on the end of the line. 'Thank God. You must go to find him.'

Those were the words I'd been dreading since I'd opened my uncle's envelope. Long seconds passed before I replied. 'I can't, I'm not ready.'

'Not ready, Jacob, what does that mean?'

'I … I'm not strong enough yet.' He knew I'd had a hard time, but not grasped how much the torture and attack had hit me. 'There's something I need to tell you.'

'What is it, son?'

'I'm no longer a detective.'

'You've left the police?'

'No, at least not yet, but I've not been on my normal duties for a while. I've been off active cases and working on setting up a system to help with paperwork. Superintendent Dyer hoped it would help, but it hasn't. Not much, anyway. I expected I'd be ready to go back by now, but I'm not.'

I told him of the dreams and of the fear that wouldn't go away. My father listened the whole time while I unburdened myself, then he paused so long I checked he was still there.

'Why didn't you tell me, son?'

I mumbled something about not wanting to worry him and Mama.

'That's what parents are for, to worry over their children. You may be a grown man in your thirties, but you're still our boy. You should have said something.'

I apologised, as ever, and changed the subject. I asked after Eli and Sarah, my little brother and sister, and Meena Classen, the fourteen-year-old girl they'd taken in a few weeks earlier, who'd escaped on the Kindertransport trains.

'They're all fine, your mother too, though...'

'What? Is Mama ill?'

'No, no, it's not your Mama, it's Meena. She has been subdued these last few days. The poor girl seemed happy once she'd been with us for a week or two, but now it's like she's gone back into a shell.'

The flow of Jewish children being brought to safety from Germany through Kindertransport stopped about the same time my uncle posted his letter. Meena was one of the first. Though I'd doubts about their plans, especially with their ages and two other young ones to look after, my parents didn't hesitate to offer refuge to a child who needed it.

'With all the news from her home, I expect she's worried about her family.'

'You're right, Jacob, that's probably it. We try to keep her away from the wireless reports and the newspaper, but I'm not sure the other girls in school have the same protection. It's not hard to guess how they'd gossip. All this talk of a war will frighten them.'

'Will Herr Hitler back down?'

'Not now, son. He's gone too far. Mr Chamberlain has, I think, been too weak. The Germans have marched into Poland, and our brave Prime Minister has politely asked them to march out again. We'll be at war within the week.'

'Perhaps that's another reason for me not to run off to France.'

I expected my father to tell me not to be such a coward, that I should go to find his brother and bring the family back before the conflict began. Instead he surprised me, though I could hear how difficult it was for him to concede.

'There's no need for a second reason, Jacob, the first one is good enough for me. If you are unwell, then you must rest and get better.'

THREE

A whole generation will remember where they were on the morning of the third of September 1939. I was in the canteen at Kenilworth police station, with almost the entire local force gathered to listen to Mr Chamberlain's words on the wireless. Coppers occupied every bench and chair and were standing where they could to get the best earshot. On most days there'd be plenty of space, with breaks taken at staggered times, but today even some off those off-duty came in to listen to the news with their mates. The men and women wandered in from around quarter to eleven, some returning from their beat and some on official break, the rest abandoning work, knowing everyone else in town, including the ne'er-do-wells, would do the same. There'd be no calls for the police in the next half hour.

As eleven o'clock approached the chattering reduced, then stopped as the Prime Minister's first words broke through.

'This morning the British Ambassador in Berlin handed the German Government a final note...'

When the broadcast began the windows were open and the street was quieter than usual, even for a Sunday morning, and though we were enjoying a warm autumn it did little to lift the chill from the grey walls or from the Prime Minister's announcement that England was now at war with Germany. Some of the men, those too young to remember the last one, cheered the news. Everyone else was quiet, and I guessed they were thinking of family they'd lost or fearful for those they might lose in this conflict.

At the start of the Great War I'd been ten years old, and my father was beyond conscription age when it was introduced two years later, though there wasn't a street in Birmingham where they'd not lost friends and neighbours. Two of my father's cutters lost sons in the trenches. A patternmaker who joined up in the early months and had a leg blown off at Ypres was a constant reminder in the workshop of those days of bloody slaughter.

We stood for the national anthem when Mr Chamberlain finished, then chatted in groups until Sergeant Burns turned off the wireless and shouted above the din, trying to impose some order.

'Right lads, back to work. There's not much any of us can do about this except go about our jobs as best we can.'

Phil Trimble interrupted. 'Wait a minute, Tommy. Might we perhaps have a moment's prayer before everyone goes?' Phil glanced at me. 'No matter which God we pray to, we'll need as much help as we can get next few months.'

All the men bowed their heads and Phil, who was active in his local church, put a few words together with me mouthing a few of my own, and then he led them in the Lord's Prayer. As he spoke, church bells chimed and, away in the distance, sirens cried over Coventry.

These portents faded as I made my way back to my desk to shuffle papers for an hour, trying to shake off the waves of images crashing round in my head. Phil's words reminded me of the cross and the chapel, and a monster awoke which I couldn't wrestle into its cage. It wasn't only the death of the girl, Rose, in my last case, or even the vicar's in the latest. Everything bad that had happened in my life flickered past, like the newsreels in the cinema as the war approached. One by one they flashed by. The letter telling my parents of my brother's death in Spain. The body of the love of my life lying bruised and despoiled in undergrowth. Hangings, murder, torture, and anti-Jew thuggery. No order and no relief. I carried on the pretence of working until I knew I'd get nothing done for the afternoon.

Tom Smith looked up from his filing when I dragged on my jacket.

'Off out, sir?'

'Had enough of this lot for the day. Take yourself home soon. With this news, your family will want you close and this filing seems pointless now, don't you think?'

Smith looked at me for a few seconds then shrugged. 'If you say so, sir; I'll give it another hour then I'll be off.'

I said a final good afternoon and trudged downstairs to the street.

The Prime Minister had just told us that the world we knew was about to end, yet the sun still shone and the swallows still skittered across the park, filling their bellies for their flight all the way to Africa in the coming weeks. A man whistled tunelessly, riding his bicycle into town, and the bell on the baker's door tinkled as a woman left, a loaf under her arm. Everything had changed and nothing had changed.

I walked the long way home, avoiding the school where the crucifix featured so large in the last death I investigated, and once I was away from the town centre I met only half a dozen people on the road. A couple seemed lost in their thoughts, all the others nodded but only one spoke, a man of about my age who I recognised as working in one of the local shops.

'Bad, bad business, Mr Given.'

I agreed, he shook his head, and we moved on.

The sunshine, fresh air and relative normality calmed the storm in my head until I picked up the morning newspaper from my mat. The headlines told of the impeding declaration, already old news, supported by articles explaining why war with Hitler was necessary and with photographs of children being evacuated from cities up and down the country. One piece, in particular, lowered my mood again. It reported Hitler's intention to annihilate all Polish people to occupy the land he wanted for producing food. The journalist said he would start with the Jews and we must expect the same wherever the Germans took control.

I shuddered as I thought of my uncle in France, and my father's plea to find him.

The afternoon stayed sunny but became uncomfortable, with a warm, humid wind blowing from the south, and I sat with my window open, listening to the wireless. King George's speech to the nation lasted a little over five minutes, delivered falteringly and in a monotone as weighty as the situation. The words were sombre, trying to be calm and reassuring, though he told us only the same as Mr Chamberlain in the morning. When he said that war would no longer be confined to the battlefield, it chilled me to the bone.

The telephone rang soon after he'd finished.

'Did you hear him, Jacob?'

My father's voice brought my front room into sharp focus — a single armchair, an oak table, net curtains wafting in the breeze. A place where I'd still felt secure despite what happened a few months earlier. But that threat was a person, close, possible to fight, not a quarter of a ton of random metal and explosive falling from the sky. This cocoon seemed less safe than before the King spoke.

I shook myself free. 'Yes, Papa. A frightening day for us all.'

'He's helped me decide.'

'In what way?'

'I will go to look for Gideon. The King said we must each do the right thing as we see it, and for me that means finding my brother and bringing him to safety.'

'Papa, you can't, it's too dangerous.'

'Dangerous? How can it be? Soon there will be young men facing German bombs and bullets. Now that's dangerous. I may be too old to join the army, but I'm not too old to climb on a train and travel to France.' His voice softened. 'Jacob, we've read and listened to the wireless for weeks about what these people are doing to Jews. And now France has joined us in this war, the Nazis will soon knock at their gates. How can I not go to search for him? He's my brother. You'd have done the same for Ariel if he hadn't been…'

My father rarely mentioned my brother. His death was still raw for all of us. He'd died in Spain only a few short years ago, fighting for what he believed in, and my father was right; if I could have gone there and saved him I would have done, regardless of the hazards.

Papa wasn't often stubborn. A young Jew from Russia would only have fitted into England by being able to bend in the wind. He often told me that in business "stone walls win few customers", a phrase he claimed was a traditional Russian proverb but was more likely to be one he'd invented to win his point. Only on a few occasions in my life had I seen him take a stand, but the steel now in his voice told me this was one of them and little I might say would dissuade him. Except the one thing I didn't want to say. I closed my eyes and counted to ten, then told him what he needed to hear.

'All right, Papa, I'll go.'

'No, Jacob, that's not what I am asking — you're not well, you told me so yourself.'

He was right, I knew I wasn't well enough to take the pressure, but I lied. Perhaps I even thought it might be a good thing to get away; at least it would put a distance between me and Dyer's demands to investigate yet another death.

'I'll be fine. A holiday will help me feel better.'

There was no possibility he'd have accepted this unless he'd wanted to, but he protested for a while. Apart from his concern for my health, I think he was torn between giving up his new-found adventure and knowing my training and experience made me better equipped to find my uncle. The argument continued for a few minutes, my father insisting I stay, me insisting I go, the reasons on both sides becoming more and more obscure as we went on. In the end he gave in.

'When will you leave?'

'I'll see my boss tomorrow, then it will depend on when I can book tickets. It won't be too easy with all that's happening. Dyer might give me a week; he'll not be happy with more.'

'You're a good son, Jacob. Will you come over to see us before you leave?'

'I will, Papa.'

My clammy hands couldn't stop the telephone handset from rattling as I laid it back in its cradle.

While I waited for Dyer to finish his call I looked at the cardboard boxes now stacked against the walls in the superintendent's room, each of them labelled for their destination. The majority looked they were headed for my office. Even if the boss hadn't needed most of his predecessor's files, he wouldn't throw them away, not now he'd set up the new system. It would take weeks for me and Smith to catalogue and store that lot.

The wood panelling looked naked now the photographs, commendations and notices had gone. The boss looked up when he hung up. 'Seems like the vicar topped himself after all, James. Phil Trimble has followed up —' he raised his eyebrows — 'in your absence. Asked a few questions, wrote the report, took him no time at all. Don't know why you couldn't do it.'

Trimble had replaced Terry Gleeson when he left and was better but not brilliant. Trimble was steady and there was nothing to suggest he was bent like his predecessor, which was perhaps why Dyer had chosen him over the others on offer. I also liked him a whole lot more than I'd liked Gleeson.

'That's good, sir.' I nodded toward the boxes, lacking any honest interest in the outcome of the investigation. No surprise, Trimble going for the obvious. The easy way out. 'Another one to file.'

'Funny you should mention that. There are plenty heading your way — will you be there to receive them?'

'Sir?'

'Are you here to tell me you've changed your mind and want to be back in your old job, or will you be staying in that cellar? Demoted, of course, if you continue down there with Smith. Can't be tying up your rank in a job any grade of copper could do with their eyes shut.'

'No. Er, yes. Sorry, sir, "no" that's not why I've come, and "no" I haven't changed my mind, and "yes" I do want to be out of that place. Just not yet.'

'Well that's cleared that up.' Dyer laughed. 'So why have you come to see me?'

'I need some time off.'

'But you're on the softest job I can offer. I can't see you're so bad you need to sit at home all day. Mustn't be good for you.'

'It's not that, I just need to take some leave. Family business.'

Pointing to a seat, he told me to explain.

Black clouds covered the sun which had been streaming through the window and the room was as dark as Dyer's mood when I told him what I was planning. Thunder shook the building. I reminded him about my Uncle Gideon, how I'd been concerned for his welfare over the last year, and how, now we'd heard he'd made it to France, my father wanted me to fetch him to England.

'It'll only be a week, sir, maybe a day or two longer if I get some leads late on and need to follow them up. With luck the break will take my mind off things, then when I come back you can reassign me.'

For the first time in several minutes Dyer spoke. 'You're mad, James. How can you be going to France now with the chaos that's out there? Don't you have friends in military intelligence who could help with this?'

'I can't ask them — they'll be dealing with much bigger issues at present, like how to defeat Hitler. Must go over there myself. I don't even believe there's a cat in hell's chance of finding him, but my father insists he'll go if I won't. Anyway, Paris in September is a fine place to be.'

'I'm not happy about this, James, not happy at all. Bent over backwards to keep you in a job and now you're asking for more.'

'I know, sir, and I appreciate everything you've done, but I'm between a rock and a hard place. I don't want to go gallivanting across the Channel, not with everything that's happening, but I don't want my father putting himself at risk either. He'd not know where to start, get into trouble himself, then I'd have to go hunting for him too.'

Dyer leaned back in his chair, hands clasped below his lips as if he were in prayer.

'Seven days, Inspector, not a minute more. When you get back to England, whether you've found your damned uncle or not, I want you in this office telling me you're abandoning filing to be a detective again. No ifs and no buts, otherwise we'll need to take a long hard look at your future in this force.'

FOUR

It would take me several days to arrange transport over the Channel, if I could do it at all. The newspapers reported that the government had commandeered the ferries for troop movements as soon as they had declared war, so I'd not an idea of how I'd get to France. I thought my father might see this as a good enough excuse for me to abandon the enterprise, but he didn't when I telephoned him.

'There has to be a way, Jacob; it's even more important now that we find Gideon's family and bring them all to safety. I told you before — if you're not able to go, I'll go myself. There will be a fisherman to take me across if everything else fails; I'm sure I'd find one if I paid enough money.'

'You can't go, Papa, where would you search? Uncle Gideon could be anywhere.'

'I'd have as good an idea as you. I'm not quite in my dotage yet, even if you think I am.'

'The problem is you wouldn't. I'm a policeman and used to asking questions. France is a big country. Even Paris has many times more people than Birmingham, and I'd be able to open doors you'd not get near.'

'So you go.'

Why did we do this? Every time he'd force me into an argument then get me to do what I'd argued against in the first place. It was a gift. With very little thought, I gave in and told him I'd see what I could do. I hoped my next call would settle the matter. A call I'd been avoiding, but now there was no alternative.

'Inspector Given, how are you?' There was a false brightness in the man's voice. 'Not phoned me to find that uncle of yours again, have you? Far too much going off at the minute.'

'Not exactly, Mr Mitchell. I do need a favour though.'

Mitchell and I had known each other for around a year. Although we'd not met in the best of circumstances he'd been helpful when I needed him, but I'd stretched his goodwill to the limit when I'd twice asked for help to locate my uncle in Germany.

The line went quiet long enough for him to make clear he didn't want to hear the request that was coming. 'Go on then, Inspector, spit it out. There's a war on you know.'

At least he was still willing to listen. He'd already spent more time than he could spare, and I knew his patience would wear thin.

'I need to get to France.'

'Join the army then, Inspector. There's lots of soldiers going over, even as we speak.'

If I hadn't been so desperate I'd have told him what to do with his sarcasm. Instead I kept my voice calm. 'That wouldn't help, would it, Mr Mitchell? My Uncle Gideon's family might be in Paris and I need to find them. I can't get there because the ferries aren't available to civilians, and I'd not bother you if I had any other way of doing this.'

He gave a bitter laugh. 'The Continent is in turmoil, Inspector. You must be crazy to even consider such a venture.'

'You're right, but what can I do? My uncle is there, and my father considers it my responsibility to bring him to England.'

'You're heading for trouble, but give me a minute and I'll see what I can manage.'

The clunk as he put the phone down on his desk left me listening to a muffled discussion on another line. In less than a minute he finished his other call and came back on.

'Best I can do is try to get you on a troop carrier. But don't blame me if you get your head blown off, and don't expect me to send in the cavalry if you've bitten off more than you can chew. I'll telephone you tomorrow when the ducks are in a row, then I'll tell you what I want in exchange.'

New Street station was as deafening and busy as ever when I arrived the next morning, its massive ceiling almost hidden in the smoke pouring from the half dozen trains sitting at the platforms. I was glad to get out onto the relative quiet of Birmingham city centre streets to look for a taxi, but even here the noise and traffic was too much for my liking. Buses, cars and delivery vans queued on both sides of the road and the city dwellers packed both pavements, moving in all directions. Shop girls and pin-striped bankers went about their business, mothers and uniformed nannies pushed prams, and boys, still too young to drag off to war, struggled with barrows piled with fresh vegetables destined for greengrocers, restaurants and hotels throughout the centre.

I could have taken a more direct route to the south coast, but I'd wanted to see my family before I left. Though I normally walked to their home when I travelled by train, I didn't fancy lugging my suitcase that extra mile, so I waited in line for the next available taxi.

The cab journey took less than five minutes, but that didn't stop the driver passing on all his thoughts about what we should do to Hitler when we caught him.

'Learned a bloody lot from the last one I reckon. We'll be in his back yard within a month.'

I couldn't decide if this was the usual British feelings of superiority or his ability to see hope where there was little, so I didn't argue and said I wasn't so sure but hoped he was right.

'Mind you, he's the right idea when it comes to them Jews.'

I didn't reply.

'Can't have them running the country, owning the banks and the like. Send them home, I say.'

I didn't bother to explain that many Jewish communities had existed in Germany for two hundred years or more, that it was their home. That they'd been there longer than Adolf Hitler, and he was only doing what many other rulers had done over the centuries — blaming those who were different as the cause of their country's difficulties.

The cabbie must have taken my silence as agreement with his views, because he continued to pour them out for the rest of the journey until he returned to his earlier theme just before we pulled up outside my father's workshop. He stopped gabbling when he saw the sign proclaiming "Dov Geffen, All Manner of Tailoring, Bespoke Suits Our Speciality" on the door. I paid him his bare fare, with no tip.

'You mark my words. Within a month,' echoed again from his window as he drove away.

I pushed open the door and made my way past the silent machines, then up the two flights of stairs, bracing myself for the inevitable fuss my mother would make. Sabbath was due to begin in the next half hour, and she looked up from her table preparations when I walked in.

'Jacob! Come in, come in. Take a seat. I'll pour tea.' She planted a huge kiss on my forehead and rushed to the bedroom door. 'Eli, Sarah, come see. Jacob is home.'

My brother and sister came through and greeted me with a little less passion than our mother. Sarah was growing but still enough of a child to give me a hug. Eli, at fifteen, thought he was above such things and shook my hand. Every time I visited he was taller, thicker set, his voice more broken, and it surprised me how he was changing. The face of the girl standing behind showed he was attractive to the ladies. Meena was a few months younger than Eli, though looked older, and pretty. Her blond, wavy hair might have saved her from the Nazis' attentions if it hadn't been for skin darker than they cared for.

All three turned to the door with a chorus of 'Gut Shabbos, Papa' when my father came in. He tousled Sarah's hair, nodded to Eli, and took my elbow, guiding me into the sitting room.

'So, Jacob, what do you have to tell me? Good news I hope.'

'I'm leaving for Paris in the morning; I've a passage arranged to Calais and the train onwards.'

He smiled and nodded. 'You're a good boy, Jacob.'

'James, Papa, it's James now.'

The smile disappeared. 'Not to me, it isn't. I still don't know how you can deny what you are in such a way.'

We had the same argument almost every time I visited, because he couldn't see that to fit into my world I needed to lose some of his. I wasn't in the mood for another merry-go-round of reasons why I should move back in with the family, join him in the tailoring trade and re-adopt our faith, so I switched back to the details of my trip. My father was soon listing the names of contacts in the French capital he'd collected from friends. I explained I only had a week and my first stop would be to the local police, then I'd follow any leads they might give. We continued to discuss the search until Eli popped his head round the door.

'Mama says we're ready to go.'

As my father stood he rubbed his back and, for the first time, I saw him as an old man, struggling to deal with a changing world.

After dinner, Eli and I stayed at the table while Mama, Meena and my sister went through to the kitchen to wash the dishes needed for next day and our father ambled out to the street for a cigarette. He didn't smoke much, but when he did Mama wouldn't let him do it in the house. Our new sister, as Sarah called her, appeared to be fitting in well with the family though she seemed reserved, in the way my father mentioned. Earlier I'd asked how she was settling, and she'd replied that she was very grateful to my parents for taking her in, but she missed her own.

There were twenty years in age and tens of thousands of miles travelled between Eli and I, so our conversation was never easy. I could talk to Eli about school and we did this in a relaxed way for a while, though I sensed he was much more concerned about something, maybe upcoming exams, than he was admitting.

I asked how he was getting on with Meena, and he flushed then mumbled she was "nice enough". He spoke much more clearly when he demanded I took the smirk off my face or he'd punch it off. This, of course, only made me grin more and Eli sat with knitted brows for a few minutes. I was unsure if he was just angry with me or struggling with his thoughts. When he spoke again I had my answer.

'Jacob ... James?'

'Yes?'

'What do you think of the war?'

The question stopped me in my tracks. 'Well, I don't imagine it matters a jot what I think. We've arrived and that's that.'

'But is it a good thing? Not the war I mean, but fighting Hitler.'

'I was in Germany when he came to power, and he seemed an evil man then. Nothing he's done since has made me change that view, but war itself is evil; millions died in the last one. People we knew.'

'The rabbi says Hitler's trying to get rid of all Jews in Germany. Isn't that something we should fight against?'

We talked for another ten minutes in this vein and it surprised me how well informed he was, some of it from school gossip though much from the wireless and newspapers. I wondered if he'd also discussed this with Meena, even though our father was trying to keep her protected from it.

'I want to join up.'

'What? You can't, Eli, you're too young.'

'Everyone says I look older than I am, so I'll have no trouble getting in.'

Ariel, our older brother, had been the same. Strong beliefs and willing to die for them in Spain. I don't have this trait and, listening to Eli, wasn't sure if I was pleased or sad about it. As a police officer, I'd not be called up so had a choice whether or not to go to the front, and I was certain I'd stay at home to fight the war in the way I knew best.

'Don't do it. There'll be plenty of time to do what you think is right if this goes on for long. Go now and it will kill Mama.' That was a low, unfair punch, but I hoped it would do the trick.

Eli paused and looked at the floor. 'Is that a good enough reason not to do the right thing? Rabbi Smart says we should always ask our hearts, not our heads, when faced with a decision. It wouldn't kill Mama anyway; she'd be worried, but she'd soon get over it.'

'Don't be ridiculous, Eli. She'll be terrified the whole time you're away. As will I and your sister.'

Eli jumped to his feet. 'Well, there's no need. I can look after myself and won't stay around here forever. Papa's already talking about me starting in the workshop as soon as school finishes.'

Before he became angrier, the front door swung open. My father stepped inside and looked at Eli then at me.

'And what are my boys arguing about?'

Eli shot me a glance and sat down.

'Nothing at all, Papa. Eli was telling me about his school friends. He was explaining one of the silly games they play.'

'He has good friends, all nice boys, good families.'

So the conversation turned, with our father in full flow about these families: their businesses, their histories, and their place in the life of the Jewish community. Mama and the girls joined us again at the table and peppered me with questions about my trip, every one of them making me clearer it wasn't one I wanted to take.

FIVE

Platform Two at Victoria Station heaved with passengers looking for their carriages — most, like me, carrying a suitcase in one hand and consulting a ticket in the other. Almost all had a gasmask slung over their shoulder. Those accompanied by porters made their way through the melee with ease, while the railway staff dragged enormous trunks, or three, four, five cases on trolleys behind them, crying ahead for passengers to move out of the way. The snatches of conversation I overheard were in French and Dutch, between people who I assumed were hoping that there were some routes still open. Several army officers stood outside one carriage, smoking and looking serious. Inside were row upon row of soldiers, some looking out of the window with grim terror etched on their faces, others were laughing in groups, oblivious to, or disregarding, the horrors they might soon encounter.

I'd left Birmingham on Saturday morning after Synagogue and my father, for once, refrained from telling me off for not observing Shabbat. Even Rabbi Smart came after prayers to offer his blessing on my search for my uncle.

'It's a good thing you are doing, Jacob. These evil men in Germany won't stop until they've wiped us off the face of the earth, so if you can bring back your uncle safely that will be one small victory for goodness.'

'I'm only doing as my father's asked, Rabbi; there are no high morals on my part.'

He smiled and laid his hand on my arm. 'Too modest. I am sure you would not be putting yourself in danger if you did not believe this the right thing to do.'

'Hardly dangerous. The Germans are still being held at the French border, a long way from Paris, so I think I'll be safe enough for a good while, Rabbi.'

'Travel on the land would not concern me, Jacob, but you'll be crossing the Channel, and their navy has already claimed many lives at sea.'

I could have done without his reminder so thanked him for his support and made my escape before he found it necessary to go into more detail. The family walked home, talking to friends and neighbours, their general sombre mood taking me even further down each time one of them wished me well for my journey.

When I left the house for the station, there had been tears from my mother, hugs from Eli and Sarah, and a firm handshake from my father, telling me he was grateful for what I was doing.

The journey to London had been uneventful, though a thunderstorm over Rugby was spectacular, drawing gasps from my fellow travellers until we rumbled out into the autumn sunshine a quarter of an hour later. I busied myself with the newspaper, attempting to get some idea of what was happening in France, and going through the names of contacts my father had provided, adding them to the notes I'd made on how I might tackle the task ahead.

On the two occasions I'd been to the capital before it had been on police business, once a course, and later, a case. Each time a car had met me, so I'd not needed to use the underground. As a result, I didn't trust myself to negotiate my way from Euston to Victoria through the maze of tunnels so queued at the rank outside the station in the pouring rain and took a taxi for the second time in as many days. Unlike the Birmingham cabbie, this driver kept his opinions to himself and he remained silent for much of the journey until we came close to our destination.

'Last trip, thank God. Soon be home with my feet up.'

'Been a long day?' I asked.

'That it has — I do a milk round before this. Up at five then this lark in the afternoons. Glad to be driving back to Balham after I've dropped you off.'

Birmingham was busy compared to my quiet streets in Kenilworth, but London was on a different level. I pitied this man, stopping and starting every minute of every day, weaving his cab and customers through constant traffic. In the years I'd spent at sea, sometimes weeks on end staring at the horizon, there were no sounds other than the throbbing of the engines, my workmates' banter, and the occasional cry of gulls in search of an easy meal. That's the life I'd prefer, and I was looking forward to breathing in the sea air again for a few short hours.

I reached Victoria Station, boarded the train and before long most of my fellow travellers on the train were sleeping or reading. There were two soldiers, one snoring, the other writing a letter, and I wondered how he kept his hand neat with the train rocking from side to side. The other passengers in the carriage, two men and three women, didn't appear to be travelling together because they'd not spoken since we left Victoria. I'd no sense if they were English or some other nationality, but one woman was pretty and so fashionably dressed I assumed she was French, though nothing confirmed or disproved this for the entire trip. The men wore pin-striped business suits, one sporting what looked like an old school tie so might have been a diplomat or civil servant. There were no clues to the status or profession of his neighbour.

I'd finished the *Evening Standard* by the time we chugged into Kent and, once I'd played the game of trying to fit lives to my companions, there was nothing else to do but gaze through the window at the countryside. In the evening sunshine I glimpsed acres of orchards almost ready for harvest. It threw me back to the days before my present life, a time of my greatest happiness and of my worst horror, when I first realised the joys and depths that humanity can reach. This memory and its link to my last case crashed into sharp focus.

My chest tightened and my breath came in spurts until my whole body shook and images of my murdered girlfriend, Heather, spun before me, lifeless, covered in blood. I stretched to grab for the emergency cord, desperate to escape into the fields, go back to Birmingham and beg my father for forgiveness. I couldn't do what he was asking.

'Is everything all right, sir?'

The letter writing soldier standing over me dragged me from the edge of the precipice.

'Yes … yes, I'm fine, thank you. Just a dose of flu. Temperature up and down with it. If I fetch a cup of tea I'm sure I'll be right as rain in no time.'

He tapped the brim of his cap. 'If you say so, sir, you'll get one just two carriages towards the engine; the lads are brewing along there. Are you sure that's all it is?'

'Yes, yes, thank you. I'll be fine in a minute.'

Slumped in my seat, I closed my eyes and breathed deeply, trying to slow my racing heart, and wondering if I'd ever survive this trip.

I eventually arrived in Paris after crossing the Channel by boat, and on the city streets children were being shepherded onto buses to take them to relative safety in the west. The contents of a museum on Rue Saint-Martin were being loaded onto covered trucks when I walked past, to escape the anticipated bombardment. But everyone seemed organised and business-like, going through all of this as though it was an everyday event. No-one displayed any sign of panic. The German army was lining up on the country's border, but the city was as unruffled as London had been when I passed through. Everyone at home believed France would be the front line once the shooting started, just like in the last war, and it amazed me its citizens were taking it so calmly.

The atmosphere in the French capital was in complete contrast to how I'd found Dover. There, soldiers decamping from the train did so in disciplined, military style but then their officers didn't seem to know what to do with them, leaving me hoping the lads would fare better on the battlefield. Vehicles queued on the quays, drivers unsure if there would be transport to the other side of the Channel for their passengers. At one point the cry went up that they'd reinstated a ferry service at Folkestone, and all hell broke loose with much revving and reversing until harassed port officials quashed the rumour. Suitcases and trunks lay everywhere, with a melting pot of well-dressed and down-at-heel men and women milling around them. From time to time a group would dispatch one of its number to find someone to give them information and he'd come back shrugging his shoulders or shaking his head because none had been forthcoming. I couldn't imagine how scared they were they might not get back to Germany, Italy, France, or wherever they called home.

I'd watched all of this from the comfort of the lounge where the officials ushered me when I'd flashed the papers sent by Mitchell. The man on the train who I'd assumed might be a diplomat was already in there when I arrived. He'd tipped his hat in recognition but didn't speak, so we sat in silence watching the pantomime outside the window until we received the message to board. He went below and I stayed on deck until we sailed out of harbour only a little later than planned.

My father's friends had provided the addresses of several hotels in Paris, and I worked my way through the list until I found an affordable one I liked. It was in the Marais, the largest of the Jewish districts and close to the centre of the city. Part of the attraction had been the pretty restaurant on the ground floor and the 'English spoken' sign in the window. At reception sat a grey-haired woman in black who answered my clumsy "*avez-vous une chambre pour quelques nuits?*" with a smile and confirmation in decent English she had a room. She led me up tight, dark stairs to the second floor and waited to ensure it suited me. Madame Després told me she was a widow whose son, Maurice, served as an officer in the Police Judiciaire, the unit looking after criminal investigations in the Paris area. I think she wanted to practise her English and chattered about his achievements for a few minutes.

My vague plan was to call on the contacts I'd gathered, show some photographs of my uncle and his wife, and enquire if anyone knew of them. I'd then ask questions in all the places the family might frequent, like the synagogue, markets, shops and schools, though I'd no clue how big a task this might be. The French I had picked up at school and only a little improved in my years at sea wasn't likely to get me by, so when Maurice Després, whose command of English was even better than his mother's, made me an offer over dinner on my first night I accepted with open arms.

'If you come to the police station, on Rue Maupassant, we can talk to my colleagues to find if they know anything. Not tomorrow. I'm busy on a case. Come the next day in the morning.'

I only had a few days to spare and didn't wish to waste one waiting to meet with the police, generous as Maurice's offer had been. So, with the name of an English speaking Rabbi provided by Daniel Shine, a family friend, I set out in sparkling sunshine for the synagogue where I found Rabbi Abrahams, an imposing figure, some inches over six feet and broad-shouldered. He would have been frightening if his welcoming smile hadn't been as wide as those shoulders. However, that smile disappeared when I told him why I wanted his help.

'These are difficult times, Inspector. Very difficult. Hundreds of families, if not thousands, have fled over the border in recent months, and they're still crossing. Some have come to the cities but many to the countryside. Wherever they feel safe. Here in the Marais many have taken sanctuary with friends, relatives and good-minded people.'

'So have you had any contact with my uncle?'

A shake of the head. 'I am afraid not.'

I've been a policeman for too long to let my emotions show too much, but I admit my heart sank. It had been a vain hope, though a hope it was, that my first port of call would reveal where my Uncle's family settled in Paris. Then I could jump back on the train to tell my father the good news. Better still I would send a telegram and then spend a few days exploring the delights of the city, away from the pressure of work and my parents.

The Rabbi understood his own trade enough to appreciate he'd blown my boat out of the water.

'I'm sorry, Monsieur Given, it is not pleasant for me to disappoint you. As I said, these are difficult times. But there are other synagogues, many places where our people gather. I'll put out the word if you can leave me as much information as you have. And I'll offer prayers you find them soon.'

I thanked him and we chatted about how things were in England and how long I thought the war might last. He told me he couldn't understand how long it took Mr Chamberlain's government to realise that Adolf Hitler was an evil man who needed to be stopped. The Rabbi admitted he was pessimistic of France's ability to survive a German onslaught, and the consequences for his community if it didn't. Before we parted, both of us depressed by our conversation, I left him with details of where to contact me in Paris and in Kenilworth, then wandered off to search for leads.

The streets around the synagogue were a mix of older houses, small shops and businesses, many of them wearing Jewish names. I'd bought a street map from the Gare du Nord to find the hotels, and after I'd left Rabbi Abrahams I sat in a café with my list of contacts to identify any that might be nearby. Only four of the addresses were within walking distance, so I set off in search of them. The first two were in the same street, neighbours, and, by the surnames, related, but when I knocked the doors they told me the families had moved on. Gone to Brittany. The lady at the third house, Madame Bloch, asked to see some identification then welcomed me in, offering tea and seeking news of her friends in England. I passed on what information I had and asked if she'd met my uncle or aunt.

'I do not know them, Monsieur Given. My family has lived in this neighbourhood for thirty years, but now there are so many changes with new arrivals and people leaving for the country it is hard to keep up.'

The photograph didn't help. She peered through her glasses and shook her head.

'There is no-one here I recognise, I am sorry. It was taken such a long time ago and people change so much, do you not think? Who else do you have on your list?'

I passed it to her, and she confirmed the ones I'd visited had left the area, then ran her finger over the final one and laughed.

'Good luck with Mr Adler. Very suspicious. Keeps himself to himself.'

Madame Bloch was right. A maid answered his door then disappeared inside when I asked in my very poor French to speak to him. When she returned she said her master wouldn't come to the door and didn't want to talk. I showed her the name of Mr Adler's friend in Birmingham and gave her the photograph and indicated she should take it inside to him.

A minute or two later, the door was flung open by an elderly man wearing pyjamas and a dressing gown. He thrust the photograph back at me.

'I don't know these people. Why would I? That fool Spelman would be as well minding his own business and not sending men over here to bother me.'

Before I could reply he'd flung the door in my face, leaving me bemused and frustrated on his doorstep.

This left me with no alternative but starting from scratch. There would be no point knocking on random doors; there were far too many of them. Instead, I looked for rooming houses, anywhere a family in transit might stay until they found something more suitable. There were plenty of these. In any emergency, those with foresight and spare capital can find ways of making a little extra money. Such people had purchased run-down three- and four-storey houses and converted them to pack in as many families as possible. Ready for renting to the hordes of people fleeing from the spectre of Nazi persecution.

Most of the people I spoke to were from different parts of Germany to where my uncle had lived, or from Austria, Poland, Czechoslovakia, all now under Nazi control or serious threat. All were disorientated, all concerned about revealing too much about themselves to a policeman, and none of them confessed to having met Gideon on their travels. As I talked to them, I thought I understood why Mr Adler had acted the way he had. These people had faced terrible times. Many had fled their homes and others, like Adler I suspected, thought they may have to do the same before long.

After an hour or so of searching, one man said he was from Bremen and knew my uncle though hadn't seen him on the road. I wasn't sure I believed him. There was a wild and somehow eager look in his eyes, as though he was desperate to please me. Or anyone.

As I walked from building to building I picked up, when I could, the names of the landlords, adding them to the list of possible sources of information. Each time I passed a boulangerie or boucherie I'd show the photo my father had sent with me, and each time there was an emphatic "Non".

Paris is a city of over 2 million souls, recently swollen by thousands of Jews, and it was like looking for a needle in a haystack. After five hours of this, followed by a late and mediocre lunch on the Rue de Rivoli, I trudged back to my lodgings.

Madame Després dashed from her kitchen as soon as I walked in.

'Monsieur Given. There has been a...' She gestured, putting her fist between her ear and her chin.

'A telephone call?'

'Oui, a telephone call. From England. A Constable Sawyer. The constable said to telephone him as soon as possible.'

She showed me into her sitting room and pointed to the table in the corner. I found it fascinating how French the room was, so different to my parlour in Kenilworth, though it was difficult to put a finger on the difference. The turn of a chair back? The fabrics? A much darker wallpaper than we'd be used to, offset by gold on the mantel clock and table legs? Everything as functional yet more elegant than its English counterpart.

'You may call him from there.'

I didn't fancy wrestling my way through a French telephone operator with an international call, so I asked Madame Després to help. When the ringing started at the other end, she handed back the receiver and tiptoed out of the room.

'Sawyer? Is that you? Why on earth did you telephone me here?'

'Sorry, sir, Superintendent Dyer told me to do it. Said you might see sense if I rang.'

I resisted the urge to explode. John Sawyer was only following an order from the boss.

'And what am I to see sense about?'

'This Reverend Beattie case, sir. Looks like we may have to open it again.'

SIX

Dyer made his message clear. Return to England and investigate the new evidence about the vicar's death or stay in France then spend the rest of my days filing old cases. If I'd wanted to stay in Paris, there's not a chance his order would have sent me running home. But I didn't, and it did. It gave me an excuse to abandon the hunt for Uncle Gideon. One which my father couldn't deny, a murdered clergyman. Even though he followed a different faith, my father would respect the need to find the killer of a man of God. It should also satisfy him I'd tried, and I'd set in motion some local searches which might reveal more than me tramping the streets of Paris for days on end.

The earliest possibility for my return was two evenings away. It had been easier to set up than my journey out because England-bound troop boats were almost empty. Mitchell provided me with a contact at the British Embassy in Paris, along with a letter of introduction and said the man would "oil the wheels" to get me home.

When I climbed the steps into the impressive building, a queue spilt out from the lobby. The guard at the gate told me to ignore it when I'd showed him Mitchell's letter, and instructed me to make my way to Room 37 on the second floor. These poor people, with such belongings as they'd been able to pack, would have surrendered their eye teeth for the access my documents granted me. Many of them were dishevelled, unwashed and unshaven, as though they'd been waiting several days.

The second-floor corridor was more mundane than the grand entrance hall and staircase, and the secretary inside the designated glazed door asked me to wait a moment, made a brief call, then returned to her typing. The telephone rang a few minutes later. She answered then led me into an inner office at least three times bigger than mine. I recognised the tall young man, tanned and smiling in a pin-stripe suit, who stood and stuck out his hand.

'Inspector Given, nice to meet you properly. Howard Champion. Bumped into each other on the ferry. Understand our mutual friend Mr Mitchell has asked if we can get you home, eh?'

I nodded.

'Good, well that should be no pose no difficulties.' He lifted and tapped Mitchell's letter. 'Useful to have friends in high places, eh? There's a good many others not so lucky. Expect you saw some of them downstairs. Absolute bloody chaos. Still, not your problem, eh?'

Champion rifled through the second drawer of a filing cabinet, pulled a pink document from a file, stamped it, and handed it across.

'Here, present this when you get to Calais tomorrow and you'll be back in Blighty in no time.'

I thanked him and made my way out onto the street, passing the queue of hopefuls which didn't seem to have moved in the last half hour. For the next few hours, I wandered the Marais and even ventured further afield to other Jewish areas, but the result was the same as my first day. Nothing. So on my last night I treated myself to an excellent meal, which only added to my inability to sleep. In the morning, tired and almost crippled with indigestion, I met Maurice Després at his office where he organised copies of my photographs and made notes of all the information on Uncle Gideon and his family. He promised to pass it on to his colleagues and to get in touch if the found anything. Before I jumped on the Calais train to leave the city, I continued my fruitless search. At least I could tell my father I tried.

As far as possible, troopships were crossing under cover of darkness to limit the chances of U-boat attack, and this meant I didn't arrive home in Kenilworth until late afternoon, then drove to Warwick after I'd dropped off my luggage.

Throughout the journey back I'd been thinking about how I might deal with Dyer's request. It wasn't unreasonable: we had a case to solve and I was a senior detective based in the area where the death occurred, with recent experience of handling such investigations. In his position I'd have been demanding the same. But this new case with the cross and all its connotations almost made me wish to be back on the beat. When I reached the boss's office I'd missed a night's sleep and weariness put an end to any chance of putting forward a decent argument for why I didn't want to take on the case. My plea that I wasn't ready fell on deaf ears and sounded pathetic. The boss was insistent.

'It's time, James. If you're able to investigate in France you're well enough to do it here. I've been lenient, but now you need to decide what you want to do. I can turn your current assignment into something permanent, or you can do what you do best and be a bloody detective again. Your choice.'

We glared at one another for an uncomfortable minute. At the end of that minute I saw no good reason not to do as he was asking. If he left me working with Tom Smith long-term then I'd be handing in my notice before the year was out anyway. I might as well pick up the Beattie case, see how I managed, then decide about my future after that. I tried one more time to say 'no', he said 'yes' again, and I capitulated. We shared a frosty handshake, with him saying how pleased he was I'd seen sense, and me lying through gritted teeth it was good to be back.

Arguing with Dyer put me in bad sorts, and after I pushed my evening meal around the plate for a while I scraped it into the bin, left the dirty dishes in the sink and plonked down in my armchair by the window. Even the sun sparkling off the red sandstone of the castle didn't lift my spirits like it usually did. I stared at its ruined battlements without seeing for an hour, trying to work out any way I might have approached the boss to get the result I wanted. I wasn't even sure what I wanted except more time. Even then, I wasn't sure that more time would make any difference.

The light was fading when I left the house, hoping a walk in the early evening air might settle my head. I wandered up the hill, avoiding the urge to call in to The Queen. The temperature was dropping as the sun dipped lower and I was glad I'd slipped on my scarf and gloves. Aimless turns through lanes dotted with thatched cottages brought me to a street I recognised far too well. In his garden, digging, like the first time I'd been here, was Bill Webb, father of the dead girl in my last investigation. I hung around on the corner watching him for a few minutes as he turned over sod after sod, stretching his back as he reached the end of a row. As he did so he spotted me across the road, then peered for a second or two to through the deepening gloom.

'Inspector?'

'Good evening Mr Webb. Well, I trust?'

He laughed. 'Me? I'm well enough. Fit as a fiddle you might say. Have you time for a cuppa?'

I'd nothing to lose and knew he'd perhaps be the company I needed for an hour, but still I was hesitant, certain it might dredge up everything I was trying to put behind me. I refused, saying I didn't want to pull him away from his garden.

'Not at all, I'm about finished here for the night. I'd welcome a chat. Please come and join me.'

He soon had the kettle singing and the table laid with what I guessed was his best china, at odds with the large brown teapot he used to fill the cups when the tea brewed.

We talked of the weather and his garden for a while, then he asked me what was wrong.

'Wrong? Nothing, why?'

'Come on Mr Given, I can tell you're not happy. Why else would you be wandering up this end of town at this time of night?'

There was something about the gentle concern of this man, burdened by enough sorrow of his own, that helped me talk. Leaning back in my chair I rubbed my forehead.

'Rose's death has made me look at my work in a new way, Mr Webb.'

'Call me Bill. Please. We should know each other well enough by now. In what way are you thinking differently?'

'Frankly, I'm not sure I want to do it at all. I've seen a lot of bad things in the last few years and it's getting me down. Even the reason I joined the police in the first place has now gone, so there doesn't seem much point in doing the job any longer. No-one could expect to investigate half a dozen deaths in the last eighteen months without it taking its toll.'

This vein bled for another five minutes with Bill listening as it all spilled out, nodding and throwing in the occasional word of sympathy. When I'd finished he stayed quiet until I apologised for laying all my troubles in front of him.

'Not at all, Mr Given, if I hadn't wanted to hear I wouldn't have asked. No chance I can advise you what to do. I'm sorry, I wish I could. What I will say is this. When Rose was taken from me I was lost. You, by digging and digging until you found what happened, showed me there is still decency in this world. Ordinary people like me need men like you to help us make sense of troubled times. To bring us justice when it seems there's none left.'

The kind words were good to hear, but I still felt I'd already played my part; seen things I didn't want to see again. That now it was someone else's turn. I thanked him for listening, said my goodbyes and began my walk back down the hill. When I reached the stile across the field from my cottage, his last comments repeated in my head like a stuck gramophone record. I turned on my heels, headed back past his house and up into town to the police station.

Two things lay on my desk when I arrived in the station, most of which was now in darkness. The first, a note from the boss, half-apologising for the row we'd had earlier in the day and telling me to "take it steady", the second, the case file which Sawyer left for me. It was in a real mess. Phil Trimble scribbled notes on scraps of paper in no particular order, having, more or less, concluded a suicide before he asked questions. The file only confirmed what I already knew. The vicar left home on Wednesday at teatime and was last seen at eight o'clock that night by the exotically, and I suspected falsely, named Amethyst, who reported he was a regular customer and dressed in "ordinary clothes" when he was with her in a room in the house. If Beattie wasn't in his vicar's outfit when he left her then when, and why, did he change? Did he leave on Wednesday and return sometime later? Also, where were the clothes he'd worn before?

They discovered him on Friday afternoon. Everyone interviewed appeared shocked to hear he was a vicar. Only on the last page of the file was there anything new, and this turned up while I was in France. Jacqueline Flowers, who had been away visiting her sister from Thursday morning, the day after Beattie was last seen, returned. Trimble then interviewed her. She said she saw a man leaving the outhouse about half an hour after the good reverend left his "escort". The evening had been dark by then, and even though there was a lamp a dozen yards away, her description wasn't helpful. Not young but not old. Brown or black hair, perhaps grey in parts. Not tall, but not short either. Clothes? Not a clue. So Mr Average who might have been a banker or a builder's labourer. Miss Flowers hadn't been working at this establishment for long, so didn't "know for definite" if the man she had seen was a regular, but she didn't think so.

With that description, Sawyer and Trimble had no luck tracing the man in the two days since Jacqueline had surfaced. Those questioned in the brothel hadn't seen him, and although my colleagues asked in the streets around they had nothing to jog neighbours' memories. I recalled the number of passages behind the terraced row leading into the streets on either side. A man or woman leaving through the back could find their way to a different part of the town in minutes and no-one seeing him, or her, would consider anything amiss. As a result, Phil Trimble went to the boss without a result and he'd told Sawyer to phone me. I wouldn't imagine that our superintendent thought I was a better copper than Trimble, only that I was different. He'd be sure I'd cast a new eye on it, one less structured, maybe see something Trimble hadn't spotted. It has been my experience that investigating teams are more effective when the members have skills which are not the same. Sawyer and Trimble are too alike, they both take one step at a time, in a straight line. I sift, and reflect, sometimes taking a tangent and following where it leads. If, as often happens, it leads nowhere, I'll pick up the thread where I left off and continue until there is another fork in the road. If it's a useful diversion, I can trust Sawyer to catch up, and to have double-checked all the facts along the way. I don't believe I've ever told him how useful he is, even though he's saved my hide, and my life, on occasions. One day I must get around to it.

Armed with this testimony from Jacqueline Flowers I went through the file again, looking for anything to reinforce an assumption it might be more than suicide. Tucked between the outhouse description and a receipt for Trimble's lunch was a list of everything found in the room, including Reverend Beattie's effects. The same items I'd been going through when I found his cross. I read it three times, then once more to make sure of what I'd spotted the first time. There was no key to the outhouse door on the list. Nowhere in the notes was there mention of a key on the inside, nor anywhere in the room. If there was no key with Beattie, then he couldn't have locked the door and our mystery man must have done it. The vicar might still have hanged himself but the missing key, alongside a man seen leaving, made it less likely by a country mile. How could Trimble have missed something so basic? It was possible Beattie left then returned having changed, but why would he? Where would he have done it? His wife had said she'd last seen him on Wednesday, so he hadn't been home.

The Reverend Duncan Beattie had been hanging in the room at the back of a brothel for a day or two and no-one had reported him missing. Not his wife, nor any of his flock. How could that be? And who would want to murder a vicar?

I took two minutes to compose a farewell note to Smith, another ten to throw the contents of my desk into a box, and before a half hour was up I'd decamped to my old office on the third floor.

SEVEN

The vicarage lay back from a country road, separated from a pretty church and ancient graveyard by an avenue of shining mature yews running down to the River Avon. It had taken me a pleasant half hour to drive to Stowham in the warm sunshine, less than ten miles from Kenilworth but the twists and turns of the lanes meant I got lost more than once. The large house was built when Victorian wealth wished to display itself and when clerics had big families and servants. A thin woman in black skirt and black cardigan opened the door when I knocked. Her shoulder-length, brown hair, looking clean though lifeless, framed pinched cheeks and a pale complexion. The horn-rimmed glasses spoke of an earlier generation and made her appear fifteen years older than I suspected her to be. Being generous I'd have described her as plain, and not a woman who cared much about her appearance, an idiosyncrasy I've found not uncommon in those of a certain class.

'Mrs Janet Beattie?' A nod. 'I'm Inspector James Given. I need to talk to you about your husband's death.'

For a moment she pressed her palms on to her cheeks and eyelids, not breathing. When she removed them she exhaled, whispered "I knew it" and drew the door wider.

'Come in, though I can't tell you anything I didn't tell the other officer.'

I followed her into a sitting room furnished with two tapestry-covered armchairs and a leather settee. An oil painting of a woman in regency costume above the dead fireplace bore such a striking resemblance to my host she must have been an ancestor. The walnut side table topped with a silver tray and china tea set completed this scene of respectable gentility. Mrs Beattie pulled open the closed curtains an inch and peeked out.

'Such a lovely day, Inspector. What a shame to be in here in the dark.'

No grief in her voice, only sadness at being deprived of the sunlight. When she stepped away I asked if we could sit down. She took an armchair with a sewing box at its side and I wondered if the other chair had been where her husband usually sat. The woman stared past me at the bay window, as if now trying to see through the curtains to the ungrieving world outside.

'Duncan was murdered, wasn't he?'

'How…'

'If my husband had taken his own life it wouldn't attract a second visit from a detective inspector, would it? In any case, Duncan wasn't one to take the brave way out. I've never accepted suicide, not deep down. So unlike him. Then there was the note.'

'What's wrong with the note?'

'The writing isn't his. Not to my eye anyway.' Mrs Beattie ran a hand through lank hair. 'Something about it wasn't right. I thought perhaps he was in such a nervous state it had affected his handwriting. After all, the other Inspector was so insistent Duncan had killed himself it made me fancy I might be mistaken.'

'Do you have any reason to believe someone murdered him?'

Surprisingly, she hadn't asked me the question. Incredulity is the usual response, that someone known or loved had enemies who hated them enough to take away their life.

'My husband was a man with, how shall I put it, certain interests. Sometimes they took him to places which weren't safe, and I've always felt it only a matter of time before he'd bump into an unsavoury type who wouldn't succumb to his sweet talk.'

I'd just told this woman someone had murdered her husband and she'd shown no emotion. There seemed little point pussyfooting around my next question.

'You know they found him in a brothel?'

Her face turned to the curtains again. 'Yes.'

'And we understand he was a regular visitor.'

She turned back and smiled grimly. 'Look at me, Inspector, I'm no vision now am I? And, as I said, Duncan had particular tastes I didn't feel comfortable with, so we agreed he wouldn't make demands and I wouldn't enquire.'

'When did you last see him?'

'Lunchtime on Wednesday, and afterwards he went to his study for an hour while I worked in the garden. He shouted to me at about three o'clock he was going out and not to wait up for him.'

'Were you worried when he didn't come back that night?'

'Not overly. He'd stayed away before. When he wasn't here for breakfast it annoyed me he hadn't warned me, but that was all.'

'And when he didn't return the next night?'

'I began to worry a little. Duncan would have telephoned me if he expected be out longer than the one night; it has happened before, and he'd a parochial council meeting planned. I had to postpone and give his excuses.' Mrs Beattie's voice cracked, and I thought her resolve was about to break. 'I suppose that's how it will be now. The old order broken and everyone finding out he wasn't the paragon they hoped he was. Terrible really because he was a good man, he just had this weakness for attractive young women.'

'Can I ask where you were all the time he was away?'

'Vicars are busy people, Inspector, and their wives are sometimes even busier. I can't imagine why you'd think I'd want to kill my husband, but you clearly have it in your head that it's a possibility, so I'll tell you this. Apart from the time I was gardening and the hours I slept, I was in the company of others, either on the telephone or face to face.'

She left the room and returned with a large desk-diary, then dictated a list like one I might have collected from any cleric's wife or assistant. Sick members of the congregation, church elders, committees, and so on. I noted them all and was certain everyone would confirm her story. Not because I thought her innocent but because she was too intelligent to give me names who wouldn't. I tried to picture her in a man's coat and hat, wondering if she could be the nondescript leaving a body hanging in a brothel outhouse. Janet Beattie stood tall enough and hard-featured enough to pass as a man in the half-light. It seemed unlikely but I filed it anyway.

Funds weren't available for us to employ specialists to help with investigations, but Mrs Beattie told me that one of her husband's flock was an amateur handwriting expert. Several police forces used his services and she was sure he'd help. She telephoned him and he agreed, without hesitation, to examine the suicide note.

The trek to Kenilworth and back to collect it wasn't welcome, but I was keen to complete this part of the picture. To make sure I wasn't on a wild goose chase.

Arnold Pemberton's house was only half the size of the vicarage, though of a similar age. The gardens looked immaculate and two stunning climbing roses framed the front porch, their leaves now fading but most of the yellow and peach blooms still glorious. A man about my height and build came out when my tyres crunched onto the gravel drive, although he looked considerably older, in his mid-fifties if I had to guess. I introduced myself and he ushered me inside to a study with shelves from floor to ceiling, laden with books whose titles would have revealed his hobby even if I hadn't already known. In pride of place, on one end away from the others, was a pamphlet entitled "William Shakespeare the Man: What we can learn from his handwriting" with Pemberton credited as the author. It gave me confidence he knew his subject.

'It's good of you to take a look, Mr Pemberton.'

'Not at all, Inspector, only glad to help. Despite what's come to light about the vicar I have nothing but respect for him. When my wife died two years ago he offered remarkable support. His words and his prayers got me through a terrible time.' Pemberton's eyes, momentarily sad, suddenly sparkled. 'Besides, we graphologists like nothing better than a good puzzle.'

I gave him the suicide note and a sample known to be Beattie's writing. He lay both on a desk blotter and examined them through the largest magnifying glass I'd ever seen. Pemberton turned the papers this way and that, held them up to a lamp to peer through them from the back, and was all the time murmuring and scribbling on a pad. From time to time he'd pull a volume from a shelf, flip through it, then curse as he crossed out one of his conclusions.

After half an hour of this he leaned back in his chair and massaged his neck.

'Definitely not Reverend Beattie's hand, Inspector. A good imitation but that's all it is.'

'Are you sure?'

'Without doubt. Handwriting is as unique as fingerprints if you know what you're looking for, and I've spent the last forty years looking.'

There followed a detailed explanation of things he called loops, flourishes, disconnections, and a dozen other unfathomable terms until he saw my eyes glazing over, then he laughed.

'Sorry, it's the way of all enthusiasts. We never quite gasp how other people don't get as excited about our subject as we do. Suffice it to say there are small elements in some of the letters which are forced. Not natural.'

'Can you work out who wrote it?'

'Unlikely. Even if I had an example of their natural writing, this has been so heavily disguised it would be different.'

'Man or woman?'

'Hard to tell. The lettering has the weight of a man's, but if a woman practised it would be simple to disguise her natural traits. What is interesting, Mr Given, is that the vocabulary is in keeping with the vicar's own. Whoever forged this note was well educated.'

I thanked Pemberton for his time and asked if he'd send his findings to me at the station. As I pulled away into the sunlit afternoon I felt we'd moved a step forward, only a tiny one, but forward, nonetheless.

John Sawyer popped his head round my door. I'd left a message I wanted to see him about Beattie as soon as he came in the station. He looked sheepish, and this didn't hang well on his large frame.

'Good morning, sir. Is there something wrong?'

'Only this file Constable. Look at the state of it.' I leafed through the assorted scraps then tossed it back on my desk. 'How did you let it get in such a mess?'

Poor Sawyer blushed.

'I tried, sir, I really did, but Inspector Trimble just kept throwing more bits and pieces in there. Every time I tidied it he'd shuffle it all again and add even more notes. The Inspector wouldn't listen. Said it wasn't important because the vicar had topped himself so it would never go to court.'

With every sentence Sawyer became more flustered until I laughed and waved Trimble's lunch receipt. 'Don't worry, John, I'm only pulling your leg.'

His shoulders relaxed.

'On the other hand, I need you to do some work on it. Get it all written up, nice and neat, and put it into order. Now we might be faced with murder we need to go through it all again, bit by bit, and make sure we have all the relevant facts to hand.'

'Onto it straight away, sir. So you're now satisfied someone killed Reverend Beattie after all?'

'Not altogether, but there's the lack of a key at the scene or in Beattie's pockets. I can't believe you and Phil missed that.'

Sawyer reddened.

'Double check with the people at Beeches Lane, but I'd imagine no-one there has it. The other thing is the suicide note. Beattie's wife had her suspicions about the handwriting and his parishioner, Arnold Pemberton, who's something of an expert, has confirmed it's unlikely to be her husband's. Tied in with Jacqueline Flowers seeing the person sneaking out the back it seems conclusive. Shame you overlooked these earlier, wouldn't you say?'

To his credit he didn't rise to the bait.

'Flowers described a man, you said "person".'

'Miss Flowers was far too woolly, no more certain than I could be, and I didn't see them. It would be easy enough for a woman to put on a disguise, then who'd know the difference, especially in the dark? Let's keep an open mind for now.'

Sawyer had lived near Kenilworth all of his life, close by Edie Bridgnorth, who'd worked for the vicar, so there was a chance they'd have crossed paths.

'Did you know Reverend Beattie, John?'

'Not really. I'd met him once or twice but couldn't have put a name on him.'

'You didn't attend his services then?'

'Oh no, he'd have been church and we'd have been chapel.'

'Sorry?'

'Reverend Beattie was Church of England; we're Methodists, at least my mum and dad are. Don't go too often myself these days.'

'Why not?'

'Suppose I got out of the habit. When I left school, my parents said if I was old enough to put bread on the table I was old enough to decide where I'd worship. Being not much more than a child and offered a free choice I decided I wouldn't bother with any of them. A mistake. You do something else with your Sunday mornings for a while and then you're embarrassed to go back. I still believe in God and everything, just not sure how to put it into practice.'

I hadn't appreciated that Sawyer shared the same doubts as me. If I'd considered his religious persuasion at all I'd have pictured him trotting off to church every week, perhaps even leading a bible study class afterwards. I also found his surprise at my suggestion he worshipped within the same church as the vicar interesting. It made it clear my ignorance of splits in

Christianity was at least as bad as Sawyer's would have been on Judaism.

Sawyer took me through the interviews he'd conducted and showed me where they were in the file. Trimble had restricted my partner's involvement to interviewing the brothel's neighbours, the thankless plodding round the streets trying to find someone who may have seen something.

When we reached the end of his material I could see he wanted to ask me something.

'Go ahead, John, ask away. I can see you're itching to.'

'France, sir, did you find anything?'

'No, I didn't. People are moving all over the place and my uncle is only one in thousands. I've made some contacts who are putting out feelers but there's not much hope.'

'Is it bad there?'

'Not yet, but it will be. Why?'

He paused.

'Come on, spit it out.'

'I'm going to join up.'

'Great God, John, why on earth would you do that?'

'It just seems the right thing to do. I could stay here and keep the peace or do something worthwhile for my country.'

'But you are doing something worthwhile. Any idiot can shoot and be shot at, it takes someone special to protect their community. You're good at your job and can only get better.'

'That's kind of you to say, sir, but I'll never be as good as you. I just don't have it. Besides, I want to see the world. When you were my age you were travelling everywhere, to places I can only imagine. I don't want to spend my life walking the streets of Kenilworth and looking after my dad's farm. I used to think I did, but now I'm not so certain.'

I sympathised with him. I'd left home and gone to sea when I was young, to escape the constraints of my family, and it was one of the better decisions in my life. Who was I to tell Sawyer he shouldn't leave? But the idea of him joining the army filled me with horror. The Germans killed too many good men on the Somme, and I didn't want him to go the same way in this war. There was nowhere for this conversation to go, so I muttered a few strong words of discouragement like "mindless" and "stupid" then sent him off to work on the murder file.

EIGHT

Benny Grainger would be considered handsome if not for prolific acne and a mouth fixed with a sly grin, enhanced at some point by a knife blade. One copper at the station told me a gang, not happy with the way he ran his girls, chased Benny out of Coventry. He'd had this house in Kenilworth for about four years and was only now in his mid-twenties so must have started the "business" young. He picked at his nails and shot glances in every direction all the while we talked, and I wondered if this was because of drugs rather than inherent nervousness.

'So Benny, tell me, the vicar, regular customer?'

'Can't give out that sort of information, Mr Given, wouldn't be right now would it?'

He winked, his grin widened, and I laughed.

'What is this, some code of honour? The man's dead and he came to your establishment once or twice a month. Let's be clear. What you're up to is against the law. You might think you're providing a public service, but the judge would have a different view and send you down for a few years. So give me the truth and I won't have to bring my boys down here to clean up the place. Understand?'

The grin disappeared as far as it was able.

'No need to be like that, is there, Mr Given? Only saying I've people's reputations to worry about. Ask me what you want, and I'll help if I can.'

'Very sensible, Benny. Now, we've already agreed that Reverend Beattie used your place frequently. How well did you know him?'

'Hardly at all. Didn't know he was a vicar, that's for sure. Bit of a laugh that, isn't it? Tarts and vicars.'

The grin flickered again, but he clearly thought better of it.

'So you didn't know him outside, how shall I put it, your commercial arrangements?'

'Nah. Never does to mix business and pleasure. That's what I'm always telling my ladies. He turned up when he felt the urge, paid his money, did what he needed to do, then left. And you'd be guessing I'd not be hot-footing it to church on a Sunday morning, would I? Didn't even enquire too much about his name, none of my business.'

This man was a rogue, but he knew his place in the world. Everything was straightforward to him and though I couldn't condone what he did, he did it with an integrity of his own making.

'His wife said he had particular tastes. Any violence? Anything would make someone want to kill him?'

'Most of the gentlemen who come here have tastes, Inspector, but I never let them hurt my ladies. Turf them out on their ear I would. Did it to one feller not long back. Came in full of drink then slapped young Diana about. She screamed and we sent him home with a good kicking. Shame really, he'd been a good customer until then. As for the vic, I never heard tell of him wanting anything out of the ordinary. He liked them young and pretty, but he wasn't alone in that.'

'The room where they found him, expanding were we?'

'Now that's a funny thing, Inspector, it's not a place we'd use much. When we first set up here it seemed a good idea to have a place where our gentlemen could do some business if they needed to. If they were just in town for a meeting like. Give the place a bit of class. Never caught on. Waste of time and money. Even though it was behind the house with its own entrance, I expect they thought it would still come out what we do out front. No-one had been inside for a few weeks and don't know how the reverend would have found out about it unless one of my ladies mentioned it. As it happens I'd had an enquiry from a gentleman that day.' Grainger looked left and right, crooked a finger and lowered his voice. 'Quite well known around here, wanted somewhere private on his next visit, so I sent young Mary to tidy it up.'

'What about the key? Miss Selkirk told us the door was locked when she found him, did you have it?'

'I've a spare on my keyring I think, but there was always one left in the door; if it's not there now, I don't know where it's gone.'

'Sure?'

'Course I am.'

I let him continue fidgeting while I consulted my notes, leafing through the pages longer than needed.

'Inspector Trimble's file says you were in the house the whole time between Reverend Beattie arriving and the body being found. Is that correct?'

'That's what I told him, yes.'

'But is it correct? Two days? Seems unlikely. Didn't nip to the shop for some cigarettes? Didn't go for a pint in the evening?'

'It's the truth. I'm here all the time. Have to be sure the business runs right. If I need anything I'll send a girl or Eddie. Plenty of booze in the sideboard if I fancy one but it's not often I do.'

'Huh. You must consider me none too bright, Benny, if I'm expected to believe that.'

'Well there's nothing else to say, Inspector. I'm not lying. Why would I?'

'Maybe because there was a dead vicar found on your premises and you could have killed him.'

The look on Grainger's face was priceless. It's strange that people can shake with nerves when interviewed but are still shocked when they realise we do suspect they've committed a crime. It isn't any indicator of guilt though, just the way they are. So I went through the rest of the interview he'd had with Trimble. I found nothing new, nor any discrepancies, so thanked him for his time and asked him to send Jacqueline Flowers through to see me.

'Jacqueline? Is that your real name, miss?'

The woman, barely over twenty, brushed a blond curl from her forehead.

'No, it's Mary, but Benny likes us to sound exotic. Mary Selkirk didn't fit the bill.' She coughed, crushed a cigarette then lit another one. 'Makes no difference what they call me.'

'You told Inspector Trimble you hadn't been here long. Where were you before?'

'In Coventry. Grew up in Birmingham and Mum threw me out when I was sixteen so her fancy man could move in. Caught the train and a ticket to Coventry was all I could afford.'

'And were you Mary or Jacqueline there? Or something else?'

'Just used my own name; the bloke in Coventry didn't care about anything if you did what you was told and earned him his money.'

'So why move over here?'

'Heard Benny was setting up a new place and he approached me a while after to see if I'd join him. Some of the girls said he could cut up rough, but I always found him decent so packed my bags and came. Not a job to be in if you're fussy about the company you keep.'

'I might say the same thing myself.'

Mary laughed and brought on another cough. I'd heard that sound before, on old smokers in the dark corners of pubs, and I didn't like it. This girl might be young and might be pretty, but I doubted she'd live a long life. I began to check her previous statement, but she stopped me after the first question.

'Why are you going through this again? I told the other policeman all I know. While I'm sitting here talking I'm not earning, and Benny won't be too happy.'

'Don't worry about Mr Grainger —' I made a note on my pad — 'I'll have a word and he'll be fine. When Inspector Trimble came to see you, he was just tidying up loose ends and you'd been away when he did his first interviews. After he'd spoken to you he thought there was a possibility it might be more serious, so our boss has asked me to have a look. Happy?'

She smiled and nodded, seemingly satisfied that if I squared it with Benny Grainger then she'd stay as long as necessary. I thought it a strange relationship between the prostitutes and the pimps, both dependent on the other for their livelihood. The women taking protection from a man they feared, the pimp caring for 'his ladies' but not averse to beating one of them if they stepped out of line. Mary Selkirk was one who'd not suffer from Grainger's violence because she'd do as she was told.

'You said in your earlier interview that there was nothing unusual about the person you saw leaving. Not enough to make you remember them. Is that right?'

'It is. I've tried to think if there was something about him but nothing's coming.'

'You're certain it was a man though?'

She laughed again, grimmer this time.

'I've known enough men in enough places, in daylight and in dark, to know one when I see one. They move different somehow.'

In the same way Arnold Pemberton saw the subtleties of handwriting, this woman read the subtleties of men. A specialist in her own way, though I doubted I could bring her into a court of law as an expert witness. For the time being I was now prepared to accept we were looking for a man.

We trudged through answer after answer she'd provided to Trimble, without a single one becoming clearer, some even more muddled than before. I began to lose patience, raising my voice more than I intended.

'Come on, Mary, give me something. There must be something.'

She cowered in her chair, perhaps fearing a violent assault to come.

'The only thing I can think of is his shoes.'

I softened my voice and measured my next words.

'Shoes? What about them?'

'Good quality, that's all. Polished so bright the light reflected when he passed through the gate. My dad was a cobbler and when I was little, before Mum got rid of him for his drinking, he'd sit me on his knee in his workshop and explain about the ones he was fixing. Tell me which belonged to gentlemen and which to working men.'

'Why didn't you tell this to Inspector Trimble?'

Again she flinched, and I shuddered to think of the pain she must endure every day from the men she went with.

'It's all right, Mary, I'm not angry with you, it's just that any little detail could be important.'

'I didn't remember when I spoke to the other policeman, only when you were asking again. The dark hid most of the man, but I can now see the light glinting off those leather shoes clear as anything.'

Since my original, disastrous, visit to the mortuary Walter Naismith had gone off for a holiday to a fortnight of golf and walks with his dogs in the sunshine somewhere on the south coast. I needed to speak to his colleague about the latest information and drove over with dread, fearing that being there again would bring everything back to the surface.

I wasn't sure I liked George Porter. He greeted me in a business-like manner but with no warmth, though this was the first time we'd met, and I was hoping he might improve. Walter and I were, if not friends, then close professionally. We'd never met outside work, but we'd shared stories of our low times when drinking and he'd stood by me when the job was getting on top.

Porter pulled his notes from a filing cabinet beside the desk, then skimmed the opening page.

'Beattie. Reverend Duncan. Church of England vicar. Male. Five feet eleven inches. Fifty-six years of age. No scars or distinguishing features. Found hanged in a brothel. That your man?'

I said it was.

'Death by asphyxiation. Conclusion suicide in Dr Naismith's autopsy, reported to the Coroner by me a few days ago.' He looked up. 'What's changed?'

I explained it had emerged there was a locked door with no key, that we'd now found someone who'd witnessed a man leaving the scene, and that Arnold Pemberton had concluded the suicide note wasn't Beattie's.

'Ah. Seems like we might have jumped the gun then doesn't it, Inspector?' The pathologist raised an eyebrow. 'But not information you provided earlier, was it?'

'That's because I wasn't here.'

'Pardon?'

'I said I wasn't here. I never concluded suicide, I was in France when your office and Inspector Trimble looked at the evidence. If you got it wrong then it's not my fault.'

'Please don't take that tone, Inspector.' Porter flushed now. 'I wasn't accusing anyone.'

'It certainly sounded like you were accusing me.'

'Well someone in your department wasn't doing their job were they?'

'That's as maybe, but it wasn't me. You know damned well that new evidence comes to light constantly. It's nobody's fault when someone who can point to an alternative conclusion goes away for a holiday soon after the vicar's disappearance. Without her, they had nothing to suggest it was any more than a straightforward suicide.'

'I agree, and so you can't expect us to have come to any different conclusion with what we had in front of us.' He sighed and leaned back in his chair. 'Let's start again shall we, Inspector. As well as the new witness, you're saying someone had locked Reverend Beattie in after his death with a suicide note which now turns out to have been forged. Correct?'

'Yes.'

He ran his finger through the notes until settling on the line he was searching for.

'That might explain the barbitone in his blood.'

'Barbitone? Isn't that a sedative?'

'It is. A medium strength barbiturate. I'd assumed he'd just taken a pill or two to calm his nerves before doing the deed. I've seen that before.'

'Where would someone get hold of it?'

'Well almost anywhere, Inspector. It's commonly prescribed for women with a nervous disposition. In crystal form it dissolves in water, and the capsules are easy to take with few side effects. I'd suggest that in this case it may have been used to knock out the victim before the killer hanged him. Bit easier than trying to do it when he was alive and kicking. In small doses barbitone is intended to calm the nerves, but double that dose and it's night, night, sleep tight. A significant amount might kill a person, but I wouldn't guarantee it.'

I inquired if there was anything else they had discounted as not relevant. Perhaps there was the merest hint in my voice I thought he'd been sloppy.

'Listen, Inspector Given, I think we may have started on the wrong foot. If I annoyed you in the way I responded to the new information then I apologise. Mistakes happen, it's the nature of the work. Yours and mine. We'd have ignored the drug because it's common and could have been prescribed; at the time everything pointed to the man topping himself. One thing I do know is that we're both on the same side. Both of us wants to make sure that the people who cross our paths get the justice they deserve. Am I right?'

I looked at him hard for a few seconds, trying to decide if this was just some kind of conciliatory speech perfected for when he'd rubbed colleagues up the wrong way. I decided, for the moment, that it was a genuine and extended a hand.

'Apology accepted. Sorry if I over-reacted.'

Porter smiled graciously and I asked if he'd arrived at a time of death yet. He skimmed the findings.

'We found it difficult to estimate an accurate time other than knowing he'd been hanging for more than one day. If I had to hazard a guess, off the record, I'd conclude Beattie died sometime on Wednesday evening, not too long after the record says he was last seen.'

'Anything to back that up?'

'The weather was mild, and he was indoors. In those conditions his body temperature would have taken about a day to drop to the same as the room, then wouldn't go any lower, so he'd been dead more than a day. That takes us to Thursday evening if they found him on Friday afternoon, doesn't it?'

I nodded.

'Rigor mortis had set in but not been through all its stages so suggests death somewhere between thirty and forty-five hours beforehand. Following?'

'Yes, thanks.'

'In addition, the body had become pretty whiffy, so I'd say Wednesday evening is as close as we'll get. Odd though, don't you think?'

'What's that?'

'To hang him. If you're putting a drug in someone's drink, which is how I assume they did this, then why not go the whole hog and just poison them? Why go to the trouble of knocking the vicar out then string him up? Seems like the killer was making a statement, doesn't it?'

Tied in with Beattie wearing his clerical outfit, something he'd have been unlikely to do for a night in the brothel, I had to admit this made perfect sense.

I phoned Sawyer from the pathologist's office and said to grab the evidence file.

After a few minutes he phoned me back.

'Got it, sir. What are we looking for?'

'Go through the list of stuff in the outhouse. What was there other than the furniture? Any cups, glasses, that kind of thing?'

I heard him flicking the pages, stopping when he found what he wanted, then murmuring the contents.

'Here it is, sir. Two empty beer bottles and two glasses, both half full.'

'Good. I thought I remembered something; get down there and collect them. Have them sent over here to Mr Porter as soon as possible. Is there a record of any other clothes?'

'Give me a minute.'

The pages turned again.

'No, sir, not that I can see. Why?'

'Because the pathologist thinks someone drugged Beattie before they hanged him, and I don't believe he'd have gone to Beeches Lane in his church outfit. Why would he? He wasn't known there as a vicar and it would have exposed him to blackmail. It's more likely that his killer changed the clothes after Beattie was unconscious.'

'Seems a tiny bit weird, doesn't it, sir?'

'Certainly does, John, but it stands up as a theory. Now you'd best get off and collect those glasses.'

'Yes sir.'

'And John.'

'Yes?'

'Don't spill any. And don't be tempted to take a swig, else you won't make it back.'

NINE

George Porter rang back next morning, when he'd had time to test the items I'd had sent, confirming one bottle and one glass contained traces of barbitone. Not a high dose but enough to put someone out for a few hours.

I hung up and told Sawyer.

'And this sedative is mainly prescribed to women, sir?'

'The doc says it is. Used to treat nerves.'

'So —'

'I know, I know. We can't now trust the testimony from Jacqueline, or Mary, or whatever she calls herself, one hundred percent. I was convinced she had enough expertise in these matters, but this shows our killer could be man or woman. Only thing to make a man more likely is the strength needed to hoist Beattie from his chair. Even that wouldn't be beyond the realms of possibility with a strongish woman and the rope slung over a beam.'

'What if two people were involved? That would make it easier.'

I shrugged. 'Possibly, though the girl only saw one heading out of the gate.'

'Depends on how long she looked outside, doesn't it?'

'Granted, it does, we'd better ask her again, but what about the fact there were only two used glasses, not three, in the room?'

'Perhaps one didn't drink.'

Once Sawyer gets an idea in his head he sticks with it. His tenacity can be productive and means he'll look at anything that supports his current theory. This thoroughness helps develop a case, pulling random strands together which in the end convince a jury. On the negative side, it can blinker him to other options, and it annoys me because he's a good copper in many other ways.

'I've said it's a possibility, John, and we'll keep it in mind, but I don't think it's likely. I'm having enough trouble trying to figure out why even one person would want to murder a country vicar without complicating it by adding another one into the mix. Let's stick with the one for the time being. If that doesn't hold water we'll come back to your suggestion.'

Sawyer gave a slight shake to his head and flipped his notebook closed. 'Fine, sir, you're the boss. Anyone in mind?'

'Not yet, male or female. It would be someone the vicar knew well enough to share a drink with. Also someone he wouldn't suspect wanted to do him harm. My gut tells me they'd know the house was a brothel but, then again, they might not. The outhouse where he was found has a separate entrance, and you can't tell what goes on inside the house from the back. Not unless you peek through the window, and even then it's not obvious.'

'So what do we do next?'

'You'd best see if any of the girls at Beeches Lane are prescribed this barbitone. I'll drive over to ask the widow.'

'Will do, sir. I've been thinking about what Dr Porter said about the hanging being some kind of statement.'

'And?'

'I wondered if it was a warning.'

'Good point, John. But a warning to who? And what about? I'm not sure it answers any questions but certainly something to keep in mind.'

I let Sawyer leave to get on with his interviews and jotted a note on my pad.

Why hanging? Ritual? Revenge? A warning? Cover-up?

Janet Beattie scowled when she opened the door.

'Good afternoon, Inspector, I didn't expect to see you again so soon. I believe I told you everything last time.'

'I'm sorry if you're finding our investigation of your husband's murder tiresome, madam.'

'That's not what I meant.'

'It certainly sounded like it, but no matter. Whether you like it or not, I'll carry on doing my best to identify his killer.'

Janet Beattie stared me in the eyes for a moment then invited me inside and we went to the sitting room again. The curtains were now open, flooding the room with light. There were half-filled boxes in the corner.

'Are you moving away?'

'There's no choice, is there? The vicarage is for the vicar, not the vicar's wife. Don't get me wrong, the parish has been generous, they're letting me stay in the gate lodge until I find somewhere more suitable. Another inconvenience caused by the death of my husband.'

'Inconvenience? That's an odd word to use.'

She looked at me blankly for a few seconds.

'Oh. I expect it is. But that's what it amounts to.'

'The two of you don't seem to have been close.'

'No.' She stood and looked out of the window. 'Actually, it's more complicated than that. We were never what people would describe as a devoted couple. Met late in life, both in our mid-forties, and liked each other's company. My family insisted I should marry, and I had some money to support myself. Duncan wanted a wife to get a parish of his own. Some might see it as a marriage of expediency, but it was much more; we needed each other.'

'Needed?'

'I imagine that's the right word. Apart from achieving the practical benefits, we'd become friends before we married, and this grew afterwards. There were, as I've said, practical benefits and he didn't make any, how shall I put it...' She looked away. 'Demands. You said we weren't close, but we were. Just as friends, no more. There's a lot to be said for support and a listening ear at the end of each day. It wouldn't surprise me if many marriages are like that, no romantic love, no great passion, just muddling along helping one another when necessary.'

I had no doubt she was right.

'He hadn't been a vicar long when you met him?'

'He'd only been ordained a few years before and wasn't even a vicar, just a curate. Duncan had his eye on this parish, and they appointed him soon after we married. My husband told me little of his earlier life except that he'd travelled a lot and spent some time working for a company in Egypt. He always said the poverty and inhumanity he'd seen on his travels brought him to Jesus, hoping he might bring a little good into the world.'

'Is there anything he told you from that time which might make you suspect his life could be in danger?'

Mrs Beattie breathed deep and shook her head.

'Nothing. He'd not been himself in recent weeks, but when I asked him about it he'd said he was struggling with his faith because the world stayed as full of pain and sorrow as it had ever been. He'd been most concerned about Herr Hitler and what he'd been reading in the newspapers. Duncan also had a new curate and was wondering how best to support him.'

'Did your husband have life insurance, Mrs Beattie?'

'Thank the Lord he did, otherwise I'd be near enough destitute.'

'But you said you had money.'

'"Had" is the operative word, Inspector. Duncan imagined it important to keep up appearances, so we lived well beyond his means. Little by little my nest egg has disappeared. In some ways it's a blessing he's gone; we'd not have survived financially for much longer without him having to cut back.'

'So you stand to profit by his death.'

A laugh exploded.

'Hardly. There's enough to bury him and the rest might cover my rent until I find a job.'

I couldn't fathom this woman. She'd said she and her husband were close friends, and that she tolerated his infidelities, but I detected bitterness every time she spoke of him.

'Are you still trying to suggest I had something to do with Duncan's death?'

I wasn't convinced either way but had to find a way of discounting her or pushing her up the list of suspects.

'You know as well as I do, Mrs Beattie, that we need to explore every possibility in a murder case. Until I'm certain you, or anyone else close, didn't kill him I must keep asking the questions. Tell me, do you take a sedative of any description?'

'I do. Veronal. Why?'

Veronal was one of the trade names of the barbiturate found in Beattie's bloodstream.

'Because someone drugged your husband with one before they killed him.'

The hand clasped to her mouth didn't stop the gasp escaping.

'I … I don't understand. Why would anyone do that?' Her eyes clouded and took her, bewildered, to another place. After a moment she drifted back. 'And you think I drugged him?'

'You had the means.'

'But so do most of my friends. Doctors perceive women as more nervous than men, more in need of medicine to calm them down. Sedatives are prescribed as if they are bon-bons.'

I asked if she'd fetch hers. She left the room and I heard her climbing the stairs then, in a few minutes, coming down more slowly, empty handed when she returned.

'My pills are not there, Inspector.'

Edward Winston was a tall, elegant young man, with aesthetic features enhanced by wire-rimmed spectacles. The curate occupied a self-contained wing of the vicarage and invited me in when Mrs Beattie explained who I was. The space was smaller, less homely than the one lived in by the vicar and his wife. Perhaps this was purposeful, intended to demonstrate the hierarchy and showing the transience of men in his position, the rooms never being occupied by one person for long enough to stamp some personality on them. Winston had also been packing. I pointed to his boxes.

'Will you be taking over from Reverend Beattie, Mr Winston?'

He gave a violent shake of his head.

'Oh no. Well, only for a short while because the parish asked me to.'

'Why not permanently?'

'Reverend Beattie meant a lot to me. He taught me so much and we were almost friends. I can't believe he's gone. I … I could never step into his shoes.'

'Had you known him a long time?'

'Only six months. I came here straight after finishing my training but he and Janet, sorry, Mrs Beattie, were so kind to me. We spent occasional evenings together, especially on Sundays after the services finished. Over a bottle of beer, we'd discuss the news or his book collection. Sometimes he'd help me.'

'In what way?'

'I'd become unsure I was cut out for a life in the Church after all. When I entered the ministry, I imagined I would fill my days with prayer and learning, not church fetes and visiting old ladies. The vicar would talk to me about what I'd done each week and try to explain how those little things still served God and did His work.'

'He sounds like a caring man. Are you aware he was murdered?'

Winston closed his eyes and squeezed the lids with his thumb and forefinger. I hoped he wouldn't break down.

'Mrs Beattie told me after your last visit. Who would do such a thing?'

I shrugged.

'We have no idea yet. Have you any thoughts on who might want to harm him?'

There was a long pause. So long I had to prompt him again.

'Mr Winston?'

'Sorry, Inspector Given, I've been racking my brains since I heard the news and it's beyond my comprehension how one human being can kill another, let alone one as kind and generous as Reverend Beattie.'

'So there's nothing.'

'I don't know, Inspector. As I say, I struggle to understand but he'd upset two people recently. I doubt it would impel either of them to murder him, but I expect I'm not equipped to judge.'

I asked him who they were and what it was about.

'He sacked the handyman, Robbie Wilkes. I didn't see it happen, but there was a small problem with the lock on my door and when I asked the vicar to get Robbie to look at it he snapped at me. "That damned fellow has gone" he said. I could see he was in a bad mood so didn't ask any more.'

'Didn't you say the vicar was a kind man?'

'He was, but he wasn't perfect. None of us are. Reverend Beattie had good days and difficult ones just like you and me. If someone upset him then he would give as good as he got.'

'So this man Wilkes had done something to put him in a temper.'

'As I said, I didn't see what happened between them.'

'And the other person?'

The curate screwed up his face.

'Oh, a most unpleasant young lady. I popped my head out into the hall when I heard raised voices and saw Reverend Beattie arguing with her on the doorstep, though I only caught the end of it then he slammed the door in her face. His final words were "Get out of here Miss Bridgnorth before I call the police" and I'd never seen him so angry. Shaking he was, and usually such a quiet and caring man.'

'Any idea what they were arguing about?'

'No. I asked if everything was all right and he said it was nothing, just some silly girl trying to take advantage of his good nature.'

'When was this?'

Winston thought for a moment.

'I'm trying to be clear in my head. I'd be almost certain it was three days before they found him, the same day he sacked

Robbie.' This fey young man looked on the verge of tears once more. 'The last day we spoke.'

I cursed Phil Trimble's slackness again. If he'd interviewed the curate, it might have thrown at least a little doubt on suicide being the only conclusion. Any doubt at all might have led the pathologist to make more of the drugs in the vicar's blood and led to Beattie's wife revealing her thoughts on the validity of her husband's note. We could be two weeks further forward in our investigations. Two weeks in which the killer had time to cover their tracks or escape the area altogether.

TEN

Back at the station I'd spoken to two of the town coppers, Bert Willis and Graham Speck. Only Speck recognised the curate's description of the woman who'd argued with Beattie.

'If I'm right, her first name's Edie. Drinks a lot. Can be found hanging around the town pubs almost any time, day or night. Never been in trouble to my knowledge, but we've had to help her home from a park bench once or twice.'

Sawyer recognised her and provided her surname.

'Edie Bridgnorth. Strange woman. Quiet and respectable when she was younger. Not well off but in a steady enough job at the timber yard. Seemed to go off the rails after her father died. There was talk it was because of a man she got involved with who threw her over, though I wouldn't be certain, you know how these rumours get up. Anyway, she started going to the worst pubs in town, places where a woman shouldn't be seen. Soon the drink got to her and she was out night after night, boozing and having a good time.'

'I'll go looking for her later when the pubs open. It would be useful to have someone with me who knows her, someone she'd trust more than a stranger. Do you fancy coming along?'

'I had planned on being out tonight, sir.'

'Oh. Well that's not a problem, don't change your arrangements for me.'

'Are you sure, sir?'

'Certainly. I thought it might be an opportunity for you to be involved with different aspects of the case; you'll never learn if I keep you on the mundane stuff. Expect you had a bellyful of that with Phil Trimble.'

Sawyer thought for a moment before grinning.

'It was only a night drinking with the mates, there'll be others. If you want me to join you I will, and thanks for the opportunity.'

The knot dissolved from my stomach because having him along would keep me off the bottle. Ever since the call from my father asking me to go to France I'd had a hard time staying on the wagon, barely able to fight the urge to drink so I could smother the reminders of past cases and a dead girlfriend. So far I'd succeeded but spending a night wandering round Kenilworth pubs on my own might be a step too far.

Sawyer finished talking to Graham Speck as I arrived outside the police station at six o'clock. He'd picked up that Edie Bridgnorth was often found in the Duke of York in the early evening, so we tried there first. On the way I told him I'd been out to Robbie Wilkes' home.

'Did you speak to him, sir?'

'There was no sign. I knocked front and back but got no answer. Place is a dump.'

'Not known for his cleanliness, isn't Robbie. Bit too fond of the bottle.' He shot me a look. 'Sorry, sir, I … I didn't mean anything.'

'Don't worry, John. Thick skin.'

We found Edie in the second pub we visited, having had no luck at the Duke. She was sitting at the bar with a whisky and water in front of her. Not the first of the day. Edie was well under thirty but could be mistaken for ten years older. If the drink and years hadn't been so unkind she'd have stayed an attractive woman. The man on the stool beside Edie nudged her elbow when we came in, a superfluous action as the entire room fell quiet the second we stepped through the door. I can't believe policemen smell different or look different out of uniform, but this is something we expect in the seedier pubs. Edie's companion made himself scarce when it was clear he wasn't the one we were after.

Sawyer made the introductions.

'What do you want?' Her voice was slurred. Her brown, woollen coat was stained, and she carried the whiff of booze which would always be around a heavy drinker. 'Ain't done nothing.'

I suggested we took a table in the corner and the barman nodded when she looked at him for guidance.

'Don't I know you?' she said to Sawyer when we sat down.

'You used to live near me, Edie, with your mum and dad. Down the road, near the crossroads. Remember?'

She stared at him through the alcohol fog, rubbing her chin for a few seconds before slapping her thigh. 'Now I've got you. Bank Farm. Near the crossroads.' She began to snivel. 'That was before my dad died.' As quickly as they'd come, the tears stopped. 'You a copper now?'

Sawyer confirmed the obvious and told Edie we needed to talk to her about Reverend Beattie. She spit on the floor.

'Didn't like that man. Shouted at me he did, and all I wanted was a bob for a drink.' She looked at her empty glass then at me.

I shook my head. 'Not now, Edie, maybe later when we've had our chat.'

'All right, officer, fire away. Let's get it over with.'

'How well did you know Reverend Beattie?'

'Used to work for him. Well, for his missus really. He never had anything to do with me, but I seen him coming in and out of the kitchen.'

'What work did you do?'

'Only a skivvy. Cleaning. Lighting the fires. That kind of thing. Shouldn't have been working at all really, should have been at school. A kid I was, but Dad said we needed the money and schooling was a waste of time for girls.'

Sawyer butted in.

'Sorry, Edie, I don't understand. If you were a child when you worked for his wife, and Reverend Beattie didn't know you, why were you arguing at his house?'

She laughed. 'Not listening were you. Didn't know me when I worked there I said. Knew me well enough later.' She looked down her body. 'When I'd filled out some.'

I picked up the thread. 'So you met him again after you left?'

'In the pubs. Every couple of weeks he'd turn up at one. No-one guessed he was a reverend though, 'spect he lived too far away. I didn't let on. Not many in these places would be at church anyway. Didn't use his real name either, Albert Green he called himself. Always eyeing up the ladies he'd be. Most nights left with one as well, them as not too fussy and glad of a few shillings. Tried it on with me once or twice, but I said to sling his hook. Could be I drink more than I should, and enjoy a laugh with the fellers, but I'm not that kind of woman. Not to go off with a married man, no thank you.'

She lifted her empty glass and peered inside.

'In a minute, Edie, you're doing well. Tell me, why were you at his house shouting the odds on the doorstep?'

'Do I have to say?'

'No. Not if you don't want to. But we'd have to take you down to the station and put you in the cells until we get around to asking you again. Much easier all round to tell us now, isn't it?'

Edie lifted her eyes to the ceiling and tutted.

'Not something I'm proud of. I was skint. Flat broke. Otherwise I'd never have done it. Mr Beattie had been in the pub a week before and started chatting me up, telling me how pretty I was and how he'd like to take me somewhere. Told him again I wasn't interested, and he left in a huff. Expect to that house where they found him, I heard he went there a lot. Anyway, as I was saying, I needed money and the idea came into my daft head to go out to his place and say I'd tell his wife if he didn't come up with some. Thought he'd pay to keep me quiet and that would be the end of it.'

'But he didn't.'

'No, he didn't. Laughed in my face at first, said I was a silly little girl and his wife would never believe me. I told him I'd bring witnesses if that's how he wanted it, and he bellowed to clear off or he'd call the police. With all the racket that other vicar looked in and Beattie slammed the door in my face.'

Sawyer had another go. 'I bet that made you angry.'

'It did. Made me hopping mad.'

'So you lured him to Beeches Lane and killed him.'

Edie Bridgnorth jumped up from her chair, knocking it backwards to the ground.

'What? No! I'd never do that.'

I grabbed her forearm. 'Sit down Edie. Everyone is looking at you.'

She stood shaking for a minute then did as I told her. 'Honest, Mr Given, I didn't kill Reverend Beattie. I swore a lot when I marched off, borrowed the cash from a mate and poured it down my neck to forget about him.'

'You're telling me you let it go?'

'It's true.'

'Well we'll need to think about that. Where were you the night after you visited his house? It was a Wednesday. About two weeks ago.'

She snorted.

'How'd you 'spect me to remember something like that? In the pub I 'spect. Usually am.'

'Any pub in particular?'

'Been spending a lot of time in the Cat and Fiddle. Landlord's a gent. You could ask in there.'

'Don't you worry, Edie, we will, and if it turns out you're lying we'll be after you quick as a flash.'

I left Sawyer to buy Edie the promised drink, but before I did I pulled him to one side.

'See she gets home safely after that one; afterwards go around to the pub she mentioned to check her story. If you get any witnesses make sure you can believe them, if they're drinking as much as she does.'

He looked at his watch.

'Sorry John, it'll only take you half an hour. I'll follow up on Robbie Wilkes tomorrow morning and later we'll meet to discuss progress.'

There are pretty country cottages occupied by elderly spinsters, with immaculate gardens and roses round the door, and there are labourer's cottages, run-down and neglected by tenant and landlord, a place to sleep when a hard day's work is done. Robbie Wilkes' cottage was the latter type, with moss covering the roof and paint peeling from the doors and windows. A small garden was piled with the debris of a farming life: wire fencing, timber posts and tools that would have been old when Adam was a lad. Wilkes rubbed the sleep from his eyes when he opened the door at half past eight in the morning. He looked in his late-thirties and as grubby as if he'd crawled out from under the mounds of rubbish.

'What're you knockin' for? What you want?'

'Police, Mr Wilkes. Can I have a minute?'

He expressed no surprise, merely turned on his heels and wandered into the murk.

'Better come in I suppose.'

The inside was only marginally tidier than the garden. Every surface, other than one armchair, was stacked with newspaper, cardboard, empty food tins, bits of rope and lots of other rubbish I couldn't identify. The fire hadn't been lit and dirty dishes filled the sink. Wilkes cleared a second chair and invited me to sit down. I wasn't sure I wanted to.

'Not working today, Mr Wilkes? Robbie, isn't it?'

He nodded and coughed, deep and full of phlegm. The kind of cough a man gets when he's abused cigarettes and alcohol for too many years.

'Not feelin' too good. Might go in later.'

'You've got a job then?'

Wilkes looked down at his feet. 'Not exactly.'

'That's what I heard. Why I'm here you might say.'

His brow furrowed.

'You've some work for me?'

'No, not at all, it's about your last one. Reverend Beattie sacked you. You picked up he's dead?'

'I heard that.'

'Did you have a grudge, Robbie?'

The furrow deepened.

'A grudge, surely, but I wouldn't 'ave killed 'im. Wouldn't 'ave got my job back, would it, so what'd be the point?'

There was a perfect logic in what he said, but murderers seldom act with logic. It's often either a fit of temper or perhaps a minor insult most people would brush away. One which festers away inside until it explodes into violence against the offender.

'You'd better tell me what happened.'

'The Reverend was always a good man to me, but he could 'ave 'is moods and he 'ad a fine one on 'im that day. You can see, Inspector, I'm not at my best in the mornings, take a bit o' time to get going, but Mr Beattie never seemed to mind in the past. Even joked about it sometimes, 'e did. I turned up late as usual that day, just after young Edie 'ad the door slammed in 'er face. She used some words a decent woman shouldn't be usin' when I asked 'er what was goin' on.'

'You're friends with Edie Bridgnorth then?'

'Known 'er since she were a young 'un workin' for the Beatties.' He sniffed and wiped his nose on his sleeve. 'Can't say we're friends though. Don't get on.'

'Why's that?'

Wilkes squirmed. 'Don't know. I like 'er, but she don't seem to like me.'

I told him to continue his account of his sacking.

'Well, I carried on to work round the back. Mrs Beattie wanted a second shed building at the bottom of the garden, a "summer 'ouse" she called it, and I'd got to the point of puttin' the roof on. I'm just liftin' the ladder out and next thing, the reverend storms out of the vicarage, face as red as you like, and tears me off a strip for bein' late. Told me I'd done it once too often and no-one was goin' to take advantage of 'im. Said to collect my things and get out.'

'So what did you do, Robbie?'

'What could I do? I apologised and said it wouldn't 'appen again, but 'e was havin' none of it. Just pointed to the front gate and said 'e'd 'ad enough. He slipped an extra bob in my pay packet though, so maybe 'e was sorry afterwards.'

'It still seems to me you'd be angry after being treated like that. Anyone might.'

Wilkes nodded.

'You're right, Inspector. A body shouldn't be treated that way. It's not fair.'

'And you thought you'd get your own back, did you, teach the vicar a lesson?'

'No, no, I didn't. As I say, the Reverend was decent with me until then. And in a way 'e 'ad a point, I was takin' advantage of 'is good nature. I might 'ave done the same if I'd been 'im. It was only a job. I'll get another when I'm ready. Not worth killin' a man over, you can 'ave my word on that.'

Wilkes seemed like he might be telling the truth, but I've seen villains who'd steal the gold watch from your pocket and tell you straight faced they'd nothing to do with it. It's almost as if badness and the ability to tell a good lie are two sides of the same coin.

'That's easy enough to say, Robbie, but we'll need more than your word. So, the night after he sacked you. Where were you? All night, mind, and next morning.'

Sawyer had been down to the canteen for a break and pushed open my office door then kicked it closed behind him. I carried on from where we'd left off.

'So, Wilkes told me he'd been to Coventry for the night. Had a few pints with pals. Apparently that's where he always drinks.

Said he doesn't like the Kenilworth pubs. Took one too many, he says, and missed the last bus so had to walk home.'

He laughed as he placed two steaming mugs of tea on my desk. 'That's Robbie.'

'Took him nearly two hours. Claims he was so tired when he got back he took straight to bed and didn't wake until next midday. He's provided the names of his friends but, of course, none of them would have seen him after he left. So he's no-one to vouch for his movements until he turned up at the pub again the next evening.'

'But Robbie Wilkes wouldn't kill anyone, sir. Older than me but I've known him for years. We went to the same school,' he laughed again, 'when he bothered to turn up.'

'Same school? He looks much older than you.'

'Oh, not at the same time. He left years before I started. Always hanging around the gates though. Never heard tell of him being violent or fighting. And as for figuring out how to drug and hang someone, he wouldn't have the brains.'

'Oh dear, John, what are we to do with you? Your faith in people is touching but misguided. You'll learn soon enough in this job that anyone can be a killer. Even you.'

His face reddened. 'Me? Is that what you really think?'

'Calm down, John, I'm simply saying that if particular circumstances arise anyone can kill.'

'Not me.'

'Yes, you. Didn't you tell me you're considering joining up? What will you do then? Talk nicely to the Germans and they'll give back Poland?'

'That's not the same and you know it.'

Now he was on his feet. I'd touched a nerve.

'It is. The only difference is that we call it war and not murder. They'll give you a rifle, teach you how to aim it, and expect you to kill as many of the enemy as you can. And you'll do as they tell you. Admit it.'

'It's not the same.'

'Yes it is, John. Anyway, this is getting us nowhere, sit down and let's get on. Did you check Edie Bridgnorth's alibi?'

I expected him to go into a sulk, but he did as I asked, slurped the hot tea and pulled himself together.

'I did and there's a problem. It seems the landlord of the Cat and Fiddle had a family emergency that evening and had to close the pub at half past seven for a few hours until he found his wife's precious cat. He opened again later and confirms Edie was there before and after but doesn't know where she was in between. He said she was pretty drunk when he closed the first time, so she might have been sleeping it off somewhere.'

'So we're no further forward. Two people, both drunks, argue with the vicar not long before he's found dead and neither have alibis. But neither of the arguments looks serious enough to have sent them into a murderous rage and neither of the suspects seems to be bright enough to have come up with a complicated plan to do away with him.'

'What do we do then?'

'Well first thing you'll do is check that your friend Robbie is telling the truth. Get in touch with Coventry and ask one of their lads to talk to his mates, then check the times of the buses and what time he'd have got home if he left when the pubs closed.'

'But that's just a waste of effort, sir. Robbie wouldn't have hurt the vicar. I'm certain.'

I walked over and swung open the door. 'Please don't ever tell me I'm wasting your time, John, or that you're certain. You don't have the experience for it. You need to learn that nothing is certain until we're sure the right person is behind bars and even then we get it wrong often enough. Now not another word. Off you go and see what you can find out.'

Sawyer pulled himself to his not inconsiderable full height, glared at me then shook his head and left. I sat for a few minutes trying to figure out what was going on between us. Something in his manner was getting to me and I was reacting. Was it him or was it me?

ELEVEN

The spat with Sawyer put me in poor humour so I stayed in my office until the pubs opened, dealing with paperwork I didn't want to deal with. I wanted to find the places Beattie had frequented and talk to the regulars. I needed to understand more about this man who, by most accounts, was caring and kind, yet something made the vicar a target for murder. This was no random act. Beattie had been killed by someone he knew. Someone he'd take a drink with and trust enough to meet at the brothel. But someone who'd hate him enough to drug him, change his clothes, forge a note, and stage his suicide by hanging.

As I walked away from the police station it struck me how normal life continued in the town. Apart from everyone carrying gasmasks and the reduced numbers of young men on the streets, you'd not appreciate we were a country at war. There were the hastily built air-raid shelters and an observation tower on Knowle Hill, where you could see the barrage balloons and gun placements in Coventry, but that seemed another world. In Kenilworth, people were going about their business as usual.

You'd steer clear of five pubs in the centre of town if you were in any way respectable. I'd have stayed out if I'd had a choice, but I needed to get this job done and mustn't keep asking Sawyer to protect me from myself. Edie Bridgnorth told us the vicar used the Duke of York, so I decided to go there after I'd checked the others. The landlords of two, The Mason's Arms and The Fletcher, swore they'd never seen him in their establishments when I showed them a photograph of

Beattie and reminded them of the fake name he used. I didn't believe either but I'd no proof of them lying. In the next pub, The Black Swan, they told me he called in perhaps once every couple of months, using the name Green, and would take just one pint then leave with one of the prostitutes who hung around the bar. Dan Ellis, who ran the pub, said he only noticed Beattie because he was better dressed and seemed to have a posher accent than most of his regulars, though he'd never spoken to the vicar except to take his order and give him his change.

This left me with the final pub on my list, The Talbot, one I'd never been in before. A small place with a public bar on one side of the front hallway and a locked lounge, when I tried the handle, on the other. Four men sat at the counter, all over conscription age, two nursing their pints in mutual isolation, and two in heated conversation about Hitler and the Jews. This theme was becoming discussed more over recent months and it was easy to see how the veneer of tolerance was being stripped away. The underlying dislike of Jews by many people surfaced in pubs and cafés across the country, and the vitriol expressed by the bar flies made me glad I kept my heritage hidden most of the time.

Another man sat in the corner, two drinks on the table. He jerked his head in the direction of the woman cackling as she came out of the toilets.

'Oh, Inspector, you looking for me? Didn't know you cared.'

'Hello, Edie.' She sounded the worse for wear again. 'Not this afternoon, but I'll talk to you when you're feeling better.'

She muttered something unintelligible and tottered over to the man at the table, the pair whispering and watching me all the time I stayed in the pub.

I'd done well to visit four pubs without Sawyer to keep me on the straight and narrow, but now I felt the thirst. The barman came in from his cellar, apologising as he walked towards me that he'd had to change a barrel. He stopped in his tracks and squinted over the top of his spectacles.

'Mr Given?'

'Good afternoon, Mac.' Phil McIntosh had worked in The Queen, round the corner from my cottage, and left about a year earlier but I hadn't heard where he'd moved. 'How are you?'

'Not so bad. Back playing up a bit but that's nothing new. Yourself?'

'Can't complain. Well I could but who would listen?'

Mac laughed. 'You're not wrong. Not seen you in here before, Mr Given, so I suppose this is business rather than pleasure?'

I showed him Beattie's photograph.

'Beattie, you say? Not what he called himself in here.' He pointed to the dog-collar. 'Didn't wear that thing either. Knew him as Albert Green. Soft spot for little Miss Bridgnorth over there. Anyway, what am I thinking? Can I get you a drink? Vimto isn't it?'

As he poured the blackcurrant liquid into a long glass he spoke to a loner at the bar, a man in his mid-fifties with greying hair and weathered skin.

'Henry. This is James Given. A police inspector now but used to sail the world like yourself.' McIntosh turned to me. 'This here's Henry Sturges, Mr Given, would have been in the merchant navy the same time as you. Bet you've been to the same places. Maybe even on the same ships.'

Sturges and I corrected him in unison. 'Boats, not ships.'

We laughed and the ice was broken.

I asked Mac if we might have a word in private and he led me behind the bar into the locked lounge, telling the man Sturges to shout him if anyone needed serving.

'What can I do for you, Mr Given? That lot in there will be fine for a while, but I don't have too long.'

'The chap you knew as Green, any idea who might want to do him harm?'

The barman scratched the back of his head.

'No-one comes to mind. Green would wander in now and again, looking for a woman, but I got rid of that sort when I moved here. Sometimes he'd stay and take a pint, trying it on with what I'd call the amateurs.'

'Amateurs?'

'You know, single women looking for company, or married ones fed up with what they've got at home. Sometimes he'd get lucky and take one off with him but mostly he'd get the brush off, like he always did with Edie. No love lost there I can tell you.'

'Why not?'

'Never heard tell. The girl just always seemed annoyed he'd try it on. Like they had some history.'

'Any idea when he was last in?'

'Couple of weeks ago, wouldn't be certain what night. Annoyed me because he only came through the door, noticed there were no women in and left. Didn't even bother to buy a drink. Never came back, so I presumed he'd moved on to pastures new.'

Mac turned his head when a raised voice and a bang on the bell demanded service. He stood up and apologised.

'It's all right, Mac, we're finished but if you think of anything, give me a shout.'

I followed him to the public bar and settled on a stool next to Henry Sturges.

He nodded at my glass. 'You don't drink then?'

'Not anymore.'

We swapped stories for a while, finding we had been in many of the same ports, though not the same boats. Sturges spent his last few years at sea on the route between India and England.

'That was on the Cameroon Star, James, a right old rust bucket moving any old cargo on offer. The owners paid peanuts and employed as few men as they could get away with. I didn't bother climbing back on board when we'd docked in Naples and stayed in Italy until I came back here last month.'

'Were you on freighters out there?'

He smiled. 'No, as I said, I'd had enough of the hard work with no pay. Moved to Sorrento and helped rich men sail their yachts round the bay. Later in the year I'd head to the vineyards to help with the harvest.'

The story sounded rehearsed, but I assumed he'd needed to tell it a few times to satisfy the nosiness of the locals. Small towns can accept you or reject you based on such things.

'Sounds idyllic.'

'Not quite —' this time he laughed out loud — 'but pretty damn good.'

I joined him in his laughter. 'Must bear it in mind. When I packed in the sea a few years ago, I did some fruit picking myself. If I wasn't doing this job I'd do it again somewhere in the sun. France appeals, but it sounds like Italy would be good. Why did you come back?'

'Well, this damn war was on the cards and I started to miss the old place. I've a sister in the town who, like me, isn't getting any younger and it seemed the right time to put the past to bed and settle down.'

We talked for a while longer, now comparing stories about the fruit picking life, until the afternoon closing bell rang.

I said my goodbyes, promising we'd get together again soon and as I turned at the door to give a final wave, Edie Bridgnorth was still watching when I walked out to the street.

Everything reported about Duncan Beattie suggested a man of serious contradictions. Deeply religious but a regular drinker and a user of prostitutes. Kind and caring but having "particular tastes" as his wife had put it. Plus, two sources said he was prone to bad moods. A person who'd spent most of his working life in the commercial world only to become a church minister in later years.

It had bothered me each time I'd met his wife how dismissive she was about his time with these women. Was she putting on an act? She'd shown no surprise he'd been murdered so there was a chance she'd killed him, tipped over the edge by his lifestyle. I'd nothing concrete to treat her as a serious suspect and took a gamble she wasn't going anywhere. When I'd returned from my tour of dodgy pubs I'd phoned Janet Beattie and asked her to call in to the station when she was next in town. The woman snapped that she'd be in next morning after church if I'd be able to see her then.

The vicar's widow now sat stony-faced on the opposite side of my desk.

'So what is it now, Inspector? I thought I'd answered all your questions.'

'I'm afraid not, Mrs Beattie. Until we catch your husband's killer, we'll keep asking them of everyone who knew him. Or at least anyone who might have wanted him dead.'

This last comment had the desired effect. She half rose as if to leave but sat down again, wringing her hands.

'I had a no reason to kill Duncan. Our marriage wasn't perfect, but he was fond of me in his own way, and I was fond of him.'

'The insurance alone would be a motive.'

'We've been through this already, Inspector, the money was nothing. A pittance that will last a few weeks —' she almost spat her next words — 'a fraction of what I had when I married him.'

'Then there's your attitude about your husband's death, Mrs Beattie. And on the way he lived his life.'

'I beg your pardon?'

'I've not yet seen one semblance of grief from you and, to top it off, you're aware he was going with other women and don't seem concerned by it in the least.'

She lay back her head and closed her eyes. When she sighed and returned, her reply was almost a whisper.

'That doesn't look good, does it? But I need you to understand this, Inspector, our marriage wasn't what you'd consider normal. Not in leafy middle England. I grew up in India, my father was a senior Government official out there, and it was a closed community. So closed it was almost incestuous. Affairs were rife and marriages of convenience were not at all unusual.

'Duncan spent many years as a bachelor, travelling in foreign parts and he developed the habit of buying his comfort when he needed to. It just seemed to make sense to us both to marry when we did. He got his hands on some money to indulge his lifestyle and a wife who'd let him do it in exchange for the security of hearth and home. If his activities didn't bother me, and they didn't, why should it be the concern of anyone else?'

Deep down I agreed with her. What goes on behind the facade of many marriages would shock some people. In my view, if both parties are happy and doing no harm, they're entitled to their privacy. This, however, was a special case, a murder investigation. If Janet Beattie was unhappy with her husband's constant philandering, unhappy enough to kill him, then the details of their marriage were very relevant.

'What you did within the confines of your marriage is of no interest to me, Mrs Beattie. Not unless you're lying, and you'd become fed up enough to take action.'

'I'm not sure how I can convince you, Inspector, but Duncan did his womanising if not with my blessing then with my consent. He'd been doing it for years, long before he met me. What are you suggesting changed to make me want to hang him?'

She had a point. Nothing indicated his relationship to any of his women was more than a financial transaction. A payment made for a service delivered.

'You're aware someone was threatening to expose him?'

'I'm not aware of that, no. Who was it?'

'I can't tell you but there was.'

'Well if I had known, I'd be more likely to kill them to keep his secret, wouldn't I? His death has already caused more embarrassment in the parish than I'd be looking for. Now am I able to go?'

I'd nothing solid on the vicar's wife, and until I did I'd no alternative but to let her leave. As she was going out, she turned and spoke with emotion I hadn't heard from her before.

'Please, Mr Given, find who did this. Duncan and I may not have been as close as we might have been, but I cared for him in my own way and didn't wish him any harm. Please believe me.'

Two minutes after she left my telephone rang. It was Sawyer.

'I went looking for Robbie Wilkes earlier, sir. Covered all his usual haunts but he's nowhere to be found.'

'We'd better get out to his place; I'll see you at the car in five minutes.'

I rapped on Wilkes' front door and it echoed around the cottage. Sawyer peered through the front window.

'Can't see him in there, sir.'

'Let's try the back.'

What may once have been a garden was now as overgrown and scattered with rubbish as the front had been. The door swung open, unlocked, when Sawyer tried it.

'Robbie? You there?'

No reply.

I followed Sawyer in, and he jumped as a mouse scurried from under a sheet of cardboard he kicked aside.

'Jesus, look at this mess, sir.'

The kitchen looked even more disgusting than when I'd been there the day before. The dishes still hadn't been washed and now the cupboard doors were open, contents scattered on the ground in front. Other rooms were in the same state.

'Either someone's been looking for something or Wilkes has left in a hurry.'

'Does it look to you as if there's been a struggle?'

'Impossible to tell with all this stuff thrown around. For my money I'd guess your friend decided he needed to get out soon after I visited him, and he's been searching for what to take along.' I looked around. 'Hardly the tidiest of individuals at the best of times, is he.'

'Doesn't make him a murderer though, does it, sir, and I wish you'd stop calling him my friend. He's not a friend, I know him, that's all, but well enough to think he's innocent.'

'That's as maybe but it looks like he's done a runner, so something isn't right. You go around and ask if the neighbours have seen him.'

I poked around for another minute or two until the stench forced me outside to wait for Sawyer. When he came back into the garden he shook his head.

'Mrs Cathcart down the lane said she saw you drive away yesterday, and Robbie left soon afterwards. He came back after an hour or so, but she hasn't seen him since.'

TWELVE

On my way to Edie Bridgnorth's a troop of a cadets from the school marched past, all smiling with their uniforms clean and pressed. The youngest would have been around eleven years old, but the oldest looked like it wouldn't be too long before he'd march in the real army and head overseas. I called in to the butcher's to pick up a lamb chop for my tea, and on the wall behind the counter hung a photograph of a young man with two stripes on his sleeve.

'Your son, Mr Tennant?'

'Aye. Corporal he is. Joined up before this lot started.'

'Where is he based?'

'Well up to now he's been at Aldershot, but they shipped him out to France last week.'

'You must be proud of him.'

'That I am. Proud as hell and worried to death. All we can do now is pray he'll be home soon.'

'I can't argue with that, him and all the others.'

Edie's rooming house was as untidy as Robbie Wilkes' cottage, the main difference being the rubbish. Instead of farming detritus there were baby carriages, bed frames and rusting bicycles in the garden and on the landings. I climbed to Edie's room on the second floor. I'd wanted to ambush her before the pubs opened, hoping to catch her sober, but looking for Wilkes had put paid to that, so I'd had to wait until early afternoon. The line of discarded bottles outside told me I'd found the right place. She answered on my third knock, swayed when she opened it and steadied herself on the frame.

'Inspector Given. Again. Can't you leave a peaceful woman alone?'

'Can I come in, Edie? We need to talk.'

She swept her arm by way of invitation and almost fell over, then giggled and I almost joined in. Edie's room stood in stark contrast to outside; it was spotless. The decor had seen better days but the furniture, though not high quality, was clean and the shine on the oak drop-leaf table showed she didn't despise housework, even if she drank too much. The slate mantelpiece carried several china ornaments and a leather-framed photograph of a woman with a bicycle standing by a cottage door. I told Edie to plonk herself down there in the lone armchair. By the time she did the giggles had subsided and she snivelled, close to tears.

'Didn't do nothing, 'Spector. Nothing but take a little drink now and again. No harm in that is there?'

I'd been where she was, and I wanted to shake her. To tell her there was harm in it. But there'd be no point; she'd need to climb out of that pit under her own steam. Instead, I looked for something to feed her but found nothing, so I made her a cup of sweet tea and began my questions.

'Do you remember you told me you might have been in the Cat and Fiddle the night when Reverend Beattie died?'

She nodded. 'If that's what I said, that's where I was.'

'Well that's not true, Edie, the landlord tells us he closed up for a couple of hours in the middle of the evening.'

Bridgnorth frowned, as if struggling to drag something important to the surface, her eyes darting from side to side until she slumped in her chair and shook her head.

'Don't know, 'Spector. Was in there. Been trying to think and remembered that 'cos I'd been good that day and stayed off the juice 'til opening time. Don't remember him closing though. Must have had a few down me by then.'

'So you can't account for where you were between half past seven and half past nine that night?'

'If you say so.'

'Come on, Edie, it's important. If you can't tell me I'll have to keep you on my list, won't I, and you don't want that, me bothering you all the time, pulling you into the police station every five minutes.'

She banged her knuckles into her forehead, then buried her nails into her scalp.

'Don't know, don't know. 'Spect I was in one of the other pubs. You asked in there?'

'We have, and you weren't.'

'Maybe fell asleep on a bench somewhere. Do that sometimes.'

I'd done the same on many an occasion. I was rapidly coming to the conclusion she'd have been far too drunk to murder Beattie. If his killing had been something simple like a bash over the head, or a stabbing, she might have managed it but she'd never have chatted, drugged his drink, hoisted him into the air until the life had gone from him, then found her way back to the Cat and Fiddle.

'All right, Edie, we'll leave it at that for now, but if I find you've been lying to me you'd better watch out.'

'Wouldn't lie, Inspector, was a simple mistake, that's all. You know how it is when you've had a glass or two.'

I did.

'Before I go, tell me about Robbie Wilkes.'

She began to shake. I thought it was the drink, or the need for one, until she croaked her reply.

'Don't want to talk about him.'

'Why not, Edie?'

'Bad man.'

'Bad in what way?'

'Said I didn't want to talk about him.'

'Well I'm afraid you can't say he's bad then not tell me more. I'm trying to find out who killed Reverend Beattie. Remember?'

She settled, hands clasped round her knees and I thought of the times I'd done this, trying to peer through the alcohol fog, attempting to recall where I'd been and what I'd done. Or trying to forget. After a few moments she broke free.

'When we worked at the vicarage he always followed me round, telling me how he thought I was pretty, stuff like that. Then he started touching me, asking me to go back to his cottage with him, and me only a child and him a grown man. It's why I left the job. Dad was mad as anything I'd packed it in because we needed the money, but I couldn't tell him what happened. He'd kill me and Wilkes both. Why you asking about him anyway?'

'We want to talk to him and he's not home. You don't know where he is do you, Edie?'

She got up from her seat, walked over to the sink and poured a glass of water, downing it in one.

'Told you. Don't like him. If I meet him in the street I'll cross over, don't want him near me.'

'You've not answered my question though. You might not get on, but do you know where he's gone?'

'No, I don't. Why not ask that new friend of yours?'

'Who?'

'That Sturges.'

'Sturges? Henry Sturges?'

'That's the one. Saw him and Wilkes fighting in The Talbot I did, about a week ago. Your mate had him by the throat. Pushed him against the wall. Didn't hear why they were arguing but it looked serious.'

'You're discounting Edie Bridgnorth then, sir?'

'I think so, John, can't imagine how she'd do it. Too drunk. Seems she's like that all the time.'

Sawyer and I were back in my office, and because he'd spent the morning searching for Wilkes without success I'd asked everyone else in the station to pick up the man if they came across him. I'd told Sawyer about my session with Edie and what she'd said about Sturges.

'Do you believe her?'

'I'm not sure. Doesn't seem to know where she is half the time. Couldn't even remember where she went when the pub closed that night.'

'Funny. The poor woman wasn't always like that. Mum always said they were odd, the Bridgnorths, took Edie out of school and kept her at home, wrapped in cotton wool until they could send her out to work. When Edie was about fourteen they put the mother into an asylum. It was only after the father died that Edie moved into town and popped up in the pubs. Packed in a good job and everything.'

'What work did she do?'

'When she was younger it was just domestic, like she told you she did for the vicar and his wife. Later she worked in the office at Morrisey's timber yard. Learned to type and seems she had a good head for figures, so they had her keeping the books as well.'

'Any idea why she left?'

'Perhaps she'd felt trapped, smothered by her mother for a few years, then looked after her dad out of a sense of duty. I can't imagine he left any money, but Edie probably saved some out of her wages to get her by.'

I stood and walked to the window. All I could see were buildings and, beyond them, more buildings and for a second I longed for the vistas of the sea or the open fields of an earlier life. Sawyer's voice pulled me back.

'What about this Henry Sturges bloke, sir, do we need to interview him?'

'I expect so. I'll chase him up tomorrow, had enough for one day. In the morning you go looking for Robbie Wilkes again, spread the net wider, and you'd better interview all the women at Beeches Lane a second time. Ask if anyone else saw anything when Jacqueline Flowers spotted the man leaving. They could have and forgotten if it didn't seem out of the ordinary. Flowers' story might jog their memory and get a better description. Also ask if anybody has come across a bundle of clothes; Beattie's suit must have gone somewhere.'

THIRTEEN

'Mama? What's happened?'

I'd been eating an evening meal and listening to the wireless, full of warnings to keep lights covered at night and to carry a gasmask at all times. There was a discussion on about the possibility of imminent food rationing when the telephone rang. My mother was sobbing at the end of the line.

'It … it's Meena. She's gone.'

'Gone? Gone where?'

'That's it, Jacob.' Her return to my real name told me she was upset. 'We don't know where. Meena has been in Papa's workshop all day, and tonight she didn't come upstairs to eat. Papa said he'd had his head down with the accounts all afternoon and not seen her since lunchtime.'

'Have you contacted her friends?'

She tut-tutted in the way she always did when she thought I was saying something ridiculous.

'Of course, of course, that's the first thing I did and she's not with any of them.'

'Has one of you upset her? Anything happened that might make her want to run away?'

'We've had no arguments or falling out. Papa told you she'd seemed sad for a while, but we thought she'd become more settled in the last week or two. Happier. But now this. Please come and find her.'

'I can't drop everything and do that, Mama, I'm too busy at the minute. Go to Kenyon Street police station and tell them. Meena's probably with a friend you've not contacted, and she'll turn up tomorrow if we don't find her first.'

'But she's never done anything like this before, son, can't you come?'

'Not at the minute, I'm up to my ears in a murder investigation.'

'Always the same, Jacob. Work, work, work, is all you ever do. Never time for your family.'

Mama was always more pliant than my father. For her to take a stand now must mean she was distressed about Meena's safety.

'That's not fair, and you shouldn't say it. Who was it who dropped everything and travelled to France over a week ago to search for Papa's brother?'

Now I could hear her crying again. 'I know, I know, I'm sorry. I'm just so scared of what has happened to the poor girl.'

'Don't worry, Mama. I'll telephone the police in Birmingham myself, try to pull a string or two, though I think they'll tell me it's too soon to begin a big hunt for Meena. Leave it with me. Papa and you try to think of anyone else she may have gone to and I'll get home as soon as I can.'

The crying died away and she blew her nose.

'Thank you, Jacob, you're a good boy. We'll do as you say.'

I turned the wireless up after I'd said goodbye and caught a piece in the news which made me shiver. The correspondent reported the Kindertransports would cease in the near future. He said the outbreak of war, perhaps making them more important than ever, made it too dangerous for the refugee trains to continue. Meena was lucky to get out when she did, because there were thousands, possibly tens of thousands, who weren't as fortunate facing an unpleasant future under the Nazis.

I lifted the telephone and called my mother back.

'Jacob? You've heard something?'

'No, no. If I can make some arrangements at work I'll travel over tomorrow. In the meantime, keep calm. As I said, with luck the girl will turn up in the morning with a perfectly innocent explanation.'

My mother may have tried to remain calm, but she was frantic by the time I arrived in Birmingham in the middle of the day. I'd needed to talk to Sawyer to explain what had happened, so couldn't leave Kenilworth the previous night, though I'd rang her several times through the evening. He'd set my mind at rest that he could carry on without me for the next couple of days, searching for Robbie Wilkes and following up the meagre clues we'd gathered. When I rang Dyer he'd said, to my surprise, I must go, that family was more precious than anything. The sadness in his voice told me he was looking at the photograph he always kept on his desk of his late daughter.

When I pushed open my parents' front door, my father waved as I passed through the tailoring workshop, then held up all the fingers on one hand to show he'd join us upstairs in five minutes.

Despite her state of mind, my mother insisted I take a seat and disappeared into the kitchen to make tea. After she'd laid the table with food and teapot she joined me. The cups rattled in their saucers as she arranged them in front of us.

'Mama, calm down, you'll be ill panicking like this. Then where will Meena be when she arrives home?'

'But, Jacob, she didn't come back this morning like you said she might. Meena's been taken by someone, I know it.'

'Why would you think such a thing, Mama?'

The door opened and my father came in, looking as worried as my mother. I asked if he thought Meena had been kidnapped.

'Son, I don't know. Downstairs, one of the girls saw Meena twice at lunchtimes in the street and a man in a shop doorway watching her.'

'Might he have taken Meena?'

He shrugged his shoulders. 'It's possible, isn't it?'

Beatrice Meir, the seamstress who'd spotted the man spying on Meena, was seventeen years of age and Papa said she was a good, sensible, worker. I asked what she'd seen.

'Nothing to put a finger on. The man looked nice enough, though a bit shabby, and just seemed to be looking across the street at Meena walking by. A few days later he was there again.'

'So did you say anything to Meena?'

Beatrice looked down and blushed.

'I'm so, so, sorry. I'd decided to say something if he was there another time but thought it was my imagination. If I'd known…'

I told her not to blame herself, that it probably was her imagination, but we must consider any possibilities. Though she was adamant she'd recognise the man again, the girl's certainty didn't stretch to being able to provide a decent description. He'd a dark topcoat, dark cap and a beard, like any of dozens of men in that part of Birmingham, and he might be in his fifties. The seamstress wasn't sure about this, only arriving at an age when prompted by me asking if he was older or younger than her father.

From the front step of the workshop Beatrice pointed out the relevant doorway. There'd be nothing there giving a clue to the identity of the man, but I wanted to look anyway.

The spot Beatrice had indicated was the rear entrance to a factory, which hadn't been used for years. From there I could watch my father's workshop, much of the street in both directions and the shops where Meena went in her lunch break. Moving back just one step meant I was hidden from view, a perfect spot to observe someone without being seen.

Back at my parents' I asked to check round the room Meena shared with my sister and took my mother to confirm if anything was missing.

'Only one thing I can be sure is gone. There was a picture by the bed of Meena with her parents and it isn't there now.'

'Nothing else? Clothes?'

'Jacob, I'm not sure. There could be but I can't be certain. It's important?'

'Well, if she'd packed some clothes then she wouldn't have been taken. Meena would have left of her own accord. If she'd planned on leaving forever then she'd have packed a lot more and you'd have noticed things were missing.'

The two of us searched the wardrobe and the drawers without finding anything conclusive. I flipped through the half dozen books on a shelf with the same lack of success. When I opened a violin case standing in the corner our luck changed. Neatly folded in a compartment intended for rosin was a handwritten note in German. My mother and I managed a rough translation between us.

My dearest. Meet me tomorrow afternoon in the usual place.

'It's a boy, Jacob, isn't it? She's run off with a boy.' Mama began to pace the room. 'What will we do?'

'Let's not jump to conclusions. Are any of the boys missing from the workshop?'

'I'll check but it's probably one she met on the train coming to Birmingham.'

My mother went downstairs and returned soon afterwards, shaking her head. 'No-one is missing.'

I picked up the instrument case. 'This violin, Meena's taking lessons?'

'Yes. Since a small child. She plays beautifully. It seemed such a small thing to find her a teacher when she arrived.'

'Does she go anywhere else when she's not working?'

'Nowhere, Jacob. Meena is such a good quiet girl. What can you do?'

'Firstly, I'll go to the police station to see if they've turned up anything then visit the violin teacher in case Meena has confided in her. I'll tell how I've got on later.'

Rachel Stevens was stunning, more like a film star than a music teacher, and her looks knocked me speechless when she opened the front door.

'Yes? Can I help you?'

Still the words wouldn't come. Only when she moved to slam that door in my face did I manage to recover some wits.

'Police … I'm a police officer.'

She looked me up and down then raised an amused eyebrow.

'Are you indeed? Then you'd better come in.'

No second invitation was needed. Somewhere inside a gramophone played an opera I didn't recognise and Meena's teacher led me into a high-ceilinged room packed with the tools of her trade. Sheet music displayed on floor-to-ceiling racks covered every style from jazz to classical and on the wall, above a beautiful cello and stylish grand piano, concert posters announced Meena's teacher as principal soloist.

'The posters. You like them?'

'Very impressive.'

'From some time ago, I'm afraid. Fingers aren't so nimble as they once were. Now, Mr Police Officer, how can I help?'

The smile that accompanied the question almost turned me dumbstruck again, but I fell back on the formal introductions and a quick explanation of Meena's disappearance to get through.

'Oh my God, such a nice girl. Conscientious in practising and shows great promise. Have you no idea where she might have gone?'

'None, Mrs Stevens, I was hoping you might be able to help in that respect.'

'Me? How? And it's Miss, not Mrs.'

That smile again, and I wondered for a moment how someone so attractive and charming hadn't married. Then I realised the teacher was a year or two younger than me and I was still single, though not half as good looking, so more easily explained.

'I need to be clear from the start this isn't yet a formal police investigation, and I'm only acting as a member of Meena's temporary family. I hoped she may have talked about friends in a way she wouldn't with my parents.'

'I don't think I can help. As I said, she works hard at her violin. Meena comes to me once a week, takes out her instrument, we go through various exercises then she leaves again. Her English is good, but not perfect, so if she talks at all it's for clarification on how a piece should be interpreted or how to get through a complex section, that kind of thing. I know nothing of her personal life other than what Mrs Geffen told me when she first brought Meena.'

'She hasn't mentioned, even in passing, any boys she's sweet on?'

'Only your brother, Eli isn't it?'

'Eli? She talked about Eli?'

Meena's face glowed with admiration when I'd visited last time, but I hadn't attributed too much significance. Was there more going on than I'd suspected?

'Only once or twice, when I asked how she was getting on with your family. She told me she enjoyed Sarah's company and that Eli was funny, kind and good looking. I had an idea she'd a bit of a crush on him.'

'Nothing more than that?'

The teacher adopted the same amused expression she'd teased me with at the front door.

'Goodness me, Inspector, what are you suggesting? She's a child, well a little more than a child I suppose, but it's perfectly natural for girls of that age to take a shine to handsome young men. Meena never gave any hint there was anything serious between them. Only worshipping from afar I'd imagine.'

'And there was no-one else?'

'I'm afraid not, Inspector.'

I tried to conjure up other questions to keep me in the teacher's company for a while longer, but nothing would come, so she walked me to the door.

'We must hope you find her soon; please give me a call if … when you do.'

When the music teacher spoke, I turned and caught my reflection in the hall mirror: medium height, slight paunch and worn suit. An unflattering comparison to Miss Rachel Stevens, but I said I would keep in touch. Afterwards, walking down the street, I knew I'd keep this promise. I also realised I must have a word with Eli.

Mama had prepared a meal as usual, with some special trimmings to honour the prodigal, but she and Papa pushed the food around their plates with little interest and I imagined they'd not have eaten at all if I hadn't been visiting. The pair listened to every detail of my account of talking to both Miss Stevens and to the local police. To save my brother's blushes, I held back on what she'd told me about Meena's crush. The poor boy shot glances throughout as if he were expecting me to say something because earlier I'd taken him aside and explained what she'd said. He pretended to be shocked, though puffed his chest a little, and assured me there was nothing going on. Eli was adamant he didn't have a clue where Meena might be. I told him I believed him and we rejoined the family, agreeing to say nothing more about it.

'The police had nothing?' my father asked. 'Surely they'd be able to find her if they looked hard enough.'

'It's not as easy as that, is it? Meena could be anywhere, Birmingham is a big city and she may not even be in Birmingham any longer. The local men's view is she's run away, and I have to admit if I were in their shoes I'd also consider that to be the likeliest explanation. Far more likely than being kidnapped. My contact said to wait a few more days then get in touch again if we haven't heard from her.'

My father sat, arms folded and shaking his head, and I could see he wasn't happy.

'I'm sorry, Papa, but there's no more I can do. Other than the man who Beatrice said was watching Meena, there are no leads. Even he's a long shot and I've told the police about him, so they'll be on the lookout. It's their job to investigate this and I'll get into serious trouble if I start poking around on their patch too much. So we have to leave it to them. I've also my own case to deal with. A murdered vicar. I can't just abandon that, and I'll need to go off first thing in the morning to get back to work.'

Papa got up from the table and scurried through to the parlour, returning a few minutes later with a sheaf of papers which he tossed in front of me.

'Here, read these.'

On the table were half a dozen letters and three printed news-sheets from London Jewish organisations. All told the same tale of the increasing persecution of Jews in Germany, Austria, and Poland.

'Over three million of us in Poland —' my father was trembling — 'and they're rounding us up into ghettos. Confiscating our property. Read, son, read.' He pulled one news-sheet out and placed it on top. 'This one says Hitler plans to kill us all.' He threw down another. 'Look at this, they're saying now the Kinderstransports have stopped there are thousands of children in danger.'

'What do you want me to do? I'm one unimportant man the same as you. It's down to Mr Chamberlain and his government to get Germany under control.'

'I understand, Jacob, your job is here, keeping the peace, protecting us from bad people.' He drew a long, deep, breath. 'That's why you must find Meena. The poor thing came to us to be safe. If something has happened while she is in our care I'll never forgive myself.'

He didn't need to add that he'd never forgive me either.

FOURTEEN

The train journey back to Kenilworth had provided time to ponder, perhaps a little too much time. Here I was with three cases on the go, two unofficial, hardly a lead in any, and feeling inadequate to deal with one case, let alone three.

Uncle Gideon, his wife and two younger children missing, somewhere in France, perhaps Brittany, but I hadn't a clue where. If my search had been anywhere near official I might have been able to request more help from the French authorities but, in the times we faced, they'd be unlikely to look for one Jewish family with so many more pouring over the border. I'd racked my brains trying to work out where to get leads but nothing came. The size of the country, the language barrier, the sheer numbers on the move and the threat of German invasion all stacked against me.

Solving Meena's disappearance was no simpler. She'd left without a word to anyone, possibly with intent, possibly under duress, and hiding a letter which may, or may not, have been the catalyst. A young woman with no connections at all with anyone in England as far as we were aware, and with no real cash of her own, so where could she go?

My only hope for progress on any of them was that Sawyer had turned up something on the vicar's murder while I was away, and as soon as I got back I phoned down for him.

'Robbie was seen coming back from town about an hour after you visited him, sir. The bus conductor reported he'd jumped on board carrying a canvas bag. Only noticed it because it looked new and asked Robbie if he was going away.'

'And how did he react?'

'Just laughed, kind of nervous, and said he needed it for work. The conductor also said Robbie sat near the front and fidgeted the whole time, hiding his face whenever another passenger got on. When he got off at the stop on the main road nearest his cottage, he'd looked back over his shoulder several times until the conductor lost sight of him. This must be when the neighbour, Mrs Cathcart, saw Robbie coming back.'

Sawyer told me this in a monotone, and I assumed he was still resenting my insistence that Wilkes might be a suspect. I didn't care because I had good reason. As far as I could see, Wilkes held a grudge against the clergyman, we knew from Edie that he had an unpleasant side and now he'd gone missing, sounding like he'd gone on the run, and had a day's start on us.

'Anything else?'

'It seems he was in different places before he worked at the vicarage. As I told you, he was often around the school gates for a while after he left, but then he disappeared for a year or two and I never knew where he was. My mum did though. Apparently he'd a job in Hull at one time, looking after a hotel down by the docks. Before that he was wandering around Lincolnshire earning what he could as a farm labourer. When his granddad died and left him the cottage with a bit of land, Robbie came back and settled down.'

'Does he farm then?'

'No, not enough to make any kind of a living at it. Grows some veg for himself and keeps a pig or two.'

'Must be where he gets his housekeeping habits. Any record of him being in trouble in Lincolnshire or Hull?'

'I telephoned Hull police, but they had nothing on him. I also rang some stations in Lincolnshire, but they all said there were so many itinerant workers it isn't possible to keep tabs on everyone who spends a night in gaol for minor offences. They were sure he'd not come to their attention for anything serious. Confirms what I was saying, sir.'

'How so?'

'Robbie had nothing to do with this.'

'Sorry, John, I don't agree with you and he'll remain a suspect until I say otherwise.'

Sawyer flipped his notebook shut and stood to leave.

'Hold on, we're not finished yet.'

His face was square set and I expected him to ignore me and leave. Instead, he sat again and crossed his arms, not speaking. I didn't know if I was being hard on him, but I was becoming fed up with his moods. I'd need to tackle it sometime soon because it was getting in the way of working together. Now wasn't the time.

'Anything from the Beeches Lane girls? You went to see them I assume.'

'Yes, sir.' Strong emphasis on the "sir", that dumb insolence again. 'I interviewed them all. One, a Poppy Sinclair, I don't imagine that's her real name, remembered she'd seen someone passing through the rear gate when Jacqueline Flowers did, though it meant nothing to her and she'd forgotten.'

'Was she any better with the description than Flowers?'

'Told me she only saw the gate closing and a head bobbing out. Couldn't even say if it was male or female. Only said she thought he was carrying a bag.'

'So that's where Beattie's clothes went. No-one else saw this person?'

'Not that they remembered.'

He hesitated.

'What is it, John?'

'I don't know whether or not to believe any of that crowd. Half the girls seem drunk or doped, and that pimp of theirs, Benny Grainger, is dodgy as they come. Any of them could have done for the vicar, nipped out the gate then gone back in by the front door without being missed.'

'It's a possibility. If the women were taking drugs, could any be on the barbiturate used to knock out our victim?'

'Surprise, surprise, every last one denied it, but I could tell they were on something.'

'Let's keep it in mind, but if someone from the house killed him what would be their motive?'

'Who knows? Perhaps Beattie roughed one of them up. I know Grainger said he didn't, but maybe he did and the girl kept quiet about it, just got her revenge later. The lack of motive's true of almost everyone we've spoken to. Even Robbie. Hardly because Beattie sacked him; it was only a gardening and handyman job, something he could pick up again as easy as anything.'

'All right, I hear your objection, but we'll keep Wilkes on the list for now. Just above the wife and everyone at Beeches Lane. To be honest, I can't see any of them doing it but what else do we have? It could, of course, be someone we haven't interviewed but I don't expect it's likely. Beattie knew his killer well enough to sit down and talk to him, or her. Well enough, in fact, to trust them to meet him at a place he wouldn't want most people to know he used.'

'Could it have been one of his congregation? Found out what he was up to in his spare time so bumped him off.'

I laughed. 'Bit extreme isn't it? Why not just expose him and chase him out of the area?'

'Never know with some of these churchy types. "Thou shalt not commit adultery" and all that stuff.'

We agreed we'd add it to our list of possibilities even though I had my doubts. I considered sending him off to interview every one of Beattie's parishioners to see if they had the gleam of religious fervour in their eyes but couldn't spare him for that long. In any case, he'd not appreciate the joke.

I'd traced Henry Sturges to The Talbot again. The place had been crowded and I'd wanted to avoid spending time in a public bar, so I asked him to join me in a tea shop across the road from the police station. Sturges didn't object, even appeared to like the idea of talking to someone outside the pub.

When the waitress had taken our order, he asked how he could help.

'You knew Robbie Wilkes?'

'A little, why?'

'He's gone missing. Had you met him before you came to Kenilworth?'

'Don't think so, Inspector.'

'So what was the fight about?'

He frowned. 'Fight? What fight?'

'I understand you had him up against the wall.'

'Oh that. Hardly a fight was it.'

Sturges looked like he could handle himself and Robbie, likely as not, was drunk, so it wouldn't have been much of a fight, that much was true.

'So?'

'I'd seen him once or twice when I'd been in The Talbot and that night we'd got to chatting and drinking all evening, swapping pints. He'd run out of money and owed me one. Had the cheek to try to borrow a few bob. I refused and he got abusive. Wilkes pushed me, and I don't take that from no-one even when I'm sober. I pushed back harder, and he tried it again, but I was too quick for him. Had him against the wall, as you said, then sent him off with a flea in his ear. But it was nothing, just the booze, that's all. You must have done it yourself.'

I shook my head. In all the years I was drinking, I'd never been a fighting drunk. Chatty, yes. Amorous, sometimes. Incoherent, more often than not. Then I'd simply pass out when over the mark.

'And you're sure you never met Wilkes before moving here?'

'Look, Inspector, like yourself I travelled all over the world for years, one boat to another, one port to another, from Newcastle to New Zealand, and can't begin to remember every man I've met in that time. If I did bump into Wilkes then I don't recall, and he never mentioned it when I was with him. Why all the questions anyway?'

'We're looking for him in connection with a murder enquiry.'

'And you think I have something to do with his disappearance?'

'Not necessarily, just following a line, that's all. Had you come across the dead man, Duncan Beattie?'

He thought for a moment.

'Name rings a bell, so I might have met him but don't think so.'

'You could have known him as Albert Green.'

'Oh, him. I didn't exactly know him, saw him a few times in the pubs. Always looking to pick up a woman. Landlords all seemed to be acquainted, called him by his name when he came in.'

Sturges tapped the table and grinned.

'He was that vicar was he? Saw it in the paper. God, you can't fathom anyone can you. Always thought him too upmarket to be hanging around them sort of places.'

A waitress came to the table and started to clear away the cups. Sturges put a hand on her wrist.

'No, no, love, leave them. Bring another pot will you? Nice and fresh. And two of the fruit scones.' He looked at me. 'You'll have one, won't you, Inspector.'

Despite my continuing promises to myself that I'd try to lose a few pounds, I nodded, and we waited until she came back.

'Sorry to have to keep on with this, but can you tell me where you were on the last Wednesday of August? Thirtieth it was, just under three weeks ago?'

'Christ, you do come up with them, don't you? Three weeks? Can hardly remember where I was yesterday most of the time. I was almost certainly in the pub if it was Wednesday, but which one?'

'Try to remember, it is important. Are you always out on Wednesday?'

'Not always. I get my money on a Thursday morning, so if I've any left from the week I'll have a few pints.'

Sturges rubbed his cheeks, then counted off on his fingers, his lips moving, recounting where he'd been on previous Wednesdays.

'Got it. I'd been round at my sister's at teatime. Made a beef pie she had and asked me to stay for some. I left her place at around half past seven, walked up to The Talbot and was there until I spent my last few bob. Finished about ten o'clock, walked the five minutes back to her house and spent the night there.'

'So you live with your sister then?'

'No. I did when I first came here but I've a room on Maple Avenue, just around the corner. Like an idiot I forgot my keys and couldn't go knocking on the landlady's door that time of night. I had to go to Susie's. None too pleased I can tell you, but she's a good 'un and made me a bed up on the settee.'

An alibi provided by a brother, sister or wife is often not worth anything, but it was easy to check if I needed to. Sturges didn't seem the type to be stupid enough to lie about his movements and expect me not to find out.

Over the second pot we talked about his time in Italy, and he was full of funny stories from his life on the yachts. Some of them sounded a little far-fetched but he told them with such enthusiasm that we laughed long and hard into the early afternoon. By the time they began to clear the tables around us we were on first name terms and Henry suggested we adjourn to the nearest pub.

'Much as I'd like to, I can't manage it today, far too much work to do, but I'll take you up on it sometime soon.'

Still smiling as I crossed the road to the station, I was thinking how I'd not enjoyed any man's company for such a long time.

'Still no joy with Robbie, sir. Not a word of him around the town. I went to see all his friends, and everyone claims not to have seen him. Have to say I'm getting worried.'

Sawyer had come in to see me as soon as I got back to my office and made it clear he'd been waiting for a while.

'Why worried?'

'Robbie's not the cleverest of blokes and disappearing so completely would be difficult for him. If he was hiding, he'd probably just ask a mate to put him up for a few days but there's no-one owning up.'

'Perhaps he has a mate who wouldn't rat on him.'

'Possibly, but I've known most of them a long time and think they trust me. If any of them know where Robbie is they'd give me the nod. One or two might not tell me where, but they'd let me know he's safe.'

'And you think he's not safe?'

'I'm not sure, but that bus conductor said Robbie looked like he thought he was being followed.'

'Most likely he did, but it was probably us he thought were following him. He's still the only real suspect we've got, and the simplest explanation is he's packed his bag and gone on the run. Extend the search. Check with his friends in Coventry again, ask our lads over there, and find out if any of the other stations round the county have heard anything.'

This time Sawyer didn't argue. He might not agree with my consideration of Wilkes as a suspect, but he now wanted to find him as much as I did.

'What about Sturges, sir? Anything on him?'

'Doesn't seem to be. We had a long chat. Lived in Italy for a while, seaman before that, same as me. Gave me an alibi for the night of the murder which seemed solid, but I'll check it. There are gaps when he claimed to be walking to and from his sister's house — said it was only five minutes, but it wouldn't be much out of his way to go via Beeches Lane.'

'Shall I do more digging on him, sir? Seems odd he comes to Kenilworth then we have a murder and another man goes missing. A man he was fighting with.'

'No need. From what I can tell he's a decent bloke and, as I said, I'll check his alibi.'

Sawyer's face when he left told me he'd take no notice of my advice. But that's what he's useful for, checking my assumptions, and, even though I liked Henry Sturges, I was far from certain he was innocent.

FIFTEEN

There are times in an investigation when all you can do is slog away, and we were now deep inside one. With few leads to realistic suspects all we could do was go over the same ground, sifting and checking for anything missed, waiting for that vital clue or spark of inspiration.

I drove out to Stowham to speak to Wilkes' neighbour and dropped Sawyer off so he could interview some of Beattie's parishioners on the off chance one might suggest a motive. The neighbour told Sawyer Wilkes had looked scared and said he needed to get away because someone was after him. Despite prompting, the woman had nothing new to offer. Wilkes hadn't told her who was chasing him or where he was going, and she'd no thoughts about friends or family who might have taken him in.

Sawyer and I compared notes in the car on the way back to the station.

'Beattie's flock were as you might expect, sir. The younger members only knew him as the man who stood in front on a Sunday, they had no personal contact. The older ones had seen vicars come and go, liked this one as well as any, and even those who were a bit closer hadn't any idea why someone would want to harm him. They were all shocked about what had happened — both the murder and his secret life.'

'And none looked likely candidates I suppose?'

'That'd be a bit too much to ask, wouldn't it? Seemed decent God-fearing people, every one of them. Two said they wished he'd been more fire and brimstone in his sermons but hardly a motive to kill the poor man, I shouldn't think.'

Later in the day, I re-interviewed the Beeches Lane pimp and girls, asking the same questions, looking for differences to their earlier answers, watching for any signs they were lying. It was another waste of time. Everyone had an alibi, but any could have slipped out of the house and not been missed for the half an hour, maybe less, it would take to meet and kill Beattie.

That evening Sawyer came with me again round the pubs we'd already visited plus a few we hadn't because we'd thought them not to be the sort Beattie would have used to look for women. None of the new ones said they knew him. In the rougher ones we leaned on the landlords harder. This time, those who'd denied it on our first visit admitted that Beattie was a regular, that he used the name Albert Green, and he'd only ever have one pint unless there was a woman who interested him. None of the landlords had seen Beattie arguing with any customers. One pointed out Beryl Jenkins, who had been with our victim only a few nights before he was killed. She was young, blond, pretty and married.

'That there Mr Green was a gentleman, he was, real charming. Never asked for nothing funny, always buy us a drink first then slip us some money up front. Even bought flowers afterwards, leave them in the pub next day he would.'

We interviewed some of the women we were told Beattie had gone with and everyone gave the same story as Beryl. All agreeing he was never rough and couldn't think why anyone would want him dead.

In The Talbot we verified Henry Sturges' story with the landlord and, as far as he could remember, Henry had been there when he said, though wouldn't be tied down to the minute.

Outside the last pub, The Black Swan, a man leant against the wall and stood as we approached.

'You trying to find out about that Albert Green character?'

'We are.'

'Then perhaps you might want to talk to Maisie Butler's old man, Charlie.'

Sawyer asked why.

'Green laid him out on the ground, that's why. Maisie was in here one night, drunk as a lord, and Green tries to take advantage. Kissing and cuddling her he was. Charlie was playing dominoes in the back and someone tipped him off what was happening. Came through and went for the bloke. Got a couple of punches in but never saw the big one coming and next thing he's seeing stars.'

'When was this?'

'Few weeks ago. Didn't see Green in here again after that.'

I pressed him to be more accurate about when the fight took place, but he could get no closer than it being two or three weeks earlier. I thanked him and said to contact me if he remembered anything to pin the incident down. By the time we'd finished it was late and I sent Sawyer home for the night.

The Talbot's landlord had confirmed only half of Henry's alibi, so I walked from the pub to Henry's sister's house to check the other half. She wasn't home, but the route passed only two streets away from Beeches Lane and it would have been simple to make his way through the network of passages, having called in there on the way. If he'd been prepared it wouldn't have taken him much more than fifteen minutes to meet Beattie, feed him the knockout drops then finish him off.

Back at the station next morning, Sawyer and I went through the suspects, and agreed that Edie Bridgnorth was no longer one.

'Have we heard from Coventry police about Wilkes' friends?'

'Yes, sir, the report came in late last night. Seems none of his mates can remember seeing Robbie much after eight o'clock.'

'So what time's the last bus?'

Sawyer flipped though his notepad. 'Quarter past ten.'

'That means he could have caught the bus home after all, been back in Kenilworth in plenty of time to meet Beattie, string him up, then walk home late enough to make sure all his neighbours were tucked up in bed and wouldn't see him.'

'Still doesn't have much of a motive though, does he sir? It would be my guess he drank more than he should, wandered away from his friends then fell into another pub until closing time.'

I shared what I'd found about Henry's route home.

'So he's still in the frame, is he?'

'I don't know, John, I can't see it. My money's still on Wilkes.'

'Well mine's on Sturges.'

We argued for another twenty minutes about the two of them then, in the end, decided to keep them both on the list until we had reason not to. Janet Beattie was more problematic. Neither of us had strong feelings about her as a suspect but agreed his constant philandering and the insurance policy gave her motive. On top of this she hadn't a watertight alibi and had shown little surprise when I told her he'd been murdered. I said I'd go back to see her later and told Sawyer to find out what he could about Maisie and Charlie Butler.

Henry and I met for lunch in the Maypole café where we enjoyed roast lamb with all the trimmings, followed by an enormous slice of apple pie. The atmosphere was a little strange, as though the customers were preparing for this to be their last meal out. All the talk was of the Germans and

Russians trying to carve up Poland and how we might be next for the chopping block.

Over the meal we avoided talk of war and, instead, shared seafaring tales, each trying to outdo the other, though both agreed we'd felt safer than we would now with U-boats prowling. Six British boats were already lost, and we were less than a month into the conflict.

I tried to keep the conversation light-hearted and informal while looking for an opportunity to find out if he was aware the Beeches Lane brothel was on the route from town to his sister's. If I'd asked the question outright it would have solicited a lie or righteous indignation. In either case it might put an end to our friendship, and I didn't want that to happen until I was on firmer ground. After lunch, we shared the bill and he was walking me back in the direction of the police station when Edward Winston waved from across the road.

'Good afternoon, Inspector, nice to see you again.' The curate looked decidedly more self-assured than the last time I'd seen him. 'Any news?'

He crossed over to join us and I introduced him to Henry, who politely took his hand but looked at him strangely. Winston smiled then turned his attention back to me, avoiding or not noticing Henry's scrutiny of his face. I explained to the curate that we were following several leads, but it was a slow process. Afterwards we exchanged pleasantries for a few minutes, then he went on his way. Henry remained quiet until we reached the station steps.

'Penny for them, Henry.'

'What? Oh, sorry, just lost in thought there for a while. That curate, how well do you know him?'

'Not well, I met him when I was interviewing Janet Beattie. Why?'

'Odd, I thought I recognised him then realised it was someone else he reminded me of, someone from a long time ago.'

I smiled. 'Getting old, Henry, thinking yourself twenty years younger than you are. I did the same thing myself a month or so ago. Convinced a woman I saw in a crowd was someone I'd worked with, then realised the one I'd seen would still have been at school at the time.'

'Happens all the time these days. Just threw me, that's all, because the man I remembered is dead. Killed himself years ago.'

'What happened?'

'We worked together along the Suez Canal until he got into some trouble. A while later I heard he'd committed suicide. Don't know why, he'd always been a happy-go-lucky kind of man when I knew him, but we'd lost touch by then. Shame really, we'd become quite good mates. God, we got into some scrapes on those trips.'

There hung an awkward silence, then Henry shrugged and said he ought to let me get back to work. As I walked up the steps I looked back at him crossing the road, his shoulders lower than when we'd laughed our way out of the café.

Janet Beattie was planting bulbs in the front border of the vicarage when I climbed out of my car. She raised a gloved hand in acknowledgement then waved me over.

'Inspector, it's you again. I'm afraid you'll have to wait until I've finished this. There's rain coming and I can't be bothered tidying everything away just so you can ask me more of your pointless questions.'

'Hardly pointless, madam, but I'm in no hurry.'

'Have you made some progress then?'

I gave her the same rundown I'd offered the curate, following leads, nothing concrete, hoping for a breakthrough soon, confident of an arrest before too long, and so on.

Mrs Beattie shook her head and turned back to her task. I asked what she was planting.

'Daffodils and tulips, though heaven knows why, I'll be gone before they flower. I have to do something though; the days seem so long now that Duncan's gone.'

The vicar's widow picked up a bulb, stared at it for a moment then held it up for me to look at.

'A particularly nice sermon of Duncan's compared one of these to us. He said how wonderful it is that such a small, dull, insignificant thing, when put in the ground and nurtured, it becomes, in the fullness of time, a display of absolute beauty. He argued that we, with God's infinite love, bloom in paradise after we die. Do you think that somewhere in heaven my husband, despite his imperfections, is now that bright, shining, flower?'

I mumbled that I didn't really have a view on such matters, that most of my time was spent dealing with badness in this life without thinking too much about the next. She snatched the bulb away.

'That's the trouble with the world today; too many people think only of the present.'

With French and German tanks staring each other down on our ally's eastern border, I wanted to say there may be little advantage in thinking of the future. Holding my tongue, I waited to follow her to the back of the house where she nodded towards her unfinished summer house.

'A real shame Duncan sacked Robbie, he'd have that completed by now and I'd be able to use it until the cold weather arrives.'

'Had your husband complained about Wilkes' timekeeping before he fired him?'

'Not seriously. He knew the man was a good worker, and cheap, so put up with his lateness. Something must have got under Duncan's skin that day for him to let Robbie go.'

'Any idea what it was?'

I already knew but wanted to test her reaction.

'No. I was out in Warwick most of the day, and when I got back Duncan said I'd need to find a new odd-job man. Something I still haven't got around to.' She turned away, shaking her head again. 'I expect I can leave that to his successor now.'

'Have you seen Wilkes recently?'

'Why on earth would I?'

'He'd know your husband is dead and might have come around, hoping you'd be easier on him than the vicar had been.'

'Well I wouldn't, and he hasn't been here. Why are you asking?'

'Wilkes has disappeared, just when we started to ask him questions, so we need to find him.' Mrs Beattie laughed.

'Robbie Wilkes? Surely he's not a suspect. He'd worked for us for years and was always so gentle and polite. I can't see him killing anyone, let alone Duncan.'

'A view shared by my colleague Detective Constable Sawyer. Which is why we're still exploring other possibilities. Can I ask if your husband ever had fights — actual physical fist fights?'

'He was a man of God, not some street brawler.'

'That's not answered my question.'

She looked down and inspected her fingernails, taking half a minute before answering in a calm, quiet, voice.

147

'I told you when we first met that I wasn't surprised he'd been killed. The places he frequented and the people he mixed with weren't the highest in society, so it was inevitable he'd come to harm some time. A few times over the years he came home with bruises or a bloody nose and it was clear he'd been in a scuffle. He'd laugh it off when talking with parishioners, saying he'd walked into a branch in the garden, or some such story. The first time he came back in that state he told me he'd learnt to box in his youth so could look after himself.'

'Had it happened recently?'

'Not for a long, long time until three or four weeks ago. Duncan had been out one night, and I was in bed when I heard him rooting around in the bathroom so got up. His cheek and knuckles were bleeding and there was a tear in the knee of his trousers. So I made him a drink and put some antiseptic on the grazes but knew better than to ask what had happened. I assumed he'd been after someone's wife or girlfriend and they weren't too happy about it.'

If this was the same fight with Charlie Butler then she was one hundred percent accurate in her guess.

'Did he say who he'd been fighting with?'

'No, he didn't. Is that why you're here, Inspector? You think whoever Duncan fought with took it a step further?'

'Only a possibility we're considering. You're sure he gave you no more information about it?'

'None. In fact, we hardly spoke for several days I was so angry with him.'

'How angry?'

She stopped in her tracks.

'Whoa, wait a minute, Inspector. Perhaps angry is too strong a word, annoyed might be more fitting. I was prepared to ignore his dalliances with these women, but I did think he should be above fighting in the street over them, and I told him so. It's that kind of behaviour would get him noticed, not least by your colleagues, then all of our good life here would come crashing down.'

'So you did have something to lose by his conduct, Mrs Beattie. Did it make you angry enough to kill him?'

A flush came to her cheeks and she pointed to the gate.

'Get out, Inspector. And don't come back again with insinuations like that. Not unless I have my solicitor here with me.'

We stood our ground for a full minute, locked eye to eye, then I tipped my hat and walked round to the car. Before opening the door, I turned back.

'I'm a long way from believing you killed your husband, Mrs Beattie, but I'm also some way from being sure you didn't. Until I'm certain I'll keep coming back. Now if you think you need a solicitor with you that's fine, I'm sure it can be arranged easily enough. We might even treat him to a cup of tea when he meets you at the police station.'

She said nothing more before I watched her walk into the vicarage, slamming the front door behind her. While I sat mulling over what had just taken place, a distant lightning fork lit the fields beyond the graveyard. The storm Janet Beattie had forecast was on its way.

SIXTEEN

The rain was torrential back in Kenilworth, and I dashed through puddles from the car park to the station. When I'd squelched, panting, halfway up the stairs, Sawyer came out of the canteen, grinning when he saw me.

'Damp out there, sir?'

I gave him the evil eye.

'Careful I don't send you out there to knock some doors, John.'

The grin didn't disappear, so I waved him behind me.

'Come up to my office.' I shook a shower from my coat. 'Give me a minute to get out of this but we need to talk.'

He did as I said, keeping sufficient distance to avoid the deluge pouring from my hat and clothes. The lights dimmed when we walked into the room as yet another flash lit the sky. An immediate volley of thunder rattled the windows.

Sawyer jumped. 'My God, that was close.'

Now it was my turn to grin, hanging my soggy outfit on the coat-stand to drip a puddle on the floor. Fear is a funny emotion. Grown men who might run a mile at the sight of a spider or mouse can perform the most heroic feats on the battlefield. Even Sawyer, who was considering enlisting in the army, was worried by this thunderstorm.

'Scared are we, John? It'll be a lot worse than that on the front line. Come on, sit and tell me what you've found out about Charlie Butler.'

He flipped open his notebook and slipped on a self-satisfied smile.

'Butler might be our man, sir. Turns out he's been in prison.'

'What for?'

'Manslaughter. Killed a man in a fight. The bloke had been chatting up Butler's wife, so our Charlie smashed his skull in with a barstool. Died a few days later in hospital.'

'So he's had fights over Maisie before?'

'Oh no, sir, this wasn't Maisie, it was his first wife. Charlie got away with eight years in Winson Green, convinced the judge the dead man had provoked him. That wife divorced Charlie while he was inside, and he met Maisie when he got out. She's a lot younger than him.'

'Any trouble since prison?'

'Not that I could find but he's still got a reputation for his temper, especially after a few pints. It's never amounted to anything serious since leaving prison.'

'Violent though? Fights, that kind of thing?'

'Only the same as half the blokes who spend their wages in the pub on a Saturday night, but he's been in a few scraps bad enough for landlords to call us out.'

'Would he have followed up on the fight with our vicar?'

'Well that's the other interesting thing I found out, sir. Dan Ellis, the landlord of the Black Swan, told me that Reverend Beattie, or Albert Green as he knows him, and Charlie Butler bumped into each other in the pub the night after their fight. Beattie asked to buy Charlie a drink to show he was sorry for what happened and the two sat at a table in the corner knocking them back for a while. Dan said Beattie kept apologising, though it seemed like water off a duck's back. Charlie scowled the whole time.'

'Sounds like he didn't accept the apology then.'

'No sir, it doesn't. According to the landlord, Charlie gave the filthiest stare to Beattie's back when he left the pub. Later he told Ellis it would take more than a free pint for him to forgive the bloke for trying it on with Maisie.'

'Good work, John.'

Sawyer beamed and the self-satisfaction spread over him like a warm eiderdown.

'Do I pick up Butler, sir?'

'That would be an excellent idea, John, bring him in and let's listen to what he has to say.'

'Mrs Beattie? You wanted to speak to me?'

The vicar's wife's call came through soon after Sawyer left. She was breathless.

'There's someone wearing Duncan's jacket, Inspector. Just now. Out in the street in broad daylight. I ran around to the telephone box to call you straight away.'

'Hold on a minute. How can you be sure it's your husband's jacket?'

'I'd know it anywhere. A brown pinstripe. The best quality. The man wearing it couldn't possibly afford such a thing.'

'Still —'

'No, no, I'm certain. I walked right by him and there was a Scripture Union badge in the lapel. Duncan always wore one.'

'Can you still see him?' I grabbed my coat.

'Yes, he's sitting on a bench by the bus stop on the high street.'

I told her to keep an eye on the man and then dashed down the stairs and into the town centre. The man in the brown jacket was stepping onto the bus as I reached the stop. He looked startled when I grabbed his arm and pulled him back.

'Get off. What you doing?'

The man was short, skinny and in his sixties. I'm no fighter but he wouldn't give me any trouble. His second sleeve hung empty and limp at his side.

'Calm down, sir. I need to have a word.'

I explained who I was.

'Where did you get this jacket?'

'In my yard, in a bag. Someone must have slung it over. There were pants as well but they don't fit. Didn't think I'd be doing wrong wearing it if someone threw it away.' He stroked the front. 'Nice material, it is. Do I have to give it back?'

The man, Benjamin Jackson, looked like he needed a decent coat, but I told him I'd have to take it, at least for the time being. He lived about a hundred yards from the brothel on Beeches Lane, backing onto the passage which ran behind. He'd lost his arm to shrapnel in the Great War and he'd not have the capacity to hoist anyone into a noose and fake a suicide.

Mrs Beattie joined us and confirmed it was the vicar's jacket.

'I'll take it in as evidence after I've walked Mr Jackson home to change. You've no objection if we return it to him later?'

'No, I suppose not, Inspector, I've no use for it.'

She scanned him up and down.

'I'm sorry we bothered you, Mr Jackson. I'll see if there's anything else that might fit you.'

Janet Beattie stroked the green badge in his buttonhole, scribbled down his address, and walked away looking sadder than I'd ever seen her.

The thunderstorms hung around most of the night, and I wouldn't have been the only one who didn't get to sleep until the early hours. The telephone ringing in my study woke me after eight o'clock and I stumbled through to hear Sawyer's voice on the line.

'I've pulled Charlie Butler in, sir. With such bad weather last night, I left it until the morning but made sure to get around to his house at first light.'

'Did he give you any trouble?'

'None. Seems he's quiet as a mouse when he's sober. None too happy, mind, said he couldn't see why we'd want to be talking to him. And Maisie, she was going mad. Shouting and crying, telling me to leave her husband alone. It was only when Charlie told her to be quiet and that everything would be fine, she shut up. I thought I'd need to arrest her as well for disturbing the peace.'

'Where's Butler now?'

'In a cell with a mug of tea and a few biscuits for his breakfast. Told him I wouldn't lock the door as long as he behaves himself. Should I sit with him until you get here?'

'No need. I'm sure he'll be quiet. Anyway, if he intended to run he'll have done it while you've been on the telephone. If he has, there'll be no-one to sit with when you hang up, will there? I'll be at the station within the half hour.'

A quick slice of toast and a much-needed cup of tea later I stepped out onto the rain-soaked street into bright sunshine, the air fresh as it can only be after an autumn storm. Drops were still falling from the leaves and a layer of grey clouds floated on the horizon behind the castle, but it looked like we'd now be in for a fine, crisp day. I crossed the road to stroll beside the high sandstone walls, which caught the best of the light, and slowed my pace when I caught sight of a figure admiring Leicester's Gatehouse. I shielded my eyes and took a few steps closer to a woman who hadn't noticed me.

'Miss Stevens?'

Meena's music teacher turned and took a second or two, then smiled in recognition.

'Why, Inspector Given. What are you doing here? Not following me I hope?'

Returning her smile, I straightened my tie and wished I'd paid a little more attention to my appearance before leaving the house. I turned and pointed in its direction.

'I live just over there, across the road and I'm on my way to work. Need to be there in a few minutes. Do you like the castle?'

'It's stunning. To think, so much history. You're very lucky to live in such a lovely place.'

'Yes, I am.'

Every time I stepped across my front doorstep, or looked out of the study window, I knew I'd been right to settle here, despite how I might feel now. The eight-hundred-year-old ruined castle is superb, the countryside gentle and rolling, and the townspeople, in the main, friendly and law-abiding. The open sky and quaint cottages are a million miles from the dingy Birmingham streets where I'd grown up, so I wasn't lying in what I'd said to Miss Stevens. It wasn't my home or the town making me discontented. We chatted for a minute about the changeable weather, then she asked me about Meena.

'Listen, as I said, I'm due at the police station shortly. Why don't you walk up with me, tell me why you're in town and I'll tell you what I can about how far I've got in looking for her. That is … I mean … unless you've other things planned.'

'No, not at all. I'd love to walk with you, I can come down here again for the guided tour later.'

So we strolled up the hill towards the centre of town and I didn't give the Charity School a second look as we passed. Perhaps the images that had haunted me about the place over recent months were subsiding. I explained that there'd been no progress in finding Meena, that I'd put the word out to the local police in Birmingham but they'd had no success so far and that my parents were at their wit's end worrying what had happened.

'We're in difficult times, Inspector. The police in the city have a hard job, especially with so many of the young officers joining the army; it isn't like here in the smaller towns and countryside where I'd suspect there isn't so much crime.'

'I wouldn't be so sure, Miss Stevens; my own constable is talking of leaving to do his bit and even here we have problems. At the moment I'm investigating a murder.'

She clasped a gloved hand to her mouth. 'How awful. Kenilworth seems such a quiet place.'

'Well it is most of the time, but these things happen everywhere. Jealousy, revenge and pure badness affect people in small towns as well as the big cities. The case I'm working on now involves one, or perhaps all, of those things. A vicar killed then posed like a suicide.'

'And are you close to arresting the person who did it?'

I shook my head. 'Not really. We've pulled a man in this morning, that's where I'm going, to question him, but he might be relevant, he might not.'

We continued to talk about the case until turning the corner where the station came into view.

'I'm afraid I have to go in there now, and you haven't said why you've come to Kenilworth or how long you'll be in town. Do you have students here?'

'No, not living here, there's an old one playing in a string quartet concert in the church this evening and I've bullied an old school friend who does live here to come along. I caught an early train to take in the sights. I'm so glad I did, or we wouldn't have met.'

The flush spread from below my collar and rose into my cheeks.

'Look, Miss Stevens, I need to get inside.' I drew a deep breath and crossed my fingers behind my back. 'Would it be too much to ask for you to join me for lunch later? I should be through here by twelve.'

Her face clouded for a second, then the smile broke through again.

'That would be lovely, Mr Given.'

After I left her, the steps into the station and up to the third floor disappeared faster than they did most mornings.

I told Sergeant Burns to have Sawyer bring Charlie Butler to the interview room while I grabbed a cup of tea. A few minutes later a curly-haired man was sitting across the table from me, Sawyer on a chair behind him. I'd always seen Sawyer as an impressive figure, towering over me as he did but Butler looked to be his match. Tall and muscled, with heavy boots and the clothes and cap of a labourer, he looked like a man used to hard work.

'Thanks for coming in Mr Butler. All right if I call you Charlie?' I didn't wait for a reply. 'I'm Inspector Given ... and Detective Constable Sawyer you've already met. You know why you're here?'

A growl rumbled from deep inside Butler. 'No idea.'

'You sure? Do you remember twenty-sixth of August? Saturday it was, a little over three weeks ago.'

'Doesn't spring to mind. Should I?'

'Not particularly. Expect it was just another night on the town for you. From what I pick up, you're a man who's always getting into fights.'

Butler frowned and tightened his grip on the arm of his chair.

'Who told you that?'

'Common knowledge, Charlie, common knowledge. Let me jog your memory. You had a fight with a man called Duncan Beattie.'

'Never heard of him.'

'How about Albert Green? You know him I'll bet.'

Butler shook his head. 'Don't think so, doesn't ring a bell.'

'All right, we'll come back to him in a minute. How about the thirtieth of August, Wednesday, four nights after your fight, where were you?'

'Wednesday? I'd have been at work.'

'And after work, say around seven o'clock onward?'

Butler looked down and picked a fingernail. 'Can't remember.'

'That's convenient, Charlie, are you always so forgetful?'

'No.'

'So are you lying?'

'Why would I lie?'

'You tell me. Maybe there's something you don't want me to know.'

He snorted but it sounded like a show of bravado to hide the truth. I pressed again.

'You finding this funny, Charlie? If you won't help I must assume you've something to hide.'

'Just can't remember is all. How's a bloke supposed to keep in his head everywhere he's been? Could have been in the pub.'

'Which one?'

'Dunno, probably The Black Swan, that's my local.'

'Fine, we'll ask the landlord, see if he agrees. So, back to this fight. You're still telling me you don't know Albert Green?'

'That's what I said.'

'Oh well, we'd better ask Maisie hadn't we? She knows him, doesn't she DC Sawyer?'

Sawyer grinned. 'That's what people say, Inspector, knows him very well.'

'Actually, I expect we should say she knew him very well. Before someone strung him up. Strictly speaking he was the Reverend Duncan Beattie when he died, but Charlie here would only have known him as Green.'

Butler stiffened. 'What is this? I had nothing to do with no murder.'

'Not true that is it, Charlie? How long were you inside, ten years was it?'

He relaxed and looked me straight in the eye.

'Eight, and it wasn't murder.'

'No, manslaughter, wasn't it? Same thing though, you killed a man.'

'If you say so.'

When a suspect becomes sullen it's much harder to get information from them. I had to shake him out of it.

'Argument over your wife wasn't it? Seems you make a habit of choosing the wrong woman, Charlie.'

'Sorry, Inspector, you've got me there, I don't understand.'

'Well I'm told Maisie enjoyed Reverend Beattie's attentions. Really lapping it up, I heard.'

He was out of his chair and at my throat in an instant, strong thumbs crushing my windpipe. Sawyer dragged him off, pulled him to his seat and handcuffed the man's hands behind his back. He then punched Butler in the stomach. Hard. We both coughed and spluttered for minutes.

'Seems that temper of yours keeps flaring, doesn't it? Is that what happened with Beattie? Knocked you down in front of your mates and you couldn't forgive him for flirting with your wife? Talked him into meeting somewhere private then killed him? Is that it?'

Butler was shaking. 'No, no, it wasn't like that.'

'Like what, Charlie? He didn't floor you or you didn't kill him?'

'I didn't kill him. Why would I? I know my Maisie's attractive to men but Green… Beattie and me made it up afterwards. Had a few jars together. He was a decent feller.'

'You expect me to believe you didn't hold a grudge? A minute ago, you swore you'd never even met Green. I was also told you'd said you'd never forgive and forget. Bit of a stranger to the truth if you ask me.' I turned to Sawyer again. 'What do you think, constable? Do you believe Charlie?'

Sawyer stood and hovered behind the seated Butler, knowing what was coming next.

'No, I don't, sir. Not a word. Makes you wonder what else he's been lying about.'

I nodded and Sawyer cautioned him he was being arrested on suspicion of the murder of Reverend Duncan Beattie and we'd keep him in the cells until we could get him to court. All the way through this he protested innocence, rocking from side to side trying to free his arms, and even shouted back as Sawyer led him out into the corridor.

'You'll be sorry for this, Given. I didn't do anything, and you'll be so, so, sorry.'

SEVENTEEN

'Did you have a good morning's sightseeing, Miss Stevens?'

'Excellent. And please call me Rachel.' She laughed. 'It would make you sound so much less like one of my students.'

We'd met at what I considered to be one of the smarter cafés in the town, and even though I was ten minutes early she was waiting outside when I arrived. It was lunchtime but there were plenty of tables available, so I chose one by a window overlooking the street.

'Kenilworth is a pretty town, Inspector.'

I held up my hand. 'If I'm to call you Rachel then you must call me James — it would make you sound so much less like one of my constables.'

A waitress came across and took our order.

'Yes,' said Rachel, 'a really pretty town. I walked round the shops for an hour then down the hill again to take another look at the castle. An extremely nice lady sold me a guidebook because there weren't enough visitors to make the tour worthwhile, so I sat and read it on a bench inside the walls where I could imagine all of the rich history. On my way back here, I peeked into the gates of a school. Now what was it called? Something Charity School I think. There's an interesting-looking old chapel in there. Do you know it?'

I shuddered.

'I'm afraid I do. Hannah Robinson's Charity School was the scene of a recent case I investigated. One I'd rather forget.'

'James, I am sorry, I shouldn't have mentioned it.'

'You weren't to know, were you, and you're right, the chapel is interesting, though I hope I won't be visiting again too soon.'

Sandwiches and tea arrived, preventing the embarrassing silence which might have followed, and I turned the conversation in a different direction.

'Are you looking forward to your concert this evening?'

'It should be lovely. The cellist was my student when she was young, outgrew me a long time ago, and they're playing Haydn and Mozart, my favourite composers. I wish my friend Betty was enthusiastic, but she's more a fan of music hall than Mozart. How about you, James? Should I let her off the hook and you come with me?'

Now I was torn. Although I had listened to classical music on the BBC, I'd never been to a live concert and wasn't sure I'd enjoy it. Set against this, the prospect of spending the evening in Rachel's company was so great an attraction there was no real competition.

'Won't your friend be disappointed? Perhaps she'll want to go out with you.'

'Who? Betty? Not at all. We'll have our dinner and a good chinwag then she'll be happy to settle down and listen to her favourite programmes. Do come. It would be lovely.'

How could I resist?

For the next hour we got to know each other over iced buns and several refills of the teapot. Rachel had been a rising orchestral star in her early twenties, travelling much of the world, until she fell when skiing in the Italian Alps and damaged the tendons in her right arm. They healed over time, but she never recovered the dexterity to play violin at the top level and so became a teacher. She'd moved to Birmingham from her Cotswolds cottage because the pool of potential students was much bigger.

'A girl has to make a living you know, and there are more music opportunities in a big city than a village. I go to concerts whenever I can and I help with a local school orchestra, which is a lot of fun.'

'One of the joys of living in a country town like Kenilworth is you get to know folks from all walks of life in a way you don't in a city.'

As if to confirm this view, over the time we were sitting there, I saw several people I knew walk past the window. Henry Sturges was the first, and I almost tapped the glass to attract his attention then thought better of it; moments later Mr Fairfax and Mrs Tennant, the butcher and postmistress, followed behind, engaged in conversation. Soon afterwards I spotted the curate, Edward Winston, come out of a cake shop across the street, peer left and right then stride out of view.

I pointed out each of these as they appeared until, even to me, it became boring. At last I blurted out the question I'd wanted to ask since we'd met.

'You never married?'

A shadow flitted across Rachel's face.

'Almost. Once. He was a musician too, but we drifted apart after my accident. Philip was travelling and I wasn't, then I heard he'd taken up with someone else and that was that. Since then there's never been a Mr Right and, up to now, I've been happy on my own. What about you?'

I coughed and ran my finger round the inside of my collar like a schoolboy in front of his headmaster.

'I was at sea for many years at the stage when most young men are settling down to married life, so I've only ever been close to two women. One, who I thought I'd marry, decided to take another path. The other died before we made any plans for the future. She's the reason I joined the force.'

I wasn't certain it was still a good reason to stay in my job, but it wasn't the time nor the place to tell Rachel. It was only just dawning on me this was the case, and I wasn't sure what the repercussions might be.

'How sad, James. Perhaps you'll find someone soon.'

Was this an invitation or a kindness, something said to make me feel better? Rachel's eyes wore the same amused twinkle they had the first time we met so gave nothing away. I looked at my watch and cursed that I had to get back to work rather than carrying on the conversation well into the afternoon.

'I'm sorry, Rachel, but I have to go, much as I'd like to stay.'

'Such a shame, I'd have enjoyed a guided tour round of the town. Still, we'll have this evening.'

I left her on the café step, agreeing where we'd meet for our concert.

Rachel had been waiting by the church gates when I arrived, though I struggled to find her in the crowd.

'You made it, James, I thought you'd changed your mind.'

'Sorry, I've been looking for you for five minutes, I never thought there'd be so many here.'

'With all the cinemas and dances shut down, I expect there's not much else for people to do other than stay at home and listen to gloom and doom on the wireless.' Rachel pointed up at the spire. 'Impressive, don't you think?'

I hadn't had chance to take in the building, but she was right. Red sandstone, like the castle, and at least two hundred feet tall. In fact, the whole building was beautiful in the late evening light, which glowed off its walls and arched windows.

We shuffled in line for ten minutes before a jolly lady took our tickets and said to sit anywhere.

This was easier said than done. Saint Aubin's church was packed, largely, I suspected, with relatives of members of the orchestra and the only spare seats were individual ones, dotted around. As the point had been to spend the evening with Rachel, I didn't fancy sitting three rows away from her at a concert I wasn't sure about anyway. The face of a woman in her twenties poked through the curtain, then the rest of her stepped out and waved to Rachel, who waved back.

'Elsa, how are you? This is so exciting.'

They chatted for a few minutes with the friend glancing in my direction until Rachel realised she hadn't introduced me.

'I'm sorry, how rude of me. This is James. He's a friend and a policeman here in Kenilworth. Do you know each other?'

We said we didn't, and Elsa led us to two empty seats in the reserved section near the front.

'I had them keep these for you.' A bell sounded and she turned away. 'I need to go now, but enjoy the concert and I'll see you afterwards.'

This wasn't going at all as I planned. I had thought Rachel and I might get an hour on our own after the concert, but this now seemed unlikely. My only hope would be for Elsa to fall ill or remember another engagement.

Soon after taking our seats, they turned off the lights above the audience, leaving only the stage and the orchestra lit. The conductor tapped the rostrum with his baton and the first nervous notes from the violins began. I'd love to say the concert exceeded expectations, but it didn't. It seemed a good amateur orchestra and Elsa's solo was outstanding, but the choice of pieces bordered on the obscure, at least to me, and the whole event wasn't a patch on performances on the wireless. I didn't offer Rachel my opinion and I applauded enthusiastically after each piece, crying "Encore" at the end as loudly as anyone.

Needless to say, Rachel's ex-pupil didn't succumb to sudden illness, nor was she called away, so I had to endure her company, and a dozen other musicians, rather than an intimate evening with my preferred companion. We stayed for an hour before I said to them I needed to be away as I'd to be up early for work next morning. I half expected Rachel to stay; she'd been chatting with Elsa and discussing music with the other musicians, who were clearly in awe of her reputation. Instead, she didn't hesitate to grab her coat when I gave my excuses.

It had started to drizzle, so we sheltered under Rachel's umbrella as we walked round to where she was staying. She had been quiet, though wearing a smile, for the last quarter of a mile.

'Penny for them?'

'I'm thinking about you, James.'

It was too dark for her to see me blush.

'Me?'

'Yes, you. The concert was dreadful, apart from Elsa, and anyone would think it was the BBC Symphony Orchestra the way you applauded. You are nice.' She tapped at her friend's front door. 'Now you must go and get out of this weather. Let me know when you're in Birmingham and we can perhaps do this again; I had a lovely evening.'

I stood on the pavement until Rachel went inside, then turned up my collar to brave the damp for the walk down the hill to home. Even the poor weather didn't lower my mood, because I hadn't even felt this way when I'd met Heather. She and I had grown together over time, but this thing with Rachel was like a bolt from the blue. I was smitten and couldn't work out how or why. All I knew was she made me feel good in a way I hadn't for a long time.

The note on my desk when I got in on Friday morning asked me to call Inspector Godfrey at Birmingham central police station. I'd been introduced to him at my father's synagogue and he'd been the obvious one to contact when I'd wanted help to look for Meena. From all accounts he was a decent copper with a good reputation. I picked up the receiver and dialled his number.

'Ah, morning, Inspector Given. Has she turned up yet?'

'No, she hasn't, I was hoping you'd called because you had some news.'

'Afraid not. I only rang to see if you had. I've had the lads keeping their eyes open ever since you phoned but there's been no sign. Not a one. I even passed the word to other local stations but there's nothing. You've checked all her friends I expect?'

'She's not been in England too long so hasn't many friends outside work. We've spoken to all the ones we know, and none have heard from her. She has a music teacher and I've questioned her, but she knows nothing either. The note I found hasn't led anywhere?'

'No. Looks to us like the girl's left of her own accord if I'm honest. Will I make it an official missing person case so I can get some proper time committed to it? That note will make it more difficult, so I've kept it low profile as a favour to a colleague.' Godfrey took a deep breath. 'You know yourself; these young ones go off from time to time, then they're embarrassed when it turns out they've been having a fling with the boyfriend.'

167

I thanked Godfrey for his understanding and said I'd be grateful if he felt able to make it more official.

'You do understand, James, this won't necessarily lead anywhere? There are thousands of young women in Birmingham, and thousands of places to hide if they're so minded. Have you considered she might even have left the city?'

'Naturally, but we have to start somewhere, don't we?'

'Well if you can let me have a photograph I will, of course, pass the material round my colleagues, but I can't hold out much hope.'

We went through the necessary paperwork on the telephone and I told him I'd have my father drop off some photographs he had of Meena.

'Keep in touch, Inspector Given, and I'll do what I can. It's a good thing your family has done taking in this girl, and a real shame if she has run away. Sadly, though, we have to hope that's what's happened and nothing more sinister.'

He was right. The alternative might be much worse.

EIGHTEEN

Godfrey and I were saying our goodbyes when Sawyer knocked and came in, so I waved him to a seat as I hung up. When I put down the receiver he must have seen something worried me.

'Problem, sir?'

'Family stuff. Meena, the Kindertransport girl my parents are looking after, still hasn't come home. It's probably nothing but they're worried to death. The call was from an Inspector in Birmingham who's helping in the search. I should spend more time looking for her myself but can't spare it with this damn Beattie case on the go. Anything new to report?'

'I've been looking into Henry Sturges' past.'

'What? Who told you to do that?'

'No-one, but someone has to check him out.' Sawyer glared at me. 'And you don't seem to want to do it, though it's pretty clear it must be a person from Reverend Beattie's past who killed him.'

'Why "pretty clear", where's the evidence for that?'

'Well there's no evidence that anyone local did it either, is there? Weeks looking and hardly a step forward, just clutching at straws. Bridgnorth and Wilkes aren't serious contenders, nor any of the parishioners I've interviewed. It has to be someone who met the vicar before he came here.'

'What about Charlie Butler down in the cells? Even the magistrate said we can hold him for more questioning.'

'Come on, sir, we both know he's not a candidate either. Look at the size of Butler, he'd strangle Beattie with his bare hands without having to resort to a rope and noose to do the job. Like all the alternatives, if he killed the vicar in a fit of temper he hasn't the brains to plan anything complicated.'

Sawyer's point was a good one. This was the problem all the way through this case. The people with any kind of motive were either not physically capable or not bright enough to construct a murder like this one. None had the means, motive and opportunity to commit the crime, and until we uncovered someone who did we would clutch at straws. The only one, so far, who'd previous form for violence on the scale of Beattie's murder was Butler, so I wasn't about to release him as our prime suspect. Not until someone more credible came along.

'So what is it you think you've found on Henry?'

'Sturges has no history before March.'

'What do you mean?'

'After telephoning a few people there's no record of him anywhere for the past twenty years until he arrived here in town a few months ago. No income tax records, never been in trouble with the police anywhere in the county, no driving licence, not even a dog licence. And there's no address I can find before the one he's at now.'

I shook my head. 'Then you've nothing. Henry's already told me he was out of the country for a long time on the boats, then in Italy.'

'There's something that doesn't add up about the man, sir —' Sawyer paused, his face flushed — 'and I think you're blind to it because the two of you have become mates.'

'How dare you!' For the briefest moment I almost threw him out, telling him to mind his own business. Then the logic kicked in and I accepted he might be right, what did I know about Henry? In the course of an investigation we'd met in a pub and shared an enjoyable lunch. Hardly a lifetime spent building up trust. I took a deep breath and counted to ten.

'I'm not happy, John, about you going behind my back when I told you to leave it but, for now, we'll lay that to one side. You're right, we can't ignore potential involvement by Henry Sturges just because I'm friendly with him. I'll fill you in with everything I've learnt about the man and you do more digging.'

Sawyer's jaw dropped and the look of surprise on his face was worth every bit of my climb down.

'Are you serious, sir? I didn't expect that. Thought you would bawl me out.'

'Next time, DC Sawyer, next time.'

He stood to leave, and I pointed a finger to stop him. 'But don't let there be a next time; you undermine my wishes again and I'll rip your guts for garters. Understand?'

Sawyer continued on his path out of the door without answering or looking back. Once again, I saw I would need to deal with this growing friction between us.

Ten minutes after Sawyer left my head was still throbbing. I'd planned to spend the day going through the Beattie files, but arguing with Sawyer and Godfrey's call had stopped me before I'd even started. The telephone rang at the moment I pulled the papers across my desk. It was the desk sergeant, Tommy Burns.

'What is it now, Sergeant? This better be important.'

Luckily, Tommy wasn't one to take offence; that's why he's been on desk duties for as long as anyone is able to remember. He'd dealt with enough angry members of the public, drunks, villains and senior officers for nothing to bother him.

'Young lady down here for you, Inspector.' His voice lowered to a whisper. 'And good-looker she is too. Proper cracker.'

'What's her name?'

'Says you know her as Mary Selkirk.'

'Thanks, Tommy. Sorry for snapping, it's been one of those days. Think I need a cup of tea. Put young Mary in an interview room and I'll be down when I've popped into the canteen.'

A few minutes later, Tommy gave me a knowing wink when I passed his counter and I threatened to tell his wife he'd been ogling a girl young enough to be his daughter. I could have sworn he muttered 'lucky bugger' as I walked away down the corridor.

Mary grabbed the mug I'd brought down for her and wrapped thin, nicotine stained fingers around it, her polished nails chipped and bitten down to the quick.

'Thanks.'

She wasn't my type, but I could see why Tommy would find her attractive. Slim, good figure and a nice smile I suspected she'd turn on and off for the customers at will. I could also understand why Benny Grainger, her pimp, would want her in his stable.

'You're welcome, Mary. Is Mary all right or would you prefer Jacqueline?'

'No that's fine, Mr Given, it's not often I get to be called by my proper name.'

I looked at this young woman and thought how lucky most of us are to have the lives we live. Here was someone with few chances in her short years. Thrown on the streets when her mother found her an inconvenience, used by men from the age of sixteen and beaten by the likes of Grainger if she didn't do as he told her. I wondered what the future would hold for her when her looks faded and her figure disappeared.

'Have you some information, Mary?'

'It's about Charlie.'

'Charlie Butler?'

The fingers gripped the mug tighter and she nodded. 'Yes.'

'What about him?'

'I heard you'd got him locked up for killing that vicar.'

'Where did you hear that?'

'This is a small place. No secrets for long. Are the rumours true, you've got Charlie here?'

'We're talking to him, that's all. Do you know something?'

'Charlie didn't do it. He was with me.'

'When?'

'When I saw that man leave the backyard.'

Now it was my turn to grip my mug.

'Explain.'

'I'm certain Charlie loves his wife, but he'd not be the only one to want a little female company away from home. He visits me about once a month and was in my bed when I saw what I told you. I'd just got up for a smoke and peeked through the curtains. Charlie couldn't be in two places at the same time, could he?'

'You're not lying to me are you, Mary? Has someone put you up to this? Why didn't you mention it when we talked last time?'

'I'm not making it up, why would I? Charlie's a nice bloke but he means nothing to me, just helps pay the rent. I didn't tell you he was in my room because it's private. Benny would go mad if I did.' She chewed her lip. 'Reckon he'll go mad anyway if he finds out I've been talking to you again.'

'This is the right thing to do, so don't worry about Grainger, I'll sort him out if he has a go at you. Just pass me the word. While we're about it, tell me about him.'

'Nothing to tell. Benny's a pimp, that's all. Like all the others he has good days and bad days. Looks after us girls as best he can but takes most of our cash in exchange. Clips us now and again if we get out of line.'

I was not surprised to hear he was violent.

'Could he be the one you saw from your window?'

She glanced towards the door. 'Can I get a smoke?'

I borrowed a cigarette and matches from Tommy Burns. When I tossed them across the desk, Mary lit up and dragged deeply. She held the smoke in her lungs then threw back her head and exhaled a cloud upwards.

'So, think hard, Mary, is it possible the man you saw heading through the gate was Benny Grainger?'

'Probably not. I spoke to him in the kitchen just before Charlie arrived and he was there when I walked through again after we'd finished. Anyway, why would he go all the way round when he could just nip out the back door?'

'Perhaps to put anyone seeing him off the trail.'

'Never thought of that.' Mary's eyes darted towards the door again. 'Oh my God, I must get away. Benny might come after me as well.'

'He may have nothing to do with it, Mary, so no need to panic. I'll not tell him you've been here, but is there a safe place you can go if you want to?'

'I've a sister living near Coventry, she'll take me in. Her Bobby's a miner. Tough as nails. Bobby will send Benny packing if he comes after me.'

Mary struggled through her statement again for me to write it down then I walked with her to the front door. Tommy was still staring after her as it closed. I stopped in front of him, tutting and folding my arms.

'Stick the tongue back in your mouth, Sergeant Burns, and do the paperwork to release Charlie Butler.'

In my opinion John Sawyer and I always worked well together, but today's argument and his decision to carry out his own investigation into Henry's background was making me think again. When he was in uniform we disagreed from time to time, but this was different, it felt like he was no longer prepared to accept my authority and I wasn't comfortable with that. A good man, and loyal, he was also a decent investigator, so it made sense to respect his suggestions. None of this, though, made me feel any better.

Sawyer had also been right about Charlie Butler, and releasing him left me in doubly bad sorts, leaving my focus in shreds. With Butler out of the frame we'd no-one for Reverend Beattie's murder and it would only be a matter of time before the boss pulled us off the case. If he did so, Dyer would put me on filing duties until I retired.

I was tempted to go home for the afternoon, do a little gardening to take my mind off things, perhaps to return fresh in the morning, though I wasn't convinced that putting it to one side would help. Not that we had too many options, there were too few, so, rather than escaping, I stuck a note saying "do not disturb" on my door, pulled my chair up close to the desk and spread the material in front of me.

Sawyer had done a good job in putting the material in order. Instead of the jumble of random jottings he left for me when I came back from France, there was now a neat folder with everything dated and divided into relevant sections. There were now even typed or rewritten notes where Phil Trimble's scribble had been illegible and Sawyer created a second folder containing the photographs of the crime scene, now dated and annotated. The interviews and records of investigations carried out since I took over were in a third. It was good to see he'd even updated the material when anything new emerged.

Starting with the early stuff, referring to the photographs when necessary, there was little added to what they gathered before I returned from France, despite Sawyer's housekeeping efforts. One thing I noticed hidden in the statements was that several girls could vouch for Benny Grainger's movements in the couple of days before Beattie's body was discovered, so the pimp was off the hook. They may be lying but in court their evidence would carry some weight. Unless something obvious turned up, we'd take him off our list.

On top of this, neither Trimble nor Sawyer interviewed Beattie's curate, and hadn't asked Mary Selkirk what she'd been doing leading up to spotting our possible killer. With hindsight it's easy to find fault with a colleague's work, but it annoyed me that he'd missed routine questions to the prostitute. The answers might have saved us time and saved Charlie Butler considerable inconvenience. Not talking to Edward Winston was a much more serious omission. Someone who'd worked closely with the dead man, even shared his house and, on occasions, a drink and his dinner table. Even if they'd assumed Beattie had committed suicide, his curate might have provided some insight into the vicar's state of mind. I rang Sawyer to check.

'Sorry, sir, I didn't interview him or any of the prostitutes. Inspector Trimble didn't ask me to. He handled them himself, seeming to want the whole thing wrapped up and anyway, at the time, it looked a clear case of Reverend Beattie having done away with himself.'

'It's all right, John, I'm not blaming you, it wasn't your shout. I just wanted to make sure the interview notes hadn't been mislaid. Now I've spoken to Winston myself, so we've covered it.'

It was true I'd talked to the curate and he had nothing to offer, but it made me wonder what else Trimble overlooked through his willingness to adopt the most obvious solution. I trawled through the initial material once more to see if there was anything else which they could have followed up. There didn't appear to be, though it's difficult to spot where there should be further enquiries when a piece of the picture is missing.

I moved on to the section of the file covering the time I'd been working on the case. Slowly, slowly. Read a document, take time to absorb, then read it again. Still no suspects leapt out. Pushing the files away I rubbed my eyes. Time to go home, but the prospect of a night on my own, with this dead-end case whirling round my head filled me with dismay. Instead, I plodded down to the canteen looking for some company to lift me. There was no-one in other than a newer constable who I'd not met. So I filled my stomach with stodgy steak pie and some bread-and-butter pudding, then went back to my office to go through the whole lot again.

The possibility of the vicar's wife, Janet Beattie, being a realistic prospect had been bothering me since the last time I'd spoken to her. Mrs Beattie had been adamant she wouldn't have killed her husband for the minimal financial benefit she might get. This wouldn't be the first guilty person to protest their innocence, but I wanted to believe her. So I looked for any trifle in the notes to suggest she might be lying and there was nothing. The parishioners she'd told me would corroborate her movements at the time around her husband's death did, most of them shocked I was even asking questions about her. As a result, I telephoned her.

'Inspector Given, I asked you not to contact me again until you either had Duncan's murderer under arrest or I had a solicitor with me. I assume it isn't the former, so why are you calling?'

'Let's not get off on the wrong foot again, Mrs Beattie. I won't apologise for considering you as a suspect, it's normal for us to look at family members when something like this happens. However, I'm now satisfied, having looked at all the evidence, we can discount your involvement.'

Her response, as I expected, was grudging but gracious, and we parted, after I'd updated her on our progress, or lack of it, on better terms than last time.

When I left the station it was dark, and I was no further forward and feeling just as bad as I had before my dinner. I called in to The Queen rather than going home to a quiet and empty house, still hoping to lift my spirits. The place was dead, and as soon as I ordered my drink I knew it had been a mistake to go into a pub to end my troubles. The landlord poured my Vimto and I eyed the beer pumps and rum bottle, knowing I needed to get out while I still had the strength of will to do so.

NINETEEN

After a long breakfast reading bad news I pottered round the garden, trying to shake the war from my thoughts. The Soviets had taken a number of cities in Poland, making me wonder why we were defending the country against Germany and not them. When I read further I understood. Hitler had announced the confiscation of radios from all Jews, cutting down their ability to stay in touch with the rest of Europe, to hear how the war was going for Germany and to deprive them of any hope that a rescue was at hand.

A steady drizzle began to fall at lunchtime, moments after I'd finished cutting the grass, so my plan to spend the afternoon gardening was curtailed. Nothing in the larder caught my fancy for lunch and I considered going back to the office to read the Beattie files one more time. I decided there was no point, nothing would have changed since my efforts of the previous day. Instead, I went upstairs, packed an overnight bag, strapped on my gasmask and took off for the railway station.

To save my petrol ration and give myself time to think I took the train to Birmingham, rather than driving. My head was filled not with Beattie and his killer but other things. Sawyer and his new-found insubordination, my Uncle Gideon, and, most of all, Meena's disappearance. I should have spent more time looking for the girl, but the boss had been more lenient with my absences than I deserved and wouldn't stretch much further. Even if he did, Birmingham wasn't my patch; I'd hardly know where to begin. The same was true of my uncle; France was an even bigger mystery than Birmingham, though I'd need to go to look for him again as soon as we'd put the vicar's murder to bed. These thoughts didn't raise a glimmer of optimism, and my mood darkened the closer I got to my parents' home. Nothing improved while talking with my father about the telephone call from Inspector Godfrey.

'Meena deserves better than this, Jacob. The poor girl is a guest in our country. How can the police sit on their backsides and do nothing while she's out there, possibly hurt or worse?'

'It isn't like that. There's a war on, in case you hadn't noticed, and the police have more important things to worry about than looking for a girl who might have run away because she doesn't like the family she's with, or because she's found some boy she likes more.'

'But she hasn't gone with a boy. Why would they think that? Meena is a decent young woman.'

'How can you say that, Papa, she only came here in May. She's lived under your roof, but you've not met her family. You know nothing about her.'

'Yes I do. And she wouldn't go off like this.'

'You've nothing to back it up, other than a blind belief you can't be wrong. Like always. Were you aware she's sweet on Eli? No, of course you weren't.'

'What? Who told you that?'

'It doesn't matter who told me, but if you looked at her once in a while you'd have spotted it like I did. If she's noticed Eli in that way, who's to say she's not the same with someone you've never met?'

Rather than convincing my father, this only hardened his attitude and he pushed and pushed for the next half hour, with my mother trying to calm him, until I said I was going for a walk. I grabbed my coat and hat from the stand, threw them on and headed for the door.

'I'm sorry, Papa, this is a waste of time, there's nothing more I can say or do so I'll see you in the morning. Don't wait up.'

My mother tried to block my way.

'Please, Jacob, don't go. It's not good to leave in a temper. Stay and eat. Please.'

'I need to clear my head, Mama. Neither of us want this argument over dinner, do we? If I take a long walk, perhaps we'll all be calmer when I get back.'

Forcing my way past, I hurried down the stairs, out to the damp evening, intent on going where I hoped to find some brighter spirit.

I stood outside Rachel's gate for several minutes, unsure whether to knock at her front door. The blackout made the street darkness almost impenetrable, and she lived in a respectable neighbourhood where single ladies were not expected to receive male callers at this hour of the evening. The only light to be seen escaped from the curtains of her downstairs window, and I suspected she'd have a visit from the air-raid precautions warden before too long if she didn't remedy it. When I ventured to her doorstep I heard a piano playing and hoped it was the teacher, not one of her students, so when the notes faded I took my courage in both hands and rattled the letterbox. The door opened a few inches and Rachel's eyes peered into the gloom before she flung it open wider.

'James! How lovely to see you. Come inside. Quickly now, before the neighbours start their tongues wagging.'

In her kitchen I watched while she busied herself with filling the teapot and putting two slices of Victoria sponge onto a plate she'd lifted from a fine oak dresser.

'I can't see I'll be able to make these too much longer, what with all this talk of rationing, so we may as well enjoy them while we can. Sorry I haven't more, but I haven't baked since I came back from Kenilworth. Come on, James, take a seat and tell me why you're here.'

What was I expecting from this woman? Consolation? Friendship? More? So I lied and said I'd been walking in the area and found myself on her street.

'I hope you don't mind me calling. We had such an agreeable time when we met, and I thought … I thought we'd got on well so hoped I could ask you out sometime.'

Rachel smiled and the evening improved.

Over the cake we talked about the weather and other inconsequentials. Later she told me about the antics of her music students, and I told her about the lack of progress in the Beattie case, and how worried my parents were about Meena. I confessed that part of my reason for wandering the streets was my argument with my father. We talked of the war for a while and she listened to my concern for both my brother, Eli, and Sawyer, if they joined up.

Afterwards Rachel invited me through to her sitting room, offering me a leather armchair. She lit the gas fire and sat on a matching settee, contemplating a photograph on the mantelpiece of a young man in army uniform.

'My father. He was killed in the last war. I was twelve years old and wanted to die. I even considered killing myself to be with him. It was the saddest time in my life. Then I thought of how much he'd loved to hear me play my violin and threw myself into being the best I could. Even now, every time I pick it up I imagine he is listening somewhere.'

'That's a nice way to remember him. What happened?'

'I don't know the whole story. Dad was born here, and his parents. The family came from Spain many years ago, but he considered himself English, without a doubt, and joining the army to fight would be natural to him. Mum told me he'd been a hero, but I imagine he was part of the cannon fodder of 1916 like all of them and she only said it to make me feel better. Have you had sadness in your life, James?'

'Some, but doesn't everyone?'

'Dealing with violence and killings as you do every day can't be easy.'

'No, sometimes it isn't, but in a way I'm one step removed from the victim. I'm not a relative or a friend so, like anyone would, I regret their passing and regret that the world is the way it is, but wouldn't say I mourn them, not in a personal way.'

'Is it so different?'

'Oh yes, I think so. I lost someone once who was dear to me and it was very, very different.'

'Was this the girl you told me had died? The one you said caused you to become a policeman?'

'Yes.'

'How did she die?'

I'd not talked to anyone else about Heather for ages, so why did this woman across the room make me want to pour my heart out? A sensitivity coming from her love of music perhaps, or the quality that some people have of making others feel comfortable and secure. We'd only met a week earlier, and already I felt there was something special about her.

'I was young, just returned from sea, and trying to work out what I'd do with my life. I worked in the Kent fruit fields, loving the physical labour and the open air, as close to being on the boats as it was possible to be on dry land. Heather spent her summers doing the same and we grew close, even talked about marriage. She made me so happy. Then two men raped and murdered her.'

Rachel clasped her hand to her mouth and closed her eyes. 'Oh, James, how horrible.'

'The lowest point I've ever been, and I went to pieces for a while, drank myself stupid, but got through to the other side. That's why I joined the police, to find her killers and bring them to justice.'

'And did you?'

'Not in the way I intended, but they got what they deserved.'

We sat quietly for a few minutes. My new friend may not have known what to say next, or she may have wanted to be with thoughts of her father, but the silence helped me put my life in perspective. Rachel lost a parent to war a generation ago, like millions of other children and may soon be joined by many more in this one. I shuddered to think of this carnage and stood up.

'I should be leaving.'

'Won't you stay a little longer?'

I shook my head. We agreed that I'd telephone her in advance next time so we could go to the cinema or a meal and, before I left, I asked to go to her music room.

'Whatever for, James? Not taking up the violin are you?'

I crooked a finger for her to follow me, then walked through and closed the chink in her curtains.

'Can't have the warden knocking at your door, can we, especially with an officer of the law already inside? I'd get the sack.'

Rachel stepped towards me, putting her fingertips to my cheek and I so much wanted to kiss her. She stepped away, grinning.

'Don't go, James. Let's eat. The restaurant in the Cameron Hotel will still be serving, and that cake's whetted my appetite.'

Rachel gave me one of her dazzling smiles.

'You're a very sociable man, James.'

Was this a precursor to the brush off?

'But?'

The smile broadened further.

'No "but", James, why should you think such a thing?'

I fiddled with my pudding spoon.

'So you're not going to tell me you don't want to see me again?'

'Nonsense, you're one of the nicest people I've met in a good while. Someone who's dedicated to what they do, kind —' she raised an eyebrow — 'and you're not totally hideous.'

'Well that's something to be thankful for.'

We both laughed.

'So what brought that on?'

'Oh nothing. I met a man and it set me to thinking about myself. There are some people, male or female, who attract followers like wasps round fallen fruit. It doesn't seem to matter if they're attractive or funny or wise, they have a kind of chemistry. I'm not like that, I've never been the kind of person who people want to talk to. I don't mean I'm shunned, it's just that they don't seek my company. Perhaps I'm a little too reserved, or perhaps it's because of my job, they're scared to get too close. After I left this man, his name's Henry, I realised I have no real friends. Acquaintances, yes. Colleagues, yes. But no-one I can sit with in sociable silence.'

Rachel leant forward and covered my hand with hers.

'Maybe we can remedy that.'

By half past nine the waiters were clearing tables and shooting glances in our direction as the last couple in the place. We continued chatting about everything and nothing until the manager came over and explained politely that they were waiting to close, that we'd be welcome again any time, but he really needed to put out the lights. The man did it with such charm we couldn't help but smile when we wandered out into the cold night air.

The clock in St Paul's church chimed ten as we walked hand in hand through dark streets the short distance to Rachel's house, and at her gate I told her I'd had a wonderful evening and I'd telephone her soon. As I turned to leave, she grabbed my elbow and turned me back.

'Don't leave, James. Come inside for a nightcap.'

'I shouldn't, I need to be up early for work.'

Rachel pulled me close and kissed me full on the mouth. It lasted a long time before we separated.

'You and your work,' she said. 'Let's see if we can't take your mind off it for a little while.'

When I left Rachel's at midnight, on deserted streets, the wind had freshened and it had started to drizzle, so I pulled up my coat collar and pulled down the brim of my hat. Winter was on its way.

As I turned in to Livery Street a uniformed policeman stepped out of the darkness, making me jump.

'Evening, sir, might I ask what you're doing out at this time of night?'

'Good God, Constable, you almost gave me a heart attack.'

'Sorry about that, sir, but please answer my question.'

I explained that I was a Detective Inspector and that I was walking home to my parents' home after visiting a friend. He wanted to see my warrant card, but the gloom made it impossible and he refused to shine his torch in case it prompted an air-raid. I told him not to be so stupid.

'Come on man. Do you really imagine German bombers are hovering overhead, waiting for an unsuspecting copper to light his lamp for a few seconds?'

'Can't be too careful. Here's you roaming the streets at dead of night and could be anybody. A spy even. Just hoping someone like me will stop you and be tricked into signalling your mates up above. Next thing the whole area's flattened.'

'Well I'm afraid there's not much I can do to convince you is there.' He'd not seen my grin in the dark. 'You'd best take me down the station and we can sort it out there. Then I'll phone my superintendent, wake him up so he'll be in bad humour, and he'll phone yours. Surely the night shift isn't the worst job to put you on?'

The cogs whirred through the blackness then his torch lit my identification for the briefest moment.

'Ah. Sorry, sir. Just doing my job.'

He was just doing his job and we needed to be grateful that men like him were patrolling the streets at night trying to keep everyone safe. No-one knew what this war would bring but even in these first weeks the petrol rationing, blackout and gasmasks had changed our lives, so it was good to see coppers were staying vigilant, even if it could be inconvenient. I thanked him for the work he was doing, and we parted in opposite directions.

I found my father still sitting in his favourite armchair when I climbed the stairs and let myself in. My mood had lifted while I was out with Rachel and I was hoping his had too, but his opening words showed it hadn't.

'You're late, Jacob, where have you been? Mama was worried.'

'Not that it's really any of your business but I was having dinner with a friend.'

'Until this hour? Have you been drinking again?'

'No. I don't anymore. What is this, Papa? I'm not a child and can come and go as I please without having to explain.'

'Not under this roof you can't. And you'll always be a child to me. You arrive here unannounced, storm out in a bad temper and we don't see you until the middle of the night. Is that acceptable in your parent's house? In my view it isn't.'

I didn't need another argument to spoil the best night I'd had in ages, so I grabbed a big portion of humble pie.

'Sorry, Papa, you're right, I should have telephoned but was having such a pleasant time the evening slipped away.'

'So who is the friend we've to thank for this?'

I hesitated, then admitted it was Meena's music teacher.

'Rachel Stevens? Such a nice lady.' He winked. The apology had done the trick and the annoyance had left his face. 'And so attractive.'

Now I was blushing like a boy caught chatting to a girl outside the school gates, but at least we hadn't descended into another row.

'She's easy to talk to. Do you know her — apart from Meena's lessons?'

'I've met her once or twice; her brother is friends with the rabbi. A good scholar and very observant of scripture.'

Over a pot of tea, we spoke of Meena and about Eli's plan to join the army. I'd been in two minds whether to tell him about my brother's intentions, but my father already knew what Eli was planning.

'Do you think I should try to stop him, Jacob?'

'Of course. He's only a boy.'

'But no younger than when you left for the sea. Am I to deny Eli the chance you took?'

'But the Germans might kill him.'

'Hmm, we could all be killed tomorrow. If it's God's will he survives that's wonderful, if not ... he could die in an air-raid at home if the Almighty considers it time. Or in a bus accident, or falling downstairs. I'll talk to the boy and ask him to wait a while but he's as headstrong as you were, and I can't imagine he'll listen to an old man.'

Despite occasional differences, sometimes about my lost faith, I always knew my father was a wise, if uneducated, man. Short of locking Eli in the house, Papa wouldn't stop him volunteering for military service if it's what he wanted to do.

Later, in my room, I lay for an hour thinking of Eli and Meena. And Rachel.

TWENTY

The drizzle of the preceding night had turned to a full-on soaking rain, which lay in puddles where fallen leaves blocked the roadside gullies, and I'd my head down in a dash to the railway station, only lifting it to watch for traffic when crossing the road. At one busy junction I waited with the drops lashing my cheeks while a convoy of army trucks passed, packed with soldiers looking no older than my brother. Eli would fit in with no problem. Between the vehicles, on the opposite corner of the street, stood a young woman with wavy, blond hair, also waiting for the traffic to clear. Meena. And she hadn't noticed me.

Stepping away from the kerb, I dipped my head again but kept her in sight and waited for her to cross. She walked away and I was able to follow, about ten yards behind, keeping one eye on the doorways ahead in case I needed to dive for cover. After five minutes winding through back streets, Meena stopped, fiddled in her pocket for a key and entered a dingy four-storey building. The scrawled "Rooms to Let" sign pinned to the door announced it to be a lodging house so I took a position across the street, hoping to spot Meena at one of the windows, and I didn't have to wait long. She appeared on the second floor, stared into the street for a few seconds and turned, as if speaking to someone out of sight. An age passed before a figure stepped forward and threw his arms round her. Was this the boyfriend my father insisted Meena didn't have?

The correct thing to do would have been to find the nearest telephone box and call my Birmingham contact, Inspector Godfrey, then let the local police sort it out, but I didn't dare chance the couple leaving before the boys in blue arrived. The front door opened when I was about to ring the bell and a woman and child came out. I mumbled that I'd forgotten my key and she tut-tutted but let me in, scolding not to be so careless in future. I promised that I wouldn't, said she was very kind and puffed up the stairs to rap on the door of the rooms where I'd seen Meena.

'Who is it?' came from the other side. A thick German accent.

'Police. Open up.'

A bolt was pulled back and a painfully thin man's face peered through the narrow gap. Glasses, dark skin and a dark beard, though his hair was lighter, and he looked familiar. He was five to ten years older than me and said something I didn't understand.

I used a phrase I'd used often on my travels. *Sag es landsam bitte* — 'Please say it slowly.' When he repeated I understood he was demanding identification and to know what I wanted.

I held up my warrant card and said in my halting German I must speak to him. I cocked my head at his neighbours' doors, put a finger to my lips and pointed inside where prying eyes wouldn't be watching. Meena appeared at his shoulder, asking, in German, 'who is it?' before she saw me.

'Mr Given, why are you here?'

'I might ask you the same question, Meena. Don't you know we've been terrified something bad had happened to you?'

Her eyes darted between the man and me before she turned away. He dashed after her and waved for me to follow. In the living room, at Meena's side, he took her hand and I looked from one to the other.

'Who are you? Why is Meena in this place?'

The man frowned, perplexed, and Meena intervened.

'He's my father.'

Over the next half hour, with Meena translating, Isaac Classen told a story which chilled me to my bones. Not long after they'd secured their only child's safety by committing her to Kindertransport and the good will of foreigners, he and his wife had been forcibly removed from their home, which was handed to a Nazi party official. The couple were forced to live with four other families in a run-down part of the city.

'This was bad, but not as bad as what came later,' he said. 'First the curfew, then the rationing. Everyone was rationed but Jews received much less. The Nazis were trying to starve us to death, I think. One day they banged on our doors, demanding we gave over everything that might be needed for the war. A wireless, our valuables, even my bicycle. Without it I couldn't ride to work, and we no longer had anything to sell.'

These were the stories we'd heard many times through my father's friends though no-one wanted to believe people could be so cruel, that it must be an exaggeration, but here it was from someone who'd been through it.

'My wife, my lovely Elena, she was not able stand it any longer. A decree was posted outside the house, telling us we were only allowed to shop between certain hours and there was a list of things we were no longer allowed to buy. She read it, shook her head in disgust, then told me that I should go for a walk while she took a bath.' The tears trickled down the poor man's cheeks. 'When I returned I found her. Elena had used my razor to slash open her wrists.'

There was nothing to be said. I just let him and Meena hug and sob through their sorrow for a long time. When he recovered, he said he'd had a choice. Either take the same way out as his wife or try to find their daughter. He chose the latter.

With help from friends he obtained the necessary papers and enough money to get to England.

'Meena wrote when she first arrived and told us she was with a good family in Birmingham, so I came here. I watched outside your father's workshop for a few days, then I approached her when she went to the shop at lunchtime. I'm much thinner than I was, and I now wear the glasses, so thought she might not recognise me. We agreed to meet when we could until I found work and decent rooms, then she'd join me. I begged her not to say anything in case I'd be caught and arrested as a German spy.'

He'd pretended to be Dutch, and there are always jobs if you're not afraid of hard work and don't mind the low wages. There are also always rooms available with no questions asked as long as the rent is paid in advance. As soon as he settled he told Meena everything was ready. She packed only the minimum and left Papa's workshop as if going for lunch. I asked her why she left no note.

'I thought you'd come looking and have a better chance of finding us if you knew we were together. Then they'd arrest my father and take him away.'

Her lack of trust might have insulted me, but it was obvious why she was so frightened. With her mother dead she didn't want to lose her father as well.

'Listen, Meena, you need to trust me to protect your father's secret.' Although it screamed in the face of my policeman's instincts, I would try anything to save him going back to Germany to face almost certain death. 'But you must go to my parents to show them you're safe and well. Please explain this to your father.'

She spoke to him briefly and he shook my hand then nodded, speaking for the first time in English.

'Thank you, Herr Given, you are a kind man.'

I left the two sitting close together, holding hands, and I walked the fifteen minutes to the station to catch the next train back to Kenilworth.

The desk sergeant waved me over when I walked through the entrance.

'Please get in touch with your father, Inspector, he's been telephoning every five minutes for the last half hour, says he needs to talk to you urgently.'

I puffed the three flights up to my office and dialled his number.

'What's wrong father, has something happened?'

'Great news, Jacob. Great news. Meena has come back to us. Her father brought her this morning. He said you found them.'

'I was going to call you when I got back here; I'd no time to come around to the workshop after I left them.'

'No, no, that is fine. I understand. Thank God you stumbled on her.'

'And you've let her go with him?'

'No, no, the girl has stayed here with us, back in her own room.'

'But I don't understand. She's with you? Not with her father?'

'That's what I said. After your visit they talked, and Isaac convinced her she'd be safer with us. Despite your promise to help, he knew he'd have a hard time staying hidden from the authorities in the city, especially with a young daughter to look after as well. He's decided to find somewhere in the countryside, probably in the north. Isaac was there many years ago and loved it. A man has provided him with Dutch papers so he can keep up the pretence of being a refugee from Holland.'

'And how has Meena taken all this?'

'The girl is content. It isn't easy for her, but we have agreed Meena will write often and will visit her father when he's found a new home. Let us hope this war ends soon and she can live with him in peace. Mama is ecstatic to have Meena back.'

After my father hung up, I wondered how long Isaac Classen could stay free. A stranger in England, with no English, and zealous coppers on every corner like the one I met the previous night. Where Classen had gone they'd hardly make the distinction between a Dutchman and a German, simply hearing a foreign accent on someone new to the area. I didn't fancy his chances. Much less if they caught and interned him. Or returned the fugitive to Germany.

TWENTY-ONE

The papers relating to Duncan Beattie's murder still covered my desk where I left them. A note from Sawyer told me he'd still no luck tracing Robbie Wilkes and reminded me I'd agreed to a further chat with Henry Sturges. The choice between sitting in my office going through these files again or visiting my friend really presented no competition. On top, I needed to ask Henry questions even though I was confident he'd answer them easily. The things we'd unearthed, like his absence from records, his fight with Wilkes, and the route to his sister's house passing the murder scene, all looked circumstantial and easily disregarded. The same might be said of Wilkes, except nothing connected Henry to the vicar.

It surprised me how down-market Henry's place was. For some reason I imagined he'd built up savings from his time in Italy working for the rich and famous. If he had, he didn't spend them on accommodation when he returned. The address was a boarding house whose front door missed a lick of paint for many a year and one of the windows had been broken then boarded.

A woman in a red cardigan several sizes too big answered when I knocked. The knitting needles and wool at her side suggested the garment displayed all her own work. She let me in, taking the cigarette out of her mouth long enough to tell me she was the landlady and where Henry's room was. The crone scowled in the hall as I climbed the stairs, shrieking after me that "guests" shouldn't have visitors, though she'd overlook it this time. I'd still no notion how I was going to ask questions of Henry, or what I might discover that I didn't already know.

I was merely going through the motions to keep Sawyer satisfied. Not a good approach for a working detective, but the case was getting me down.

I knocked on his door and waited. No answer, so I knocked harder.

'Henry? Are you in there?'

Still no answer. I tried the handle and the door wasn't locked. Inside, it was so dark I could barely see a hand in front of my face, so I groped my way over to the window. A foot away I stumbled and almost came crashing to the floor, saving my fall by grabbing the curtain. Someone groaned and daylight flooded in, revealing Henry, unconscious with blood oozing from a four-inch gash in his forehead. The cricket bat I'd tripped on lay at his side.

I knelt and searched for a pulse. Weak but there.

'Henry? Henry? Wake up.'

My first-aid knowledge extends to applying a bandage or a splint, nothing as serious as this. I dashed downstairs, hammered on the landlady's door, and yelled at her to run to the phone-box to call for an ambulance. I looked at my watch two dozen times before the alarm bell swung into the street and pulled up outside. The crew wasted no time in lifting Henry onto a stretcher and expertly manoeuvring it down the stairs and into the waiting vehicle.

'Coming with us?' shouted the driver as he jumped in the cab.

'No. I'll come later. Just get him into the hospital as quick as you can.'

The ambulance roared off, bell screaming again, leaving me on the pavement staring after them and wondering who could have done this to my friend. And why. Was it connected to Beattie's death, had Wilkes snook back and taken revenge on

Henry for humiliating him in the pub, or was it totally unconnected? Thankfully, Henry was still alive, and I'd get some answers when he came around. In the meantime, I'd need to interview his neighbours.

Inside the house Henry's neighbours stood at their doors talking about what had happened. I shouted that they should go into their rooms and I would call on them shortly. A woman on the ground floor said she must leave for work soon, so I agreed to talk to her first, which left the rest grumbling.

Henry's room was so small it was a miracle only the cricket bat tripped me in the dark. A single bed, an armchair that had seen better days, a small gate-leg table and a sink unit crammed against the walls. One alcove by the fireplace had shelves of food and crockery above a cooker, a grubby curtain covered the other and a quick check revealed it doubled as a wardrobe and general storage.

A kettle lay on the floor by the sink, and I assumed Henry had been filling it when hit from behind so must have known his attacker well enough to offer a drink. He'd not got so far as lighting the gas or putting cups on the table. Had his visitor only just turned up or had they been talking for a while? I'd need to ask the neighbours if they saw anyone arriving or leaving. Other than the dropped kettle and the darkening pool of blood nothing suggested a struggle, so they'd surprised Henry.

I lifted a well-thumbed bible from the drawer of his table and flipped through. Tucked inside was a small booklet, the parish magazine for St Botolph's, Stowham. Beattie's church. So Henry may have known the murdered vicar, despite giving no indication when I spoke to him of the case. In fact, he'd acted surprised when we'd first discussed Beattie. It was possible he'd been to the church but never met Beattie, or he could have picked up the magazine somewhere, but this was too much of a coincidence, and another piece of the jigsaw. I stuffed it in my pocket, gave the room a final scan then dropped the latch on the door when I left to interview the ground floor neighbour. On the way, I instructed the landlady to make sure no-one entered Henry's room until we'd taken a proper look.

None of the neighbours saw anyone unusual entering or leaving the building in the last few hours. One on the first floor said he'd heard a bang followed by a thud, as though someone fell, about half an hour before I arrived, but thought nothing of it. I asked if he'd looked outside to find what caused the noise.

'Nah, didn't bother. Always hearing stuff like that, walls are thin and more than one of the tenants like a drink.'

A man can be struck down in his own home, with people only a few dozen feet away, and no-one thinks the signs are in the least unusual. The world was becoming a very sad place and it bothered me.

There'd not been a minute to telephone Rachel since returning from Birmingham, so I called as soon as I sorted out the paperwork on Henry. She was subdued when I told her about him, which seemed only natural, but didn't even brighten when I said Meena was safely with my parents.

'I expect she'll be with you for her violin lessons soon, though she may need a day or two to settle in.'

Again, no enthusiasm, only a quiet 'That will be nice.'

'What's wrong, Rachel? Have I done something?'

'No, nothing.'

'Said something then? Is it because I didn't telephone you straight away?'

'No, it's not that.'

'What then?'

The line went silent for a minute and I thought we'd been cut off.

'Rachel? Are you there?'

'Sorry, James, I've been wondering how best to tell you something. If you hadn't called I'd have had to telephone.'

'Tell me what?'

'Listen to what I have to say, James. Please, please, don't interrupt or I'll never get through it.'

I promised to stay quiet until she'd finished.

'After you left last night I lay awake for ages thinking about you. There's no doubt I've been fortunate to meet a person I'm at ease with, someone who cares about the same things as I do and who will look after me, always strong at my side.'

Something frightening was hurtling down the track and I couldn't keep my promise to say nothing.

'So what's the problem, you must know I feel the same. We may have something special. You're not telling me we can't make a go of it?'

'This morning my brother called round as he does every week and I told him about you. Bernard asked a lot of questions. He's a very religious man, active in the synagogue and studies the Torah in all his spare time.'

'And?'

'He phoned me about an hour after he left, said he'd spoken to some people friendly with your father.' The next words stuck in her throat. 'Bernard's asked me not to see you again.'

'Why? Because of my father?'

'Not your father. Because of you. He's heard you don't practise the faith and his position in the synagogue means he's not happy with it.'

Now I was almost shouting. 'What's it to do with him? You're not listening, surely?'

'Don't be angry with me, James. Bernard's been my rock since we lost our dad. I'd never have got through those years without him. He was everything an older brother should be, but I sometimes think this has made him believe he has the same rights as my parents. He's said I must choose between you and him. If we continue to meet he'll cut me out of his life, and I'm not sure I could stand that.'

'So you're just going to do as he asks and give up the chance of any happiness we might have together? The man doesn't even know me, and he's made this preposterous decision.'

Already my brain raced through how many ways I could make his life miserable, as miserable as mine would be if Rachel dumped me. Everyone, regardless of how righteous they pretend to be, breaks the law, knowingly or unknowingly, at times. I'd have him watched day and night and prosecuted for the slightest misdemeanour. Rachel may not come back, but it would make me feel a whole lot better knowing he was suffering as much as me.

'That's the point, James. He doesn't know you. If we can step away for a while I can try to work on him, hope he'll see that you don't need to share his fervour to be a good man. Just give me a week or two and I'll attempt to bring him round. If I can't then we'll see where we go from there.'

When we finished our conversation, she was in floods of tears, begging me to do as she asked and to be patient. I said I would, even though patience isn't my strongest suit. I told Rachel I'd wait and hung up, shaking at my desk. Throwing on a coat I stumbled out of my office, my mind racing round what I'd do next. The heart told me to drive to Birmingham and confront Bernard Stevens. The head said to go home, listen to Rachel's advice and give her time to bring her brother round.

By the time I'd walked to my cottage the logical side had won. I made a cup of tea and rang the hospital in Coventry where they took Henry. I'd telephoned a number of times and they'd said he wasn't fit for visitors. When I explained I needed to interview him in respect of his assault it cut no ice, and they said to keep telephoning. After demanding to speak to someone in authority, they put me through to the ward sister.

'Sorry, Inspector, there's still no change. Mr Sturges is very poorly. We're doing everything we can. Try again tomorrow and let's hope there's been some improvement.'

The sister wouldn't be swayed, so I was left for the evening to worry and wonder about Henry and fume at the nerve of Rachel's brother.

TWENTY-TWO

The night didn't yield much sleep and my mind was still raging at Bernard Stevens. The last thing I needed was the session planned with Sawyer to catch up, but he knocked my door not long after I arrived in and I had to put my thoughts to one side.

'I heard about Henry Sturges, sir. I'm sorry.'

'Nothing to be sorry about, John, it looks like you might be right after all.'

I told him about the parish magazine.

He sat back and, to his credit, suppressed any hint of smugness. Something had been nagging at me ever since I'd found Henry, but it wouldn't come to the fore. Only when Sawyer ran though his latest attempts to find Wilkes did it pop up.

'Did you tell me that Robbie Wilkes had been in Hull at some point?'

He leafed through one of the folders on my desk and pushed a sheet across.

'Here it is. Ten years ago. Running a small hotel, doss-house really, in Southcotes, Hull. Down the road from the prison and the docks, letting unsavoury rooms to even more unsavoury inhabitants.'

'So he may have known Henry Sturges from those days. Henry was a merchant seaman and probably in and out of Hull all the time. Denied meeting Wilkes before he came here, but the two of them were seen arguing by Edie Bridgnorth. Perhaps Henry lied. Wilkes might be the one who attacked Henry, so you must find him. And quickly.'

Sawyer shook his head.

'Don't you think I've looked for him everywhere, despite knowing Robbie didn't kill Reverend Beattie? I'm also sure he wouldn't creep up on Sturges and crack him over the skull.'

'So now you're sure he didn't do it? What happened to our earlier chat about keeping an open mind?'

'You're not keeping an open mind, Inspector, you've decided it must be Robbie. There are probably loads of people living in Kenilworth or hereabouts who've lived in or passed through Hull. That connection came up and you settled on Robbie again, even though you've admitted there are doubts about Henry Sturges telling the truth. What if your friend was in league with someone and together they killed the vicar? They fall out, argue over something, and the other feller clouts Sturges with a cricket bat which happens to be handy.'

I had to give it to Sawyer, his solution was as plausible as mine, and what I'd recently learnt about Henry had set me wondering if there might be something to his possible involvement. This didn't help though. I still wasn't happy with Sawyer questioning my judgement again. It was almost as if he'd come to resent my authority once he'd left his uniform behind. I let fly at him, more strongly than I should.

'Frankly, Sawyer, I'm not really interested in your opinion and I think you need to watch your tongue. Now get out there, keep looking and if you've not locked up Wilkes by tonight there'll be trouble.'

He stood, towering over the desk and shaking, then turned and left, slamming my door behind him.

I didn't need to wait long for the result I'd demanded. Within an hour the desk sergeant phoned and said Sawyer had Wilkes in an interview room and was waiting for me. I assumed

Sawyer didn't phone me himself because he was still mad, and this became obvious with the curt greeting when I entered.

'Inspector. This is Robert David Wilkes, otherwise known as Robbie. You wanted to talk to him in relation to the murder of Reverend Duncan Beattie on the thirtieth of August this year, sometime between seven o'clock and midnight. Mr Wilkes was picked up yesterday by a Constable Clay of Leamington Police Station where the suspect had been hiding in a shed behind a shop before being spotted by the owner. Constable Clay recognised his description when they had him in the cells.'

The whole introduction was delivered monotone, as if he were reading a statement in court. I sat down opposite Wilkes, whose clothes were dishevelled and hair was matted. He wouldn't look me in the eye.

'Now, Robbie, you have been giving us the run around haven't you? Firstly, you give me some cock and bull story about being with friends in Coventry the night the vicar was killed, going to bed when you got home. Both hard for us to disprove. Later you run off, making it look like there'd been a fight in your hovel.'

'What else was I supposed to do, Mr Given? The two of you were comin' after me even though I'd nothin' to do with it.'

'So why did you lie about missing the last bus from Coventry? Your mates told us you left them by eight o'clock.'

'Did miss the bus. By the time we split up I'd got the taste, so I called in to another pub on my own. Near the bus stop it was, to get back. Met some blokes, had a laugh, one thing led to another and I end up stayin' there until closin' time. Nothin' for it but to walk the road 'ome.'

'Why didn't you tell me this before?'

''Cos I 'ardly remembered it. Been with the other lads and just got a bit mixed up, is all.'

A smug smile formed on Sawyer's face. I pretended to flip through the file.

'Tell me, Robbie, how well do you know Henry Sturges?'

'Sturges? Don't recall that name.'

Wilkes looked puzzled enough for me to believe him. Almost.

'Come, come, Robbie, you must. Had a fight with him not long ago. Well not so much a fight, he had you up against the wall before you could do him any damage.'

'Ah, him. Only been 'ere five minutes and 'e's best seat at the bar, chattin' to the landlord as though 'e's known 'im all 'is life.'

'You met him before though, didn't you? In Hull?'

Now Wilkes looked even more perplexed.

'Hull? Why'd you think I met 'im in Hull? Can't say I didn't meet 'im when I was there, met 'undreds of fellers in and out of the house where I worked. But I don't remember 'im. Why you askin' me about this bloke anyway?'

'Are you saying you didn't go to his lodging house yesterday afternoon, argue with him and belt him over the head?'

Wilkes jumped from his chair. 'No. I didn't. Told you, don't even know the man. Not properly. I tapped 'im up for a drink one time and 'e turned funny, so we fell out. But not bad enough to brain 'im.' His objection ran out of steam and he looked towards the door, like a cornered animal seeking an escape route.

'Sit down, Robbie. If he roughed you up then I'd understand it if you had a grudge and went after him later. Is that what happened? Like with Reverend Beattie? Had a grudge against him as well, didn't you?'

He sat again, slowly, folding his arms, and leaned in towards me. 'Just realised you said this Sturges was attacked yesterday. Can't have been me. No sir.'

'And why not?'

'Because I was in Leamington nick all afternoon and all night 'til you 'ad me brought over 'ere. That Clay feller caught me at about half past eleven and dragged me down the station.'

The smirk on Sawyer's face said his triumph was complete. I told him to let Wilkes go but to check immediately with Leamington lads that he was telling the truth. In a few minutes he was upstairs again.

'Well?'

'Clay confirmed Robbie had been with them when he said. So he couldn't have clobbered Sturges.'

'You wipe that smile off your face, Detective Constable, or you'll be back on the street in uniform before you can say Jack Robinson.' The smirk was replaced by a frown. 'This time Wilkes is off the hook, but you couldn't have known he was innocent. The evidence, such as it is, said otherwise and the fact he may not have attacked Henry Sturges doesn't mean he didn't kill Beattie. Keep an eye on him.'

'Yes, sir. If you say so.'

Sawyer started to rise.

'Wait a minute, I haven't finished with you yet.'

He settled back in his seat and folded his arms.

'Are you going to tell me what's wrong?'

'Nothing's wrong.'

'Come off it, John. Since I returned from France you've been in a poor mood. Verging on the insubordinate. We've worked well together in the past and I was pleased when you took the transfer. What's changed?'

He looked out of the window without replying.

'Come on. What is it?'

Still no reply.

'If you don't start talking I'll have to take it to the boss, see if he can sort you out. So tell me.'

'It's you, sir.'

'Me?'

'You used to be so driven. Nothing would get in the way of an investigation. Since the last case though, you don't seem interested. Just get a result. Almost as bad as Inspector Trimble.'

He was right, though it hurt to hear him say it.

'You know I've had a bad time, John, I almost didn't come back at all.'

'I understand that, sir, but it's not only that is it? Your mind has been elsewhere. First your uncle and then Meena. To make it worse you're taking it out on me.'

'On you? How?'

'Well today is one instance. Knowing damn well that Robbie Wilkes was a complete outsider for this, you threaten me with the sack because I disagree with you. You've put me down that way a few times. As well, when I was looking for some support about joining the army you virtually said I was an idiot for considering it. I expected more.'

I was at a loss how to respond. It was true that I'd not been giving full attention to the Beattie murder, but had I really been taking my troubles out on Sawyer? I did the only thing possible in the circumstances. I attacked.

'It's a shame you feel that way. The comment about demotion was uncalled for, but perhaps we will need to consider your place on the team. Maybe you'd be better suited to working with another Inspector. Leave it with me.'

I expected Sawyer to take his chance to leave, but he didn't; he rubbed his forehead and slumped in the chair.

'I don't want that, sir. Obviously, you do what you think best but I agree with you, we've worked well together. You've had a lot on your plate and there are no other officers in this nick I respect as much as you. Maybe that's why I've been acting this way.'

His words took me aback, though I didn't feel like letting him off the hook.

'That's good of you to say, but it doesn't change the fact that we've been disagreeing more and more over the last couple of weeks. Let's put it to one side for now and leave me to think about it.'

Sawyer stood and left my room without another word.

After Sawyer left I jumped on the bus to Coventry to visit Henry, regardless of what I'd been told by the nurses. The same hospital had looked after me for a few days about a year earlier and hadn't improved in the intervening period. Its austere exterior gave me the shivers, and the inside was as bad. The grey-green and cream walls hadn't changed. The smell of antiseptic was just as nauseating.

A nurse I'd spoken with on the telephone accosted me on the way in.

'Can I help you, sir? Visiting isn't for another couple of hours.'

I explained I needed to speak to Henry about his assault.

'Afraid I can't let you in. I've been told he's to have no visitors.'

I asked her politely to fetch her superior. The ward sister arrived ten minutes later with the nurse in tow.

'Thank you for joining me so promptly, Sister.' I smiled and her sour face shrivelled even further. 'I need to see Mr Sturges. We're investigating the assault on him, the attempted murder you might say. It's possibly linked to another serious case and any information he might provide is vital.'

'I can't see how he'll help, he's still unconscious, but you can sit with him, quietly mind, in case he wakes up. I'll give you half an hour.'

She nodded to the nurse, turned, and disappeared down the corridor, starched uniform rustling.

My friend lay in white sheets under a grey blanket and a drip at his bedside made sure he didn't starve to death while he couldn't eat. I think I'd expected him to be sitting up in bed ready for visitors and was shocked at his appearance. The colour had drained from his face and the dressing on his head was surrounded by a blue-black bruise. Henry's breathing was so shallow at one point I thought he may already have passed away and ran for some help.

The nurse I'd called checked his pulse, shook her head, and said he was still with us. She offered to fetch a doctor and I told her I'd be grateful. A fair-haired man in his forties, wearing white coat and stethoscope, ambled into the ward a few moments later.

'You're not a relative?'

'No, doctor, Mr Sturges is a friend but I'm also investigating what happened to him.' I showed him my warrant card. 'I hoped to ask him a few questions.'

'That's not really going to be possible for a while, Inspector Given, he's terribly ill.'

'How bad is he?'

'Hard to say. At the very least he's badly concussed, but in my opinion the bang on his head may have caused a brain bleed. With luck he'll come around, but even then he won't be himself again if it's caused permanent damage.'

'With luck?'

'Oh, yes. Mr Sturges will need a lot of that. When someone's unconscious as long as he's been we're never sure what will happen. He could wake up with brain damage, or it's perfectly possible he'll not last the week.' I went cold. 'I'm sorry to be the bearer of bad news, Inspector. Let's pray your friend gets through this. The body's resilience never ceases to amaze me, and I hope I'm wrong in my pessimism.'

The doctor walked away and left me to sit by Henry's bed. A 'get well soon' card on the locker suggested someone else had visited and a woman's name, Susan, accompanied the message inside. He'd never mentioned any romantic attachments, so I assumed the card must be from his sister.

'A bad couple of days, eh, Henry? For you and me both. You're lay here like this and I've fallen out with Sawyer. Rachel's said I can't see her again and I can't glimpse a breakthrough on this case. Makes me want to pack the whole lot in. Sawyer's got the right idea, perhaps I should enlist as well, can't be much worse than this.'

The man in the next bed stared across at me as if I were mad, talking to this person who couldn't answer. The red nose and florid cheeks marked him out to be a drinker. I stared back until he turned on his other side and looked at someone else.

'So, Henry, what happened to you? Who did this and why? How well did you know Duncan Beattie? Perhaps you only met him in the pub, the parish magazine is a coincidence, and this isn't connected. But you let in someone you knew, just like he did. Was it the same person? Though this attack looks more rushed, not planned in the same way. Was he disturbed before he could do the same to you as he did to the good reverend? For the life of me I can't see what you'd have in common. You're not religious so wouldn't have met him in church, that's for sure, and you were in Italy for years so I can't think you'd know him from there. If it's not to do with him, then what have you been up to that would make someone want to hurt you so badly?'

The nurse came back into the ward, scurried in my direction, and broke up this one-sided interview.

'I'm sorry, Inspector, but you've had your thirty minutes and visiting time isn't for another few hours. Sister only let you in because you said you were investigating Mr Sturges' attack but, obviously, he's not answering any of your questions and we have work to do. Please let us get on with it and come back later.'

I thanked her for letting me stay as long as I had and gave her my telephone number to call in case he recovered consciousness.

I should have gone back to Kenilworth as soon as I could, but I dawdled down to the bus station at Pool Meadow, taking twenty minutes or more. This would have taken longer if I'd followed my inclination to dive into one or more of the pubs on the way. While I was waiting for my bus, one bound for Birmingham pulled alongside the next stand and I took the few steps then climbed on board without a hint of hesitation.

TWENTY-THREE

The strangled cat's wail of a badly played violin escaped from the window and Rachel's face dropped when she opened the front door.

'Can I come in?'

'No, James, I'm busy and I told you I wouldn't see you again.'

A freckled child's face peeked from behind the music room curtains, squinting against the sunlight to examine this man disturbing her lesson. Rachel spotted my eyes shift and stepped outside, waving the student back.

'Why are you here?'

'I just need to talk to you. Please.'

This sounded so pitiful, but I had no pride, not at that moment. Rachel rubbed her forehead and closed her eyes, sighed then switched on a gentle smile.

'Well I can't talk now, as I said, I'm busy. Meet me in an hour at the Cameron for tea and you can say what you have to say.' She leaned forward and pushed her fist into my shoulder. 'Now scoot and let me get on. God knows what Rebecca in there will say to her mother about these goings on.'

I was in the Cameron Hotel café fifteen minutes early and found the most secluded table I could then, when a waitress approached I waved her away, saying I was waiting for a friend. The place was only half full, mainly with pairs of elderly ladies sharing tiered plates of cakes and pouring tea from rose-decorated china pots. The hotel had struck me as very pleasant when I'd been with Rachel, grand but not too grand, with its high ceilings, wine-coloured walls and white plasterwork. A testament to the aspirations of its builders when the city was booming a century earlier.

On the way there I'd walked round the block half a dozen times, going over and over what I might say to Rachel to convince her we should continue to go out. At one point, when I was nearest to my parent's home, I almost abandoned the idea and made a run for the cover of their roof, but I knew if I did then I'd probably never see Rachel again.

When she arrived, it was obvious I'd made the right choice in staying with it. Rachel walked in and looked from table to table, her grin lighting up the room when she spotted where I was sitting. She peeled off her coat to reveal a beautiful floral dress that turned more than one of the few men's heads in the café. It flattered me to imagine she'd thrown her student out as soon as I left and then spent best part of the hour getting ready to meet. When I stood to greet her, my knees were quaking.

'Thank you for coming.'

'Not so sure I had much choice, did I, with a pathetic little boy on the doorstep.' My chin dropped and my cheeks began to burn, but she leant forward and kissed one. 'Don't worry, James, I'm not angry with you. Let's order tea before we talk.'

A dough-faced waitress appeared as if by magic and took our order so slowly, checking every item, I wanted to shout at her to get on with it and give us some privacy.

'So, James, what is it that's so important?'

'Surely you don't need me to spell it out?'

'But I'm not sure what I can say. I asked you to give me time to talk to Bernard and I've not had a chance to do it yet.'

'Of course you haven't, but I wanted to explain. Give you some ammunition if you like.'

So I told her a long story of how I'd hidden my religion when I'd been bullied about it on board boats as a young man, how I'd seen things in Germany which confirmed I was right to do so, and how it made sense when I joined the police to pretend I was Christian like everyone else.

'My father pushes me all the time to take up our faith again, and I do attend synagogue when I'm home on Sabbath. I even started to consider it more seriously after my last case, and perhaps it's more important now than ever with what Hitler is up to. There's no reason to hide it any longer, Superintendent Dyer and the rest all know I'm Jewish.'

'So what's the problem?'

'I don't feel it, Rachel. Deep inside. And I should. Is it enough to commit simply to please my father or your brother?'

'Or me?'

'Does it matter to you?'

'If it helps Bernard remove his objection, then yes it does.' Rachel took my hand. 'It wouldn't make a jot of difference to me what religion you are as long as we can be together, but I can't go against him. Not at the moment. I'll talk to Bernard as I promised and try to get him to see sense.'

She left her hand in mine and told me how she thought I might find greater peace if I could be more accepting of my faith.

'It isn't life or death, James, only a way of looking at our place in the universe. For me, following the rituals and making my prayers helps me be a better person, I think.'

I slid my hand away.

'And you want me to improve.'

'Don't be silly. That's not what I'm saying. Everyone needs to be better than they are. You're a good, decent man.' She laughed. 'But going to synagogue a bit more often might help prove it.'

I was about to take her hand again when the waitress came back with a trolley of tea and cakes, which she laid on the table. We tucked in, both declaring we really shouldn't, and when we finished Rachel and I walked to her home. Much as I wanted to go inside, we parted at the gate and I went to my parents' to ask my father to introduce me to Bernard Stevens when I came back on Saturday.

There'd been no further progress by Friday. Sawyer hadn't been able to dig anything up to undermine the alibis of Butler or Wilkes and was still out of sorts with me. The hospital told me Henry still hadn't improved so it wasn't possible to interview him. There was no alternative but to telephone the boss and explain we were getting nowhere with this case.

'You're sure he actually was murdered, James, not suicide like first presumed?'

'Well someone was seen leaving the yard and the door appeared to have been locked from the outside.'

'Hardly conclusive though, is it? It could have been anyone walking away.'

'And the locked door, sir?'

'Perhaps the key was mislaid when the body was removed. Neither of these would stand up in court.'

'Yes, sir, I appreciate that, but this feels and smells like a murder.'

'Don't tell me this is one of your hunches, Inspector.'

I felt like telling him that my hunches, as he called them, had been right before on more than one occasion. A hunch sounds like it's a guess, something woolly and inexplicable, dragged up when there's no proper evidence. Sometimes it's more than that. An experienced detective will subconsciously sift the circumstances and arrive at a conclusion about the events which have taken place. He may not be able to explain the reasoning, but it doesn't make it any less accurate.

'If Beattie took his own life, sir, why do it there? Why put his wife and his congregation through such an ordeal? Everything I've heard about the man is, apart from his predilection for married women and prostitutes, he was a kind, caring and considerate man. He'd also been at that game for at least as long as he'd been married, so why top himself now when a silly, drunk woman tries blackmail? The whole thing doesn't make sense.'

We argued some more but in the end the boss accepted my reasoning, saying he'd give me a while longer, so I asked if, in the circumstances, I could take the weekend off.

'You've got a damn cheek, but I suppose you might as well, doesn't seem like much more will emerge until this Henry Sturges regains consciousness. Let's hope it's soon.'

With Dyer's approval in my pocket I let Sawyer know where to contact me if he needed to.

'Will you be long, sir?'

'Back Monday morning.'

'So next week we'll get back to looking for who really did this?'

The bait stayed untouched. If Sawyer wanted to think I was abandoning the case again it was up to him. Over the next couple of days, I'd need to work out how I could patch up our relationship, otherwise I'd reluctantly have to ask Dyer to have him reassigned.

Friday evening at my parents' home was spent as usual with the Sabbath meal, only this time there were special prayers to thank God for Meena's safe return. Pink came to the poor girl's cheeks while this went on. Mama had told me they'd all made a fuss of her when she returned and hadn't spoken with Meena about why she'd disappeared without a word. I imagined she would have wanted to apologise and explain how frightened she'd been for her father. Until they talked she'd be embarrassed every time it came up.

At the synagogue Papa wandered away for a while to talk to friends. When he returned he gave me a smile and a wink.

'Sunday. Miss Stevens' brother will meet with you on Sunday morning. Here. Rabbi Smart will have a room to use. Shall I come along?'

'No, Papa, it's all right, I need to do this on my own.'

The last thing I wanted was him hovering at my shoulder, interrupting and doing his level best to paint me as a dutiful son, well worthy of Bernard Stevens' sister. My father has a tendency to bow and scrape to men he believes to be important, and I suspected Rachel's brother would be one who would expect to be treated in that way. He wouldn't get it from me, and I was determined I wouldn't allow my father to debase himself in that way.

For the next hour or so I caught up with Sarah's and Eli's lives, though my mind was elsewhere, thinking through my approach to the session with Stevens. By bedtime I'd still no conclusion so spent a while longer turning over the options before nodding off.

Rachel's brother was not a handsome man. About my age but with a crease-lined face as if he'd spent his life in the open air, though he'd worked in an accountancy office since he left school. Heavy eyebrows, a thick moustache and some of the biggest ears I'd ever witnessed completed my puzzlement at where his sister's stunning looks had come from.

He didn't hesitate in taking the chair on the business side of the rabbi's desk, intertwining fingers on top after motioning me to sit.

'So, Mr Given, my sister tells me she likes you. A lot.'

Not quite the opening I expected.

'Rachel also says you've been struggling with your faith.'

'Not struggling. Just not as certain as you.'

Stevens nodded.

'Accepted. If that's the case, why should I be inclined to give my blessing?'

'I'm not asking for your blessing, Mr Stevens. Frankly, it's none of your business. Rachel is a grown woman and able to make her own decisions. All I am asking is that you don't stand in her way.'

'An unfortunate choice of words. I don't view it as standing in her way but as ensuring she doesn't make a mistake in the man she chooses.'

'It amounts to the same thing. Interference where it's not wanted.'

'I'm afraid my sister can't pick and choose where she's protected. Since our father died I've developed the habit and I apologise if this seems a little overbearing, but it's not one I'll abandon easily. When we were young she was so badly affected by our loss it almost got the better of her and, in my estimation, only survived because we stuck together.'

219

'Rachel told me, and she's grateful for your support, but don't you consider it time to share her with someone else who'll care at least as much as you do?'

Stevens leaned back in the chair and lit a cigarette, inhaling deeply then blowing a plume of smoke towards the ceiling.

'You're right, of course, Mr Given, but I needed to make sure you were that person. I asked some questions when I knew we were meeting today. Your father, naturally, gave a glowing account of your merits. Besides him there were others, whose opinions I respect, who were equally praiseworthy. They told me that even though you don't observe, you have the best interests of our community at heart in your job. You know that I work with figures. When they add up, I'm a happy man and it seems we're almost at that point. Give me a day or two to talk to some others and to ruminate, then I'll give Rachel my decision.'

The arrogance of the man almost made me explode, but I was aware it wouldn't achieve anything. Rachel allowed him his power, he'd made up his mind, and there was nothing I could do about it.

'You have until Friday, Mr Stevens, but after next weekend, regardless of what you decide, Rachel and I will continue to see each other, and you won't prevent it. If I've not heard by the end of the week we'll talk again.'

TWENTY-FOUR

The call from the ward sister was short and to the point, and the receiver felt like lead when I dropped it on the cradle.

Sawyer looked up from his notebook. 'Something wrong, sir?'

The words would hardly come out. 'Henry Sturges is dead. Died an hour ago from the injuries.'

'Christ.'

There was nothing to add to this profanity.

'So now it's another murder, sir. Any closer to the connection?'

'I haven't spotted one but can't imagine the two aren't connected. This is Kenilworth, hardly the crime capital of the world.'

'So what is the connection? There's nothing concrete to link Beattie and Sturges. That parish magazine proves nothing, and no-one has said they even saw them together except by accident in the same pub. Could Beattie's wife know anything? We can't even make a decent stab at why anyone murdered the vicar, let alone Sturges.'

I tried to grasp the idea someone had killed this man I liked. Another pointless death in my life.

'I'm sorry, John, I can't think straight at the minute. All I know is Henry had become a friend and now he's dead. Which I might have prevented by paying more attention to catching Beattie's killer.'

'You can't blame yourself —'

'Yes I can, my mind's been elsewhere. Not concentrating on the job. If it's not my fault, who's is it?'

'The killer's. Not yours. There's not been any kind of break in this case so far, so how could anyone have stopped it? The important thing is to go through the evidence again, pull in everybody who might be a suspect and track the killer down.'

I stood. 'Well you do that, John, and let me know when you find something because I've been through it all a hundred times. I'll see you when I see you.'

Sawyer sat open-mouthed as I pushed the files towards him and stormed out. I did precisely the opposite of what I should have done in the situation. Instead of following Sawyer's advice to knuckle down and find a murderer, I went to mourn my friend.

October is a depressing month. Summer has departed and winter not quite arrived. The nights are drawing in and when drizzle seeps into every corner it hardly gets light from dawn to dusk. This was one such day, bringing me down further than I would have imagined possible.

Sawyer's attempt to absolve me of blame for Henry's death had no effect. I'd never wanted to investigate Beattie's murder, only doing so because the boss threatened desk work forever. I'd known I wasn't ready, but I hadn't expected to erect so many barriers in the way of solving the case. If I'd spent less time chasing Meena for my mother, and less time chasing Rachel for myself, I might have found a key. At the bottom grew my desire to be out of the police. To leave behind all the nastiness. Bad, bad, things all the time and the pointlessness of it all. The world didn't get better, no matter how I tried, it was becoming worse. Beattie's wife had said the vicar even held the same view.

I also wanted to be with Rachel and couldn't. No word had come from her brother and, despite my bravado, I'd have to

222

bide my time until Stevens came to a decision. The fear was it would be in the negative and Rachel would do as he asked, leaving me out in the cold. I'd looked long and hard at the notion of re-immersing myself in Judaism to keep everyone happy. It would please my father, my mother, Bernard Stevens and Rachel, but would it please me? I was no longer certain the old reasons I'd abandoned it, the freedom offered by my father and the prejudice I faced at sea, remained the only ones. Feelings about the uselessness of being in the police echoed my feelings about religion, and I'd concluded a caring God wouldn't allow all the evil to flourish in the world. The likes of Bernard Stevens and Duncan Beattie would say I shouldn't question motives in the mind of God, but this didn't work for me.

When I came of age Papa presented me with a book of daily prayer, a Siddur, which I'd kept throughout my travels all around the world, not out of any commitment to the faith but as a memento. We'd argued before I left for sea and this Siddur had reminded me of his affection despite our differences. Would I find its words pulling me back into the faith, towards him and closer to Rachel if I dug it from where I'd left it years before?

I lifted the box where I stored the prayer book, alongside the other things I'd kept from a time before Kenilworth, the police and my cottage. Reminders of my past I'd planned to unpack one day but never managed to. On top lay a postcard album, and I smiled when I saw its brown cardboard cover. In every port, I'd always bought two cards, one to send to my mother, the other as a souvenir to put in the album.

As I leafed through the pages I took a tour of my life and the places I'd visited in those years. The early ones recorded ports across northern Europe like Rotterdam, Copenhagen,

Liverpool, then the Mediterranean and Africa, and the last my final trip to America. In the very back of the album, on a page of their own, I'd stuck cards from Cherbourg and Dover, alongside a photograph I'd lost long ago.

I recalled little of the next seventy-two hours. The beginning was clear, when I took out the photograph. A group of six smiling fruit pickers, me on one end, Heather beside me in the battered straw hat I always teased her about. A basket of apples on the ground and we were holding hands. The hat lay by her side when I found her, incongruous on the bloodied grass.

Two minutes were all it took to grab a jacket and walk the hundred yards round to The Queen. Robert, the landlord, no doubt tried to dissuade me but didn't succeed and the booze soon slid down my throat like there was no tomorrow. He'd have listened sympathetically when told about Henry's death and how it was my fault, then served me another drink when I demanded one. Because that's how Robert makes a living. A scene comes to mind, in another pub, later, with tots of rum lined up on the bar and me pouring my heart out about Heather's murder, about being tortured on my last case, and how I hated my job. I seem to remember playing cards for a while, losing more money than I could afford, and talking about the time I'd been cheated out of my wages and having to hide in Cherbourg. It's like peering through fog, with almost perfect clarity when it clears before the veil closes again.

It's unlikely I ate much, I never do when I'm drinking, and I woke up at one point, rain-soaked on a park bench, before finding the warmth of another pub fireside and another landlord to tell my troubles to. It was fortunate I didn't bump into someone who'd give me a good kicking for putting them away; I'd not have been able to defend myself.

My binge must have continued at home for a while because there's no memory of surfacing through the alcohol, and all the pubs close at some time. There are a few in the town where the licensing hours are viewed as advice rather than the law, but none stay open all day and all night. The landlords accept we'll be down on them like a ton of bricks if they take too many liberties so act accordingly.

The last thing I remember is getting into an argument with Charlie Butler. I'd been playing cards, and he came over and started ranting about his arrest. I may have told him to shut up and said he still wasn't off the hook, even though he was, and he lunged at me with a bottle. It went dark.

I slipped back into consciousness in an armchair in my front room, my head thumping like a hundred steam hammers. The egg-sized lump above my left eye partly explained the pain but it was deeper, much deeper. As the room came into focus, something large was blocking the light from the window. Sawyer was staring down at me.

'Sir? You with us again?'

My legs wouldn't obey orders when I tried to stand, and I flopped back on the seat. Closing my eyes only intensified the whirling pit. When I opened them again, Sawyer was holding a teacup in front of me, the smell of sugar overwhelming from a foot away.

'Here, drink this, it'll help.'

The first disappeared in one gulp and he brought me another.

'How … how did I get here?'

'Mr Neilson, your neighbour, saw you stagger out of the house this morning and telephoned the station. Sergeant Burns sent me to find you. Charlie Butler was bashing your brains out as I got to you, so I dragged you home.'

'Why?'

'Why was he bashing you or why did I bring you home?'

I rubbed my temples, trying to stop my eyeballs from exploding.

'The latter.'

'Because somebody had to. You'd be dead in the gutter before the week was out, either from the booze or from some old lag deciding to take revenge.'

'Well what's it to you? You should have left me to it.'

The sweet tea began to work. I stood and swayed towards the door, then felt myself being propelled faster than I intended. Sawyer had caught me by the collar, pushing me in front of the hall mirror.

'This is why it's important. Look at the state of you. You're supposed to be my boss, someone I look up to, not this mess.'

The reflection wasn't good. Three days' growth of whiskers, a dark, swollen, bruise over one eye and a torn, dirty collar hardly made me look respectable. I turned and headed for the door, pushing Sawyer away. Grabbed again, this time under my arms, he lifted me up the stairs. Even though I kicked and swore he was far too strong, so I capitulated halfway up, letting him wrestle me into my room. Sawyer dumped me on my feet then, with the slightest push, shoved me onto the bed.

The two us were gasping, me lying full length and him sitting with hands on knees. I let out a stupid, drunken giggle at the absurdity of what we'd done. Sawyer looked down and joined in. When our laughter subsided he stood, tramped downstairs and brought a bucket.

'Stay in bed now for the night. Use this if you want to throw up, it'll save your rug. I'll be in the parlour and will let you out in the morning.'

With this he left, locking the bedroom door behind him, something I couldn't believe he'd done. I thumped and kicked it, roaring at the top of my voice.

'Let me out, you can't do this.'

No reply. If Sawyer heard me he wasn't listening.

'Come on, John. Open this door now or else.'

There was no sound of footsteps on the stairs. I carried on like this for a while, but he didn't appear, so I fell back on the bed and crawled under the blankets. Within minutes the remnants of the booze and half a week with no proper sleep dragged me under for much longer than my nightly eight hours.

Sunlight streamed through the window when Sawyer unlocked the door at quarter to nine, carrying a steaming mug of tea.

'Morning, sir. Get this down you. Nothing like a good cuppa first thing.'

I scowled.

'Stop being so bloody cheerful and get me the aspirin.'

'Take some after you've eaten, it'll do more good.'

I glanced at the still empty bucket.

'Don't worry, sir, nothing too strenuous. Boiled egg and toast. Will settle your stomach. Set you up for the day.'

He left the room, whistling tunelessly, and I crawled out of bed. I took off the clothes I'd slept in, washed, shaved and rooted in my wardrobe for something decent to wear.

At breakfast, Sawyer remained chirpy and I remained sour. Never at my most effervescent in the mornings, my searing headache and a sense of dread over how I'd explain this to my colleagues, and to Rachel, made me worse than usual. Sawyer's attempts at light-heartedness were making me want to punch him so I cut it off. I only began to pay attention when he said the sergeant who received the neighbour's call telephoned Superintendent Dyer's office soon afterwards.

'Why would Burns do that? I thought we were mates.'

'No choice, sir, the Super had been phoning every couple of hours wanting to know where you were.'

'That's me for the high jump then. Mind you, the way I feel now I couldn't give a damn. I've been thinking of packing it in anyway.'

Sawyer's knife clattered onto his plate, scattering crumbs over the table.

'You're not serious? Not before we've wound up this case. It's not fair.'

'Fair? What are you talking about, John?'

'I already told you I was considering leaving the force to join up. After you threw in your tuppence-worth, I weighed it up for a while and decided to wait until we found Reverend Beattie's killer. I've had such a hard time from you over the recent weeks I almost dumped my decision but stuck with it. Partly for your sake. If you go now, it'll seem I was stupid and should have left earlier.'

Sawyer's words sunk in. Time for an apology.

'I'm sorry for having been unpleasant, John, there's been a lot going on, as you pointed out a few days ago. You know I didn't want to take this case; I wasn't ready. When you started talking of leaving it threw me.'

'I knew you weren't happy but didn't think it had come to this. So what will you do?'

'In the long term, I don't know. All I can do for now is face the music with the boss and see what happens. Will you hang on until then?'

Not a second's hesitation.

'I'll stay until you make your decision, sir,' he grimaced, 'or until Superintendent Dyer makes his. But I am going when this case is solved. No doubt about it.'

We continued breakfast in silence, and I'd drunk my third cup of tea of the day before Sawyer spoke again.

'You led me a merry dance there yesterday. Everyone guessed you'd legged it back to Birmingham again until Neilson phoned. I covered a dozen pubs before I found you. The landlord of The Queen told me you'd been in to pick up more bottles, each time looking worse than the last. Jimmy Price in The Railway Arms said you were crying over some photo of a girl, then he tried to get some grub into you, but you refused, just demanded more rum. Seems like a real bender.'

'Seems like it was. Past tense and I don't want to talk about it anymore at the moment. You'd better get on up to the station. I'll finish getting ready and join you shortly. I will need to look my best if Dyer's on the warpath.'

Sawyer folded his arms and shook his head.

'Not a chance. I'll wait and we'll walk up together. If Sergeant Burns wants to have a go for me being late, we'll explain why.'

I offered my hand.

'Thanks, John, you're a good copper, and deserve better than me as a boss.'

TWENTY-FIVE

The obvious message waited at the station, to get over to Warwick double-quick. Instead, I spent half an hour checking the post and the progress notes from Sawyer, with him knocking my door every five minutes reminding me I should go to see the boss. There was also something I needed to collect before heading into the lion's den. I re-read it then tucked the envelope in my jacket pocket.

Dyer was pacing up and down his office, red-faced. I'd never seen him looking so angry, and my continuing calmness seemed to annoy him further while he blasted away. The time spent in the station and on the journey helped me plan my reaction to whatever he threw at me. In the boss's position I'd keep the victim sweating outside for a good while before letting him in, but he didn't and whisked me through as soon as I arrived.

'You're a mess, Given, a complete mess. God knows what I'll tell them upstairs. Not one iota of a clue who killed this vicar and you go on the pop. Do you prefer to explain what's going on?'

'No, sir.'

Not an answer designed to pour oil on troubled waters. The boss sat down and thumped his chair arm.

'What a bloody cheek. Do you prefer to stay in that damn cellar filling in forms for what's left of your career, because, God help me, I'll drop you down to sergeant and leave you doing it. And to think, I entertained some wild idea you might apply for my job when I go.'

I looked away.

'That would never happen, sir, I'm not cut out to be a pen-pusher.'

Dyer ignored the insult.

'Come on, James, what is going on? You're too good a copper for this kind of nonsense. I'm only here for another month, so whatever you say won't stick. Nothing will be written down and it'll go with me when I retire.'

I wasn't rational, whether caused by the hangover or the confusion about where I wanted to be, and I should have accepted the olive branch. Dyer was always a decent manager supporting me through the ranks and deserved better, but I wasn't in the mood to play ball.

'Sorry, sir, but it's personal and nothing to do with you.' I looked around the room. 'Or anyone else in this place.'

The kettle started to simmer again.

'Watch your tongue, Inspector, before you say something you'll regret.'

I stood.

'You know what, sir, I already regret not doing this sooner.' I tossed the envelope from my pocket on his desk. 'Here's my resignation.'

Dyer's face froze, and then a frown appeared. Without opening it, he ripped the envelope and contents to shreds before dropping the pieces into a waste-paper basket.

'Not a chance. You don't get away that easily. Go back to Kenilworth, pull Constable Sawyer into your office and stay at it until you solve this damn case. You're the one who made the affair more complicated than necessary and you can sort it out. Trimble put the death down as a suicide then you convinced me otherwise. Damned thing should have been off the books long ago. Now get out and back to work.'

Sometimes you need a person to tell you you're making a mistake, when you go blundering forward because you can't see an alternative and they show you a way out. The boss did that. But would his order produce a halt on my journey out of the police? Dyer or I would need to jump that precipice soon.

When I returned to Kenilworth it was so close to lunch I went home before going into the police station. Rachel was standing beside my gate when I arrived.

'James, what have you been up to? You've not contacted me for days. I was so worried when you didn't call I came over here.'

'I didn't think you would expect to hear from me. Not until the beloved Bernard sends a tablet down from the mountain. Come inside, there's something we need to talk about.'

The concern already etched on her face deepened. I opened the door, ushering her through to a seat in the kitchen.

'I have a problem, Rachel, one we should have shared before now.'

'What sort of problem?'

'I drink. Heavily. Since I was young.'

If she'd got up and left I wouldn't have been in the least surprised because I didn't know what to expect. Instead, she relaxed into her chair.

'Heavens, James, you scared me. I imagined you were ill or something.'

'Well drinking is an illness, I think. Not something easy to control anyway.'

'But you only ever take tea or a soft drink when we go out, so you must be on top of it.'

'"On top" is too strong. No-one who's drank like me is ever truly in control. Once in a while the temptation beats me, and I hit the bottle again.'

'And that's where you've been this week? Drinking?'

'Yes.'

'Why? Because of me?'

'Up to a point.'

She blinked like I'd slapped her.

'Really?'

'Because you sided with your brother.'

Rachel turned, heading for the door, but I grabbed her wrist.

'Listen, don't go. It wasn't only you. Henry's death, this case, and things from the past also crept up and pulled me down. The drinking happens sometimes, not often, but sometimes. At least it's not a problem you'll need to worry about now.'

'How so?'

'Isn't it obvious? When your brother hears about this there's no possibility he'll give his approval.'

'James, you give me very little credit. I've never said I'd obey Bernard's wishes, only that I prefer to wait to see which way he jumps. As it happens he's received nothing but positive reports about you from his friends.'

'But you'd prefer not to go out with a drunk.'

She paused for a moment.

'No, I wouldn't. On the other hand, you might drink too much occasionally but you're not a drunk are you? Perhaps, together, we can stop you falling off the wagon.'

This woman did not understand what she might be taking on. Neither did I, and she might be right. I had plenty of experience of drinking, but none of trying to stop with a strong woman's support.

'You'll also not want a man who has no job.'

'The man I want has a job though, doesn't he?'

'Not for much longer, I've handed in my notice.'

'What?'

'I'm fed up of the whole thing. Dyer's refused to accept my resignation until I arrest Beattie's killer, but he will, once he realises I'm not going back.'

Rachel took my hand.

'He's right, isn't he, James? You've got to go back. You can't quit halfway through; it would bother you forever.'

There was no arguing with her argument. The case was already eating away at my stomach and wouldn't stop. If I walked away it would always play on my mind. The mantel clock chimed a quarter to one, so I walked to the stove and lit the gas under the kettle.

'Give me a minute to make a phone call, then I'll arrange lunch.'

I called the station to tell them I'd be later than expected and when I got back to the kitchen, Rachel had already laid tea and two sandwiches on the table.

'Settling in well, Miss Stevens. I could get used to this.'

'You'd not be getting this every day, Mr Given, I've lived alone for far too long to skivvy after another person. Fifty-fifty is how we would be. Now, sit down and eat.'

I still couldn't believe she'd consider the prospect of continuing to see me despite my confession.

'Can I ask you a favour, James?'

'Of course.'

'If I tell the truth to Bernard it would be better. He's a good man, he really is, and the tale will come better from me than hearing about your binge from someone without your interests at heart. I'll also press him for an answer when I talk to him.'

'And if he says no?'

'We'll see where we go from there. If he stays opposed because of something he's heard then I'll reflect on what he tells me. If it's just this Jewishness issue then I may have to tell my brother to keep his nose out of my business.'

I told her I'd wait, though I didn't want to, and Rachel asked if I was serious about my resignation.

'Over the past couple of months there's been a lot of time to think of the good times in my life and some of the worst. When I was happiest it was never as a policeman, always when I was under an open sky, either at sea or picking fruit, warm, or when the wind and rain made me feel so alive. I can't stay in this job forever, there's more to life than rooting around in the dirt, fighting against a rising tide of badness. My stint is done, and I need to be out.'

'So what will you do?'

'I'll put away whoever killed Beattie and Henry, whether they're the same person or different, then I'll rewrite that letter to the boss. After that I'm far from certain. I've promised my father I'll go to hunt for his brother, and I talked to Henry about earning a crust picking grapes in France. Something as far away from policing as possible. Lots of sunshine and taking my mind away from violent deaths.'

'Let's hope you discover them soon. I sense Bernard will do the right thing. When he does we'll have a lot of thinking to do.'

TWENTY-SIX

After I accompanied Rachel to her train I ambled the ten minutes to my office and found a message waiting. Janet Beattie had called and requested to see me. I was on official business so pleased the petrol didn't come out of my ration, and I enjoyed the short ride into the countryside. When I knocked the vicarage door the curate, Edward Winston opened it, in cardigan and slippers. I asked if Mrs Beattie was home.

'In a manner of speaking, Inspector.'

'Sorry?'

'Janet's moved into the gate lodge.' He indicated a limestone cottage across the graveyard. 'They've asked me to run the parish until they find a more experienced man. I'd decided to move on with Reverend Beattie gone, but the least I can do is help while they do. So I've taken the main part of the house and Janet has gone over there.'

He stood watching as I made my way to Mrs Beattie's new home, and it made me think it's an ill wind that blows no-one any good. Winston had profited from the vicar's death, though it was most unlikely the gaining of a country parish would drive anyone to murder. He waved and returned inside when I pushed through the gate.

Janet Beattie asked me in, taking me through to a room piled high with boxes. The woman looked thinner and more drawn than the last time I'd seen her.

'I'm sorry about the mess, Inspector, the move came in such a rush and I've not unpacked everything yet. This house is so much smaller I don't know I ever will.'

Though much more spacious than my cottage, the lodge was a step down from what she'd been used to. The mustiness, dirty windows and peeling paint also said no-one had lived there for a while. She shrugged and put on a weak smile.

'Still, beggars can't be choosers can they?'

She smiled grimly and it was clear I needn't have worried about her still being annoyed I'd considered her as a suspect; she'd moved on and now had bigger things on her mind. She offered me tea. I refused.

'You wished to see me, Mrs Beattie?'

'I did. You were asking about my husband's past when you came last time, and I found something when I was sorting through his correspondence. He must have brought them with him when we moved to Stowham, but I've never seen them before. He kept so many papers.' A shake of the head. 'Duncan was a methodical man and hung on to everything. God knows what I'm to do with it all.'

Leaving the room for a minute she returned with a large brown envelope.

'Only when I looked inside this morning did I realise what they were. I don't know if they will be of any assistance, it all seems so long ago.'

I emptied the envelope onto the table and examined the papers. They all seemed to relate to Beattie's employments before he became a vicar. Some dated even before the Great War when Lloyds of London took him on as an office clerk.

At first glance nothing in the papers linked Beattie to anyone we'd come across so far in our investigations.

'This material may, or may not, be of use, Mrs Beattie, but thank you for bringing it to my attention. I'd like time to go through it, so do you mind if I take it away?'

'Please do, Inspector, it's no earthly use to me. There's nothing I know about that period of his life and I prefer to remember him for the years we shared, rather than a past I had no part of. As you can imagine, I'm still sorting out all Duncan's things so if I come across anything else which might help, I'll contact you.'

'It must be difficult for you, madam, it's a shame the Church wouldn't let you stay in the vicarage. You've lived there so long, and Mr Winston is on his own, he has nothing much to fill the place with.'

Mrs Beattie chuckled. 'Not Edward, he'd think it his right to take the house with Duncan's job. If I'm honest, Inspector, he's always seemed a little ambitious and selfish under the surface. Not good ingredients in a country vicar.'

She stopped in her tracks.

'I'm sorry, Inspector, I shouldn't be saying such things. Duncan thought highly of Edward, and I'm sure he is a good man underneath.'

'You don't think so yourself?'

'Not very Christian of me is it? It's just he's taken over, and I've never felt Edward pulled his weight. A curate's supposed to take some of the load off the vicar, but he was constantly saying he hadn't the confidence to do one job or the other. Edward convinced Duncan to let him go to see his mother for the weekend even when it coincided with important religious festivals.'

'I can understand how this might upset your husband.'

'Oh, he didn't bother in the main, he seemed to appreciate having Edward around, he hoped he could mould him into a good cleric. Mind, Duncan was annoyed when Edward said he planned to go to his mother's on the day the bishop was coming to bless the new font. The two argued for ages, but my husband gave in as always.'

Mrs Beattie pulled her cardigan tight.

'Take no notice of me, Inspector. As you say, it's been a very difficult time and I'm looking for someone to blame.'

When we'd said goodbye and I was walking to my car, still parked in front of the vicarage, a tiny light flickered in the back of my mind then disappeared as soon as it appeared. I'd need to go through Beattie's papers again to see what sparked it.

There was one woman at the graveside and I didn't know her, though I assumed she was the sister Henry spoke of. The other half dozen mourners were male drinking companions of Henry's from around the town, and only the woman shed a tear as they lowered his coffin into the sodden earth. As seems to be the universal truth with funerals, the rain poured down all night and had now abated to a steady, soaking drizzle. The wind came in brief gusts, scattering fallen leaves, blowing down to add to their number and causing the white-haired priest to wrestle with his umbrella. In the end it became too difficult to fight while trying to read from his prayer book, so he flung it in the mud in frustration, accepting a drenching. When the last handfuls of soil were thrown into the trench, he performed the sign of the cross, I winced, and he committed Henry's body to eternal rest. The priest closed his book and glumly invited those present to join him for refreshments in the church hall.

Only three of the men bothered to come to the hall, the others having sloped away after offering their condolences to Susan Bramwell, confirming for me she was Henry's sister. When the others left and the priest appeared to be making for the door after finishing the last of the sandwiches, I asked her to tell me about Henry.

'I'd like to say he was a saint, on this of all days, but I can't. Henry was my brother and I loved him dearly even though we'd been apart for years, but he wasn't the most honest of men.'

'In the short time I knew Henry he struck me as trustworthy.'

'Oh, he could be witty, charming and convincing, and he promised he'd reformed, so maybe he had.'

'Reformed?'

'Didn't you know? Henry was in prison on and off all his life.'

'That must have been years ago. He'd been working in Italy until recently.'

Henry's sister raised an eyebrow.

'Working? I think not. That's where he was last in prison. He told me he was well set up for a while working the yachts then ran into some bad luck and was back to his old ways. Got five years for stealing cash from a client.' Susan dabbed her eye. 'Perhaps if they'd put him away longer we'd not be here today.'

Henry a thief? So much for my intuition. If he'd lied about his past, might he have murdered Beattie after all? Had liking him really blinded me to this possibility, as Sawyer accused me?

'When we were children we lived over near Stratford and he was a lovely boy, kind and generous, but always pinched things. Only be apples or sweets, like lots do at that age, but as he grew older it got worse. Money would go missing from our mother's purse, or he'd come home with new boots, saying he'd found them in a field. It wasn't long before the local bobby was round at our house all the time. Stealing's the reason he left home and ran away to sea.'

'Were the police after him?'

'Not that time. Henry broke into the house of a man who took it badly and asked some very rough acquaintances to teach him a lesson. Lucky to escape and just as well he stayed away for a good while.'

'Did he ever live or work in Stowham, Mrs Bramwell?'

'Not to my knowledge. Why?'

'Just another case I'm working on, wondering about a connection.'

'Is it a theft or burglary?'

'No.'

'Not that vicar's murder? You can't think Henry had anything to do with it?'

'Something we're examining. We've no leads to who attacked your brother, so we're looking for links to the other case.'

The tears she'd held back since we'd come inside began to flow again, and I said I was sad for her loss. Making my excuses I headed to the station to tell Sawyer what I'd found, and to face his inevitable ribbing that my friend hadn't been as squeaky clean as I'd claimed.

As expected, Sawyer took great pleasure in me eating humble pie when I informed him about Henry's criminal past. Who could blame him? When your boss climbs on his high horse and is knocked off it, he deserves everything he gets. My only defence was I had said he should follow his hunch even though I thought him misguided, but this didn't help matters much. He strutted off with a big grin, to spread the word on how even I could be wrong sometimes.

I returned to examining the papers passed to me by Janet Beattie. Skimming through, I followed her husband's progress up the ranks, and traced his travels wherever the company retained maritime interests, which was wide. Many ports I recognised from my time at sea, but there were many I didn't. The vicar had been everywhere from Valparaiso to Vladivostok, ending up as an insurance investigator around the Red Sea and Egypt.

The documents were of three main types. The minority were general letters documenting Duncan Beattie's appointments and promotions. The second group related to postings and the third were handwritten notes, congratulating him on the outcome of particular investigations. There was no detail of the cases on those in this third group, only a simple "well done" or "another great result" type of message. Beattie's addresses read like an itinerary for a world tour.

The most recently dated item was a letter from his employers, acknowledging his resignation, thanking him for his years of impeccable service and wishing him well in his plans to join the Church of England ministry.

On a further run through, I saw some of the notes had a jotting in the top corner in the same hand on all of them. I didn't spot this similarity at first, thinking the annotation added by whoever sent the letter, for some filing purpose. On closer examination each one had the same pattern, a five- or six-digit number followed by a letter "p" and a single- or two-digit number. I wondered if these might be dates and page numbers. But from where, and was the handwriting Beattie's? A quick comparison with his signed responses on some of the letters suggested it was his.

I rang the vicar's wife and asked if she'd found any more material from her husband's previous life.

'Not yet, Inspector, I've hardly had a chance, but you're welcome to go through the packing chests if you wish.'

Fifteen minutes later I was driving through the Warwickshire lanes again, with wipers vainly trying to keep the windscreen clear of rain and wind-blown twigs, and with me hoping nothing bigger would fall from the trees.

Janet Beattie pointed to a lidded wooden box in the farthest corner of her spare room.

'If there's anything it will be in that one. It's everything from the shelves and filing cabinet in his office, other than planned sermon notes and the like which I passed to Edward, and those ledgers you took before. There's still a lot to sort and return when I have time. Shall I leave you to it?'

I told her she should, and we dragged the box to where I could delve into it more easily. The contents related to the parish: church accounts, recent diaries containing entries for christenings, marriages and funerals, minutes of meetings, and so on. The handwriting, which was Beattie's, matched that on the documents I'd examined earlier. At the bottom of the box were several ledgers, so packed first, nearest to hand when Mrs Beattie started. I assumed the vicar had been using them not long before his death.

Someone had numbered each page and ruled it into three columns. The first column was the date, the second the location, and lastly a detailed account of events. I only needed to read the opening couple of entries to realise the ledgers held a meticulous recording of investigations carried out by Duncan Beattie. A flip to the end showed me they covered a ten-year period. Page after page of cases, every one starting with the theft or fraud identified, the amount involved, and the steps he'd taken to bring it to a result. This conclusion, with a note about what happened to the perpetrator, ended each section. There were then one or two blank pages before the next case began. Several of my colleagues would have benefited by adopting Beattie's methods in recording their work.

The dates on the papers I'd received earlier might relate to these reports, and I cursed myself for leaving them in my office. I found Mrs Beattie in her kitchen and told her I needed to take the ledgers back with me to check against the other material.

'So you've found something, Inspector?'

'I think I may.'

'Duncan looked for those ledgers a few months ago and afterwards spent hours every night going through them, but he wouldn't say why, only that he needed to find something which had plagued him for years.'

With my foot hard to the floor, the drive back to Kenilworth would have gone much faster than my drive out, but the storm had become far worse, meaning several stops, reverses and diversions to avoid fallen trees.

TWENTY-SEVEN

I called Sawyer in to my office and pointed to the two sets of material laid out on my desk.

'I'll need a hand to make sense of these.'

'What are they?'

'Stuff that the vicar had in his office. His wife came across one and I dug out the other.'

'You're guessing Beattie's and Sturges' killer is in this lot, sir?'

'I don't know, John, but it's a different tack. We've had no luck following anything local, so let's follow where these lead us. It might be another dead-end but, fingers crossed, we'll find something.'

I passed the envelope containing the employment documents to Sawyer and I took the ledgers.

'Take out everything that has a date written in the top corner, then put them in order. Let's compare with the books.'

The ledgers covered a dozen locations, with Beattie economising on paper by starting one case at the first page and one on the last, both working towards the middle. He'd allocated five pages to each case, even though this sometimes left one or two blank at the end. An investigator would never know how long, or how complex, a case might be so it would be impractical to allot any less space than this. As a result, within each location the records were in date order.

Sawyer familiarised himself with the documents from the envelope, extracting those he thought relevant, and sorted them as I'd asked. I trawled through the ledgers again.

Working out the significance of the handwritten annotations on the corner of the papers was not as easy as we hoped.

When we started to compare, Sawyer leaned across the desk and pointed to marks in blue ink in the margin on one page.

'What are those?'

I flipped the pages of the ledger. 'See, there's a cross or question mark next to every entry that corresponds to one of your documents. If you check you'll find the page numbers correspond.'

I pulled across an example and showed him how it worked.

'Many of these marked sections appear straightforward and relate to investigations he'd carried out in the different locations, but there are others where I can't work out why they're marked. We'd best go through them again.'

An hour later we were no clearer and as we sifted through the more random some of the markings appeared.

'Is there no pattern at all, sir?'

'Not that I can fathom yet, though most of them are in the section recording Beattie's cases in Egypt.'

As I mentioned Egypt that spark flickered again in my head.

'So what does it mean?'

'Your guess is as good as mine, John. All I can do is go through each case and try to discover what he's connecting. I'm not sure two of us will now achieve any more than me, so you go off and deal with something else. I'll shout you again if I find anything.'

Ten minutes later he was knocking on my door.

'Any luck?'

'Good God, John, I've hardly started.'

Sawyer grinned and pulled a steaming mug of tea from behind his back. 'Thought you might need this.'

'No biscuits?'

'Afraid not. Anyway, they'd put you off your dinner.'

I laughed and thanked him before getting my head down to the job again. It was possible to discount most of the locations because there were no cases associated with the dated documents. This left a smaller pile of ledgers to work on. I started at the beginning and tried to take on board the intricacies of each marked case, which wasn't easy. There were lots of abbreviations and I know little to nothing about insurance fraud, but Beattie's records were exemplary, and I got the gist of them one at a time. When I arrived at the section on Egypt, each of the highlighted cases concerned a theft or missing goods and those with question marks appeared to be unsolved.

Towards the end of the section Beattie underlined a case heading in the blue ink, and as I read through the entry I spotted something that made me sit back in my chair. I rang Sawyer to join me. He must have bounded up the stairs because he was there almost before I put down the receiver.

'You've found something, sir?'

'Looks like I owe you another apology.'

'Sir?'

I turned the underlined case towards him.

'Henry Sturges was known to our vicar. He was a suspect in a case investigated by Beattie on the Suez Canal. Questioned but not arrested in relation to regular thefts from a freighter called the Cameroon Star. Sturges mentioned the boat when we first met but it meant nothing to me.'

'Wow. So he was lying to you about that as well.'

'Seems like it. Though I'm not certain Sturges recognised Beattie in Kenilworth. The two met a long time ago, half a world away, and the pictures in the newspaper were of a much older man, so Sturges may not have made the connection.'

'Unlikely though, sir, don't you think? Surely he'd recognise it when you gave him the vicar's real name. Still, it looks like whoever did for Beattie attacked Sturges as well. Any clues elsewhere in the ledger?'

'Nothing I can see. A man was arrested, Derek Peters, and later sacked by the company so he could have held a grudge. You should look at this.'

I pointed to a phrase scribbled down the edge of the page. Sawyer lifted the ledger and read aloud the words in Beattie's hand in blue, "two natures in one person — How They Are Fallen!!!!!"

'Any idea what that means, John?'

'Not a clue, sounds like something from the Bible though. In my mind it should be "how the mighty are fallen"; something rings a bell from Sunday School. Perhaps Beattie was already on the road to a religious life, but I can't work out what he's getting at here. Did you notice the exclamation marks? Must have been important.'

'Could he have been referring to that man Peters? If you read the account of the case it seems Peters was well-respected and never in trouble before, so strange for him to begin stealing cargo. The company didn't prosecute. Perhaps Beattie hadn't enough evidence to make it stick.'

We looked again at what we'd gathered so far, which was interesting but not much progress towards a solution.

'You might as well get off again, John. Do what you can to trace this Derek Peters. I'll write to the company he stole from, see if they can shed any light.'

After Sawyer left I penned the telegram to Beattie's employer, closed the ledgers and called it a night.

I'd spent the morning pacing my office waiting for the reply to my telegram and, when I could settle for more than a minute, trying to decipher the marks in the margins of the case ledgers. I concluded Beattie searched for something hidden amongst his past cases, with the crosses indicating rejected ones and the question marks or ticks indicating ones remaining relevant. I suspected that the margin notes and underlining in blue were much more recent than the original entries, so I rang Janet Beattie. She confirmed that her husband always used navy-blue ink for his sermons and correspondence. The shade she described matched the one in front of me.

This, alongside the ledgers being the first things packed from his desk, suggested the vicar had been going through them not long before he left home for the last time. So what occurred to make him go back to that time? Beattie argued with Edie Bridgnorth, Robbie Wilkes and Charlie Butler in the couple of weeks before his murder, but had any of them connections to his time in Egypt? Unlikely. In fact, I doubted they'd ever been out of England. Henry Sturges shared a direct link to a case Beattie investigated and they'd been in the same bar more than once. Had the vicar recognised him, and this was what rekindled interest in the case?

Just after quarter past eleven, the front desk telephoned, telling me a telegram had arrived. I was downstairs in minutes and grabbed the small brown envelope from the hand of a uniformed delivery boy. Tipping him tuppence I ripped it open.

Confirm Derek Peters sacked following thefts… Mr Beattie expressed doubt… Blacklisted not prosecuted… Peters committed suicide in England… Thefts continued… Yours.

So, even if Peters had been wrongly accused and held a grudge, he couldn't have killed Beattie, he'd been dead for years. This was yet another blind alley.

Upstairs I scoured the ledgers once more, looking for familiar names, without success. For the tenth time I stared at the quote which Sawyer said sounded biblical, the exclamation marks suggesting it was important or Beattie found what he'd been searching for. But, according to Sawyer, it wasn't accurate. Why not? As a vicar Beattie would have known the correct quotation. Then it struck me. The first letters of the last part were all in capitals.

TWENTY-EIGHT

'We mustn't go on meeting like this, Inspector. People will talk.'

Janet Beattie smiled when she opened the door, wearing a pink cotton frock, belted at the waist, and a pair of men's carpet slippers. She noticed me looking at them.

'Oh, ignore those old things, they were Duncan's. Slipped them on this morning and they made me feel close to him. Funny, as I've settled in here I've missed him more and more. Little things. Whistling. Duncan always whistled when he approached the house, as if telling me he was nearby.' The smile turned rueful. 'Definitely something I miss.'

We went inside and I asked if she'd unpacked any books.

'Yes. Most of them anyway.'

'Do you have one called *How They Are Fallen*?'

'Goodness, how do you know about that? One of Duncan's favourites. He referred to it often and talked about it all the time. He was so pleased when he discovered Edward knew of the book through his father. I think my husband bored him silly going on about it every time we had Sunday tea together. I was.'

In the sitting room she scanned a bookshelf and pulled down a volume bound in deep red leather, darkened by years of handling.

'This is the one. I understand it's a treatise on Jesus Christ being both God and Man. Sadly, Edward said they found a copy by his father's side when he died. Duncan seemed to think it would help if they discussed the book's teachings, perhaps Edward might learn what his father had seen in them.'

Mrs Beattie passed me the volume. The cover and pages were well worn, with sections separated by slips of newspaper, but it was the names of the authors that grabbed my attention.

Back at the station I called on Phil Trimble to ask about the workings of the Church of England.

'What do you need, James?'

'Who do I need to get in touch with regarding clerical postings? I expect there must be some kind of hierarchy? Someone who manages such things?'

'When my church required a new vicar a few years back, the Bishop's office dealt with the process. I assume that's how it's done.'

Within five minutes I had Sawyer on the tasks of finding the Bishop's office then phoning and asking a few questions. Twenty minutes later he rang me with the answer I was expecting.

'Caused quite a fuss, sir. Say they didn't place Edward Winston with Reverend Beattie. In fact, they've never heard of him.'

'Are they sure?'

'Adamant. They maintain strict procedures for keeping a record of these things and he doesn't show up anywhere. Asked me several times to repeat the name and we tried different spellings. Finally told me they could now see the record still shows a vacancy for a curate at St Botolph's.'

I slammed down the receiver and grabbed my coat.

TWENTY-NINE

Janet Beattie was waiting in the garden when I pulled into the gate, Sawyer having warned her I was on my way. I wound down my window and shouted across.

'Winston, where is he?'

'Edward? He's in the tower adjusting the clock. What do you want with him?'

'I'll explain later. Now go inside and lock the door. Whatever happens don't open it to anyone other than me.'

Jumping from the car I ran headlong across the lawn to the end of the church, then slowed, edging along the outside until reaching the entrance.

The door to the bell tower lay half open and I eased it further, praying that the thing wouldn't creak on its ancient hinges. The clack, clack, clack of the clock mechanism echoed far above, and I tried to match my steps to the beats as I trod the spiral stone steps.

Three quarters of the way up was a wider step with a slit window, and I paused, sucking in air, listening to the curate creaking on the floorboards above, and wishing I'd waited for Sawyer to join me. After a few moments Winston's movement stopped.

'Who's there?'

His face appeared in the arched doorway, so I climbed the next dozen steps for him to see me.

'Inspector? What are you doing here?'

'We need to talk.'

Winston beckoned me up the final flight onto the landing. As my head drew level with the floor, I noticed, for the first time, his shoes. Top quality, highly polished tan leather, probably costing the best part of a week's wages. The type mentioned by Mary Selkirk. When I climbed into the clock chamber the fake curate swept his arm round the room, gesturing at the bells and the clock's cogs and cables.

'Magnificent isn't it?' He lifted the large screwdriver in his right hand and an oil can in the other. 'Needs a little maintenance from time to time though. The clock's in good condition, considering its age, but we could do with money spending on the timbers. Full of woodworm and dry rot. Now, how can I help?'

'Do away with the pretence, Mr Peters.'

He laid the oil can back on a shelf behind him, turned and laughed.

'Have you lost your mind, Inspector, and why would you be calling me Peters? Edward Winston is my name as you well know.'

'What I do know is you killed Duncan Beattie.'

'What on earth makes you imagine that? The reverend was my mentor. You saw how upset I became when we talked about him.'

'A good act, I'll grant you, but you're a good actor. Must be to have kept up this deception for so long.'

Peters took a step forward, but I held my ground.

'I'm sorry, I haven't the faintest idea what you're talking about.'

'You can stop now, it's over, I found the book.'

'Book?'

'The one by Derek Winston and Peter Edwards. The one in your dead father's hand after he committed suicide. You clung to that book your whole life then, when you found that the man who'd wrongly arrested your father was still alive, you came looking. A new identity was needed to get near to the vicar, and the book's authors gave a good start. The combination of the authors' first names giving your father's name seemed like divine confirmation you were doing the right thing, so you took the other parts and lo, Edward Winston was born.'

'This is all a little far-fetched, Inspector.'

'I thought so myself until we spoke to the Diocesan office and they'd never heard of you. This tied in with you conveniently disappearing whenever there was a chance you'd meet any clergy who might reveal you as an impostor. It only took a little more digging and I found Derek Peters had a son, Arthur, about your age. For a few weeks you bided your time, watching Beattie and waiting for an opportunity. I bet you couldn't believe your luck when I introduced you to Henry Sturges, the man who'd committed the crime Beattie accused your father of. Sturges recognised you, you know. Well not you exactly, but the similarity to your father.'

The curate rushed at me, but I jumped aside and he tripped, diving past before crashing to the floor. He was up again in an instant, charging a second time. The man was strong, mad with anger, lunging with the screwdriver and slashing my thigh. I slipped in the torrent of blood and Winston bent over, raising his arm to deal the final blow. Puzzlement flashed across his face as Sawyer grabbed him from behind. I was never so glad to see John, who hoisted my attacker from the ground, but he was spitting teeth when Winston's head crashed backwards. Winston was up and turning.

Sawyer gasped as the screwdriver blade plunged deep into his chest.

'John!' My cry boomed around the chamber.

Sawyer looked at me, eyes glazed, and he fell to the ground, wound oozing blood through his jacket and across the floor.

Winston jumped over Sawyer's body to get to the door, but I found strength through the pain and speed I shouldn't have had and leapt on him in a second. Grabbing his right arm, I smashed it against the wall, sending his weapon spinning into space. He wheeled and took me by the throat.

'You think you're so damn clever, Given, don't you? You've no idea what we went through. Me, my father and my mother. He was a good man. An honest man. Then Beattie pronounced him guilty of something he didn't do. Judge and jury. The company sacked my father and he never worked again. Dad worked out that Sturges was the real guilty one but knew he'd never be able to prove it so took his own life because it was easier than going on. Mother turned to gin for consolation. Through all my youth she drilled those names into me. Duncan Beattie and Henry Sturges. In her cups she'd tell me I should find them and kill them. Made me promise.'

His grip weakened when he remembered his pledge to his mother. I recovered enough in that moment to push him away. He came back but I side-stepped, caught his wrist and swung him against the handrail. The worm-ridden wood shattered, and panic exploded in his eyes as he toppled backwards. The screams lasted less than two seconds before he crunched on the cold stone thirty feet below.

THIRTY

The service was packed for John Sawyer's funeral. Bigwigs in dress uniforms stood respectfully behind his parents as six constables carried the coffin from church to graveside and lowered it into the ground.

John was a copper and we don't lose many in the way he went. He'd grown up within walking distance of this cemetery and was widely respected as a decent young man. What a stark contrast the scene made to the last burial I attended, Henry's, with just a few drinking pals attending, and a sister to grieve for him.

I was in a wheelchair; strangers would soon cover John with earth, and it was my fault. John's parents told me I shouldn't blame myself when I apologised to them, but I could see the lie in their eyes. They insisted their son always looked up to me and would do anything for me. Well he did. He lost his life on my account. Because I was too foolhardy, dashing off without waiting for him. If I had, my partner would be alive and Winston, more than likely, would be behind bars instead of in the cold ground. There were so many things I could have done differently, including not taking the case on in the first place, and this was the result.

Superintendent Dyer appeared once when I was in the hospital, taking time out of his busy day to tell me I was suspended until investigations into the deaths of Detective Constable Sawyer and Arthur Peters concluded. The funeral was the first time I'd seen him since and he came up to me as the mourners moved away.

'What a mess, James. Did you see his poor parents? Distraught.' He looked down at my bandage. 'How's the leg?'

'It'll mend, sir, though doctors say I'll probably need a stick to get around when it has.'

'You discharged yourself?'

'They wanted to keep me in, but I couldn't miss this. John was more than another detective constable, he was a friend, and he didn't deserve this.'

'You're right there. Why did it happen?'

'Because I was stupid. If I'd listened to you and accepted the suicide verdict John would still be alive. We're both responsible for his death. If you'd not called me back from France none of this would have happened.'

'You can't talk that way, James. Sawyer was in the wrong place at the wrong time, that's all. Doing his duty as a policeman, and as a friend.'

'That doesn't make me feel any better, sir. It could simply have been circumstances, but they were ones brought about by my actions, and if John hadn't intervened it would be my funeral today, not his.'

I knew Winston no more wanted to kill John than he wanted to injure me; he was just a trapped animal attempting to escape. I told this to Dyer.

'His main target was Duncan Beattie and he'd have left, probably going scot-free, if he hadn't met Sturges and recognised his name. After that he needed to complete his revenge. I imagine he only remained at Stowham when he'd done it because if he'd left straight away we'd target him as a prime suspect.'

'But why the hanging, why not just find Beattie and shoot him or knife him?'

'Who knows. I've wondered about this for a long time and come to the conclusion that in his own mind, Winston saw this as a kind of justice. Dressing him in his clerical outfit, for all the world to see, and by having it appear like the vicar committed suicide, in a brothel too, it would carry the same disgrace his father carried. The shame he and his mother carried after the father killed himself. Winston was a deluded man, but a patient one too, happy to take on the role of Beattie's pupil and wait until he found the right opportunity to murder the man. What he didn't know was that the vicar recognised the same similarity to his father as Henry Sturges did, and unwittingly left a clue to his killer's identity.'

We were alone now in the graveyard, except for the gravediggers shovelling soil onto John's coffin. Dyer flattened his gloved palms against the small of his back and stretched the muscles before taking the handles of my wheelchair.

'We'd better be going, James, they'll be wondering where we are.'

As he pushed me along the path to the church hall the boss talked of his plans for his retirement, how he hoped he and his wife would move to the south coast and spend their days reading and playing golf.

'Away from all this nastiness, eh James? Away from the paperwork, from the backbiting, and from having to suspend a good copper who's only been doing his job.'

We talked more about our respective futures over tea and semi-stale sandwiches, then he insisted on taking me back to the hospital. I didn't argue. I couldn't face any more of Sawyer's mother's tears, and my leg was throbbing after the few hours out of my bed.

Dyer had been confident that the enquiries into Winston's death would wind up within the week and I'd be back on duty as soon as I was well. I wasn't sure this was something I was looking forward to.

Dyer had cleared most of his office by my first day back and I hung my shiny new walking stick on the corner of his desk then took a seat without asking.

'Almost over now, James. Out of here this afternoon. Bit of a party later, then I'm off. Just a job or two to finish before the new man takes over. Main one is to get you back in the saddle. So I can now formally tell you —' he read from a letter on his desk — 'that "there will be no further action in relation to the death of Arthur Peters, otherwise known as Edward Winston. The enquiry has concluded Inspector James Given acted purely in self-defence and is reinstated with immediate effect." There, it's finished, and you can get back to work.'

I thanked the boss and told him I'd see him later, then hobbled back to my office. The telephone rang as I sat down.

'Mr Given, it is Lemmy Adler, you came to my house in Paris.' There was a pause. 'I was not very welcoming.'

That was an understatement; he'd been downright rude, though I told him it wasn't a problem and that I'd thought he had something on his mind.

'Indeed I had, Mr Given, I had just heard that the Germans had taken prisoner my brother in Poland, along with several of his neighbours. There has been no word of him since.'

'So how do you think I can help, Mr Adler? I have no influence in Poland.'

'No, no, you misunderstand. I am not looking for help. Quite the contrary. I hope I can assist you. I found your note again after my initial shock and realised how I treated you with discourtesy. I am afraid I cannot give you news that I found your uncle but there is something.'

'Anything would be welcome, sir, anything at all.'

'I began asking questions and a family sounding like the one you search for were living here in Paris, in Le Marais, until two weeks ago, but they left. Their neighbour says they packed and went to a village near Vannes. It is in Brittany. Many of us Jews fled in that direction, hoping it will be safer if the Germans invade.'

'Does the neighbour have an address?'

'I am sorry, but he does not. He says they decided quickly when someone offered them transport to leave the city. The French countryside has no secrets, and you will find them without difficulty if you travel there to look. I would go on your behalf, but it is impossible to do so; I am leaving the city myself in a few days. I have a home in Nice and hope that will be far enough away from this war to be safe.'

Thanking Adler for his help, I wished him luck and said I might visit him if I returned to France to continue my search for Uncle Gideon.

For the next two hours I sorted through cases waiting for attention, and more than once I reached for the telephone to call Sawyer, only to put the receiver down again when the memory returned. I left it until lunchtime to contact my father because I knew he'd be busy with deliveries on Tuesday. I told him the news about his brother.

'Will you go to find him, Jacob?'

Why did he do this?

'No, Papa, I won't. I've only returned to work today and can't go on leave again so soon and, anyway, we know he's safe. He was in Paris a fortnight ago.'

'But was it him? What if it wasn't? We need to bring him to England.'

'You mean I need to bring him to England.'

'I've already told you I will go if you won't.'

'That's just silliness. It's almost impossible to travel at present, and you'd not know where to look.'

He still wasn't convinced and continued to insist.

'I'll promise you this, Papa. Give him time to settle, and if you haven't heard from him in a month I'll go. Is that fair?'

'I am sorry, son, I shouldn't push you, but I am so worried. At least it is something that your French contact thinks Gideon and his family are travelling to safety. I will give it a month, as you ask, then we can decide.'

We chatted for a few minutes before I hung up, and I already knew what I would do.

The laughter rang round the canteen as Superintendent Dyer regaled us with his stories from thirty years on the force, most of which I'd heard before and seemed to have grown in the retelling. The Assistant Chief Constable had been at the early part of the afternoon, apologising for the non-attendance of the big boss. He presented Dyer with his leaving present: a gold watch engraved with good wishes for his future. I couldn't help thinking it wasn't much of a reward for a lifetime protecting the public. All of the senior staff of the division were in the room, alongside his office members.

The latest story ended with him holding up the watch and proclaiming he had no intention of wearing it for at least five years.

'Fed up with having one of those rule my life, lads. Without it I can get up when I want, go to bed when I want.' Loud cheers. 'And eat and drink when I want.'

Phil Trimble nudged me in the back.

'Best get up there and say a few words, James, before the boss says something he regrets.'

I turned and looked at him, mouthing 'Me?' and he nodded. I sighed, shuffled up to the front, and tapped a spoon on my tea mug to grab attention. The chatter died away.

'Gentleman —' I nodded towards the two WPCs by the door, each holding a glass of sherry — 'and ladies, I've been asked to speak on behalf of the Detective Inspectors…'

I rambled on for an appropriate time about how we all respected Superintendent Dyer and how I, in particular, had found him supportive in my early years in the force. The final flourish was a toast for happiness in retirement, and this drew a round of applause. After it faded everyone looked puzzled when I didn't walk away.

'If you'll forgive me, I have to make an announcement of my own. Many of you will have known Detective Constable John Sawyer, the young man who worked alongside me and who was murdered a few weeks ago.' Murmurs and shaking heads. 'John saved my life just before Arthur Peters killed him, and I have to believe I was saved for a purpose. I don't think it was to keep chasing villains. John wasn't going to do that; he'd planned to join the army to fight for what he thought was right.'

I tapped my thigh with my stick.

'I got away lightly with this injury, but it means I can't take his place in the forces. They won't take me with a gammy leg. John's death has confirmed what I've felt for a while. The boss is a year or two older than me, but I'm as fed up as him being surrounded by badness and piles of paper. So I'm going. I'd prefer to leave at the end of today, but I'll work my notice and you're stuck with me for some weeks yet.'

Dyer was first to shake my hand after the clapping died.

'Come on, James, you've had a bad time of it over the last year. More than many officers deal with over their entire career. But you're excellent at your job, and the force needs men like you. Don't give up.'

The boss was told the same as all my colleagues who tried the same approach later.

'I'm not giving up, I'm starting again. A new life, in a new place. A life where I don't have to pick over all the sadness and badness in the world.'

I stayed for as long as politeness demanded then made my way down to the main office on the first floor to spend a few minutes by Sawyer's desk, wondering how long it would be before a fresh faced young man would take up his chair.

The party upstairs had broken up, judging by the coppers starting to return, so I climbed the stairs to my room and began to pack my possessions into a cardboard box.

THIRTY-ONE

Despite Dyer's attempt to discourage me from leaving, he'd dropped me a line saying he was pleased with my choice.

'A man can get stuck, James. Either in the mire of badness staying where he is, or in the mountains of paperwork and backstabbing if he takes a promotion. The two of us are better off out of there.'

Alongside Dyer's replacement they installed a new Chief Inspector, a career copper, only interested in results which made him look good to those up the chain of command. C.I. Stafford's comments made it clear he disliked Jews in general, and me in particular, and he didn't hesitate to condemn me back to the cellar with Tom Smith while I worked my notice. Tom continued to grin and scratch his head filing papers like he would until he retired.

After I left I put my house up for sale then filled my days with odd jobs and enjoying Rachel's company. We talked long and hard about our future when her brother gave me the all clear. Bernard still wasn't happy that he wouldn't be spending his days studying the holy books with his future brother-in-law, but he accepted we both had her well-being at heart. Rachel raised no apprehension regarding my decision to leave the police, and any concerns she had about what we would live on were put to one side when I received compensation for being disabled in the line of duty.

A month after leaving a buyer for my house came along to provide the nest egg we needed, and we married in a quiet affair with the blessing of Bernard and my parents. Mama was overjoyed that I was settling down at last with a nice Jewish girl.

I'd already promised my father I'd search for Uncle Gideon's family once we'd caught Beattie's murderer. A move to France to do this, then to follow the vegetable and fruit harvests was our plan for a new life. Rachel spoke several languages, not fluently but enough to get by, and she had confidence she'd find work as a music teacher wherever we settled.

My new wife clung to my side and her warmth radiated through her coat, despite the chilly breeze blowing down the Channel. The Calais beaches sparkled two or three miles away in the December sun and I smiled as she snuggled even closer, making me mentally thank Mitchell again for one last favour. He'd objected, as I knew he would, but when he heard my intentions he told me he'd arrange transit on one condition.

'Keep your eyes and ears open, James, and report back anything you think might be useful. We're certain the Germans are making preparations to invade Britain through France. The only way we can keep one step ahead is to have people listening to gossip in the towns and villages. We need intelligence on what appetite the French people have to fight them and on how far into the country the Germans have infiltrated. Will you do that for me?'

I had no option but to agree. The last time we met he reminded me I was bound by the Official Secrets Act and handed me an envelope.

'What's this?'

'You're going into dangerous territory. The word is that Hitler's army will go through France like a knife through butter, and you know he's not too friendly to your people. There are two sets of false papers in there, one if you need to be French, the other showing you and Rachel to be good old

English stock. In both cases you're Roman Catholics, so you'd better learn your catechism.'

There'd been only one bone of contention between Rachel and me in our final weeks in England. She wanted to rent out her house, so we'd have a bolt hole to return to if our adventure went wrong.

I was adamant it wouldn't.

A NOTE TO THE READER

Dear Reader,

Thanks for taking the time to get this far in the novel, even if you've just picked it up and are flicking through, at least you gave it your attention.

It's hard to say where inspiration arrives from. Sometimes it's an event on the news, or half-remembered from my life, sometimes simply an idea about a set of circumstances. Whichever it is, the story never comes fully formed, not for me at least. In *A Patient Man*, I'd been working on another project and struck by two things: the connection between people over time, and the contrasts and connections between different parts of the world. Without realising it, these themes underpinned my approach to this novel, then I threw into the mix a good dollop of good versus evil to make it interesting. There was another guiding thought, but I can't reveal what it was without spoiling the mystery. With these sparks working away in my head, I began to take Inspector James Given on a journey — I hope you enjoyed the ride.

The title is from William Shakespeare's *Cymbeline* and makes reference to the Inspector's predilection for card games, and his willingness to play the waiting game.

I love to hear from readers, so please contact me through my **Facebook page** or send me a message through **Twitter**. You can also see my latest news on **my website** and sign up for notifications. Reviews are so important to authors, and if you enjoyed the novel I would be grateful if you could spare a few minutes to post a review on **Amazon** and/or **Goodreads**.

Thanks for reading!

Charlie Garratt

Sapere Books is an exciting new publisher of brilliant fiction and popular history.

To find out more about our latest releases and our monthly bargain books visit our website:
saperebooks.com

Printed in Great Britain
by Amazon